PRAISE FOR
STEPHAN JARAMILLO'S

GOING POSTAL

"Capture[s] the mood and voice of a certain distinctive type of apprentice grown-up."

—*New York Times Book Review*

"Bringing a fresh humor to the old news of burnt-out 1990s' youth, first novelist Jaramillo tells an alternately sentimental and scathing tale about the hard-knock life of a Bay Area slacker . . . [A] witty narrative and motley cast."

—*Publishers Weekly*

"Judging from *Going Postal*, Stephan Jaramillo has a true comic gift, and absolutely no business being armed."

—Sherwood Kiraly

"Stephan Jaramillo's impressive debut . . . a very funny book . . . Jaramillo deserves credit for a crisp and funny style, a dead-on ear for dialogue, but more impressive, an emotional honesty that's rare and wonderful . . . This fine little novel sets Jaramillo apart from the Generation X crowd. I suspect we'll be hearing a lot more from him in years to come."

—*Rocky Mountain News*

"A fun read . . . a very witty writer . . . I did find myself chuckling audibly."

—*New University Quixotic*

"Enormously entertaining moments, reverberating with a cynical wit underscored . . . with heartbreaking poignancy and disillusion . . . haunting, honest."

—*St. Petersburg Times*

Berkley Books by Stephan Jaramillo

GOING POSTAL
CHOCOLATE JESUS

chocolate jesus

Stephan Jaramillo

BERKLEY BOOKS, NEW YORK

To my family and my mother

chocolate jesus

"Oh, what a heathendom! Oh! What lands so suitable for missions! Oh! What a heathendom so docile."

—Fray Francisco Garcés
upon first meeting the natives of
what is now Southern California, 1775

prologue

the chocolate jesus never would have happened (and many might argue never *should* have happened) except for one of those rare accidents of the cosmos, one of those synchronizations of the obscure and unlikely, the remote crossing of paths and unconscious just-right timings that one might guess would never happen at all but, nonetheless, seem to happen all the time. And it only happened because of the arrival by bus one late-winter afternoon to Valley, one of those satellite Los Angeles cities spread across the lost paradise of Southern California, of a most unlikely person. One Sydney Corbet.

Sydney sat in his seat toward the back of the bus. He was deeply involved with a bag of his favorite candy. The Wad Gomper. He could never get over the two candies in one. The finest, crispiest of all the world's known malt balls. It put Whoppers to shame. A Wad Gomper would crack (never a dud in the bunch, in all the years Sydney had never come across a *single* dud) in a satisfying malty crunch of sweet goodness, and then as you got down to the chocolate, it would transform somehow in your mouth into the finest of all Tootsie Roll–style caramels. Rich and long lasting, chewy and satiating. *What a candy!* Sydney smiled.

Sydney Corbet had never imagined what might come about because of his return to Valley. His return after fifteen years' exile in voluntary attendance at the Koala Center in the stark desert just outside of Tempe, Arizona, home of the Sun Devils and Meat Puppets. Under the capable care of Dr. Jenkins, a father figure to Sydney, who'd known neither father nor mother, who remembered his brother, Martin, and vaguely remembered Grampa Billings, the man who'd paid for Sydney's stay all those years at the Koala Center. The man who'd just died.

Sydney wasn't thinking about any of that right then, as he sat in his window seat finishing his bag of Wad Gompers. He was in the midst of firing off a serious letter concerning an article he'd read in a *People* magazine the last traveler had left behind when she got off in Yuma.

Dear Sirs:

Have you no sense of shame? Are there no longer limits to the pornography that a major magazine such as *People,* one to be found conveniently at the checkout stand of every supermarket in the entire nation, wallows in? I refer, of course, to your article so cynically titled "Sea of Love." The breathless tawdriness of the article was alone enough to have me practically reaching for my atomizer in the anticipation of a major and dangerous asthma attack.

How? How, I ask, can you defile the names and cherished memories I hold of some of Hollywood's greats, by flippantly drawing filthy, guttural "sexual" connections between them? Soon Yi and Frank Sinatra? Please! Not only is it an out-and-out lie, but an obscene thought as well. My mind still reels from the images of Mia Farrow and Woody Allen, whom you defamed to make your "connection."

If I could somehow afford lawyers, you would be hearing from them most promptly. Unfortunately, unlike yourselves, I am not made of money. No doubt due in part to the fact that I would not stoop so low as yourselves, to the peddling of smut.

Most ashamedly yours,
Sydney Corbet

Satisfied with the effort, Sydney put down his notebook and tried to again picture his older brother's face. He remembered . . . *Martin was born in November of 1959, but what does he look like? I haven't seen Martin since his one and only visit in 1988, or Aunt Sally for that matter.* Sydney's brow was furrowed and his eyes tightly shut in concentration . . . Nothing. He opened his eyes, which were bright and sharp and a deep green far more dramatic than he, and watched the scenery roll by.

The desert east—and west, for that matter—of El Centro isn't even good desert. It's bunko, low-rent, shit-brown, boring flat-ass desert. No cacti, no sand dunes, no lunar rock formations. The colors are stunningly drab. Sydney wondered how anyone ever found California in the first place. After 150 miles of western Arizona followed up with 75 miles of southeastern California? Sydney smoothed back his fine blond hair and began to nod off.

his own private utah

the reverend willie domingo liked to go out to the desert now and again. Sometimes he'd even bring Jesus, or, rather, Jesús. Jesús Torres, the Reverend's personal assistant, groundskeeper, soundman and gate guard at the Reverend's religious compound atop Miracle Mountain, on the eastern outskirts of Valley, California. Miracle Mountain was home to the End Times Museum, the Holy T-Shirt and Nic-Nax Shoppe and the broadcast booth and transmitting tower for KGOD, Channel 77, the All-God/All-the-Time cable station.

Though seventy years old, Willie Domingo was lean and nimble and had the quick step of a far younger man as he made his way with ease over the rocky, sandy floor of the desert basin. He felt that his great health, his sheer fitness alone, was proof that he had been chosen. God was his pal, and the Reverend's reward, perhaps, for their close and personal relationship, was that he had aged into someone bearing an uncanny resemblance to TV game show host, animal rights activist and sexual harassment suspect Bob Barker.

Willie unzipped his raw-ochre-colored Sansabelts, tipped

6

back his Stetson and soaked up the heat of the desert that began to bloom even in late February. You could feel it. Or what was to come. *July to September? The Reverend mused. It could kill a man. Mid-110s and that's in the shade. Not much shade around here. I like it hot. The hotter the better; give the whoremongers a taste of what awaits them. Burger-chomping sinners. Sex crazed from the unclean blood of rotting dead flesh. Jesus!* The thought near made the Reverend's stomach turn. *The Army of God eats no flesh.*

Reverend Willie Domingo was head pastor and CEO of the Church of the Returning Vegetarian Christ. The church was a strange, eclectic hodgepodge, a Californian mix of apocalyptic scripture, light workouts with free weights, a sound base of aerobics, a vengeful God, a strict vegan diet of fruit, vegetables, nuts, sprouts and fresh juices, and a Jesus who offered both the ultimate love and redemption to the true believer while promising to kick the unholy crap out of everybody else as soon as he gets back.

A vegetarian Christ? Genesis 1:29 was all the proof the Reverend needed. "And God said, Behold, I have given you every herb bearing seed, which is upon the face of all the earth, and every tree, in which is the fruit of a tree yielding seed: to you it shall be for meat."

Not satisfied? the Reverend might ask you as he sipped his morning fruit drink of fresh berries, spirulina, papaya, phenylalanine and freshly squeezed orange juice. Leviticus 3:17. "It shall be a perpetual statute for your generations throughout all your dwellings, that ye eat neither fat nor blood."

And the Reverend Willie Domingo had taken these words to heart for the latest incarnation of his church and transformed himself into a sort of Jack La Lanne (with less ethnic hair) of Biblical prophecy. The Reverend now pictured Heaven as something along the lines of a really great twenty-four-hour Nautilus with adjoining juice bar and vegetarian restaurant, serving the finest in Spa cuisine.

Willie Domingo hadn't always had this view of Heaven and God. Back in the early seventies up in San Francisco, he had run the Church of the Loving Christ. *He* even had another name. In 1972 he was known as the Reverend BunnyLove. It was back in the day when the Reverend first discovered the joys of a life free of sugar, white flour, caffeine, alcohol and meat. Back when he first experimented with a rudimentary formulation of his theories on the path to true salvation, the road to spiritual enlightenment. The surefire method to ensure selection in the first round when Jesus comes back and teams are selected for Armageddon Time.

The Church of the Loving Christ was meat-free. It was based on Peace and Love. The Reverend saw himself as a mellow and far more Christian Timothy Leary (without, of course, the drug boosterism, though back then the Reverend had sparked up behind the pulpit—a fact he hoped would never surface in the media). He had a flowing midnight-blue robe and wore a beret. Communion consisted of a Stoned Wheat Thin cracker and carrot coin. "Carrots not Guns" was enough of a philosophy for many of the sensitive born-again vegetarian hippies that made up his gentle flock.

Back in those days the Reverend BunnyLove pictured Jesus returning late one evening. (2 Peter 3:10: "But the day of the Lord will come as a thief in the night.") Jesus would honk the horn of his '65 VW bus twice—*beep . . . beep*—hop out wearing his usual loose-fitting robe, long hair and beard (which back then was actually viewed as a legitimate form of fashion) and greet BunnyLove with a smile, a warm embrace and the generous gift of a yogurt maker. They'd step into the house and catch up on things over some freshly baked whole-grain, lactose-free oatmeal cookies and chamomile tea. Discuss the coming new happy, smiley world of Peace and Love. There were going to be lots of flowers and mellow acoustic folk music.

But that was then, and the man standing in the sun this early afternoon in the Anza-Borrego Desert would hardly have been recognized by any of the old-school followers.

Six-two, lean and sinewy. The Reverend was on the yung 'un side of seventy, but you'd never guess it. His face looked fresh and rugged, his eyes alive. His full head of hair pure white. He exuded health and vigor.

The Reverend patted his toned abs as he headed back toward his car. *No, I was a deluded soul back then. Thinking the Great Redeemer would look like George Harrison. Ha!*

The Reverend had reworked his philosophy (coincidentally with the closing down of the BunnyLove congregation amid Nixonian rumors of money pilfering and false laying-on-of-hands claims) as the world worsened, as the fruit of God began to rot, as the violence screeched to amazing, stunning, impossible-to-imagine-ten-years-earlier levels, as homosexuality flaunted itself all over the place; after the twelve-year-olds started fucking and the ten-year-olds decided it was their right, too, to bear arms; when the sex plagues were at last unleashed, when crazed infidels imagined visitations by UFOs and channelizations of grand psychic proportions with historical figures—it was then the Reverend realized that if Jesus showed up simply bearing a dumb grin and some carrot cake, punk hoodlums would have his ass capped by the side of the first rest stop the Sweet

Lamb made the mistake of pulling his rental car into. It would all happen so fast that Satan would be pissed he didn't get to get in any licks after waiting some two thousand years.

No, the New Jesus, the Reverend Willie Domingo's Jesus for the New Millennium, is ready for business. This Jesus is ripped and cut. Gone are the robes (the Reverend pictured him in a much more tasteful American Gladiator's outfit). Jesus has shaved for Judgment Day. He went out and got a haircut. He's been lifting weights, doing crunches, busting the Stairmaster and treadmill till God told him to knock it off and quiet down already. Jesus (and so, too, the Reverend) knows that there's gonna have to be some serious ass-whuppin' come Judgment Day. The world has become so evil, so cesspoolian that the Reverend (and so, too, Jesus) knows Satan will not wilt in the face of a friendly hello and a winning smile.

Willie Domingo took this peculiar brand of aerobicised vegan biblical prophecy down to the southern part of the state after lying low for most of the eighties at his mother's in Alabama. He became a Brian Wilson of evangelists, not leaving the house for six years, carefully studying the pioneering TV work of the Robertsons, Robertses and Bakers. But he rallied, and after a few presidencies, the fall of the Soviet Union, New Wave music, a war named after an oil company, the cancellation of Cosby, the big fuss over that kid who fell in the well, and the advent of MTV? Who could remember a damn thing?! He was back!

And so the Reverend Willie Domingo leased a barren mountain, erected a bright white cross, built a modest radio and cable TV station, a small museum and gift shop and called it Miracle Mountain and saw that it was good.

But as the Reverend ground the heel of his Tony Lama

ostrich-skin boot in the hard scrabble of the Anza-Borrego, he was a bit worried despite his closeness to God. His extreme fitness regimen had many of the congregation scurrying for the wide open lifestyle offered by strict Catholicism. Luckily there were still the core disciples—mellow sprout-munching hippies, anorexic fitness wackoids and militant young Vegan God Warriors (who formed the most extreme wing of the flock)—but lately he just hadn't been bringing in the kind of money someone so close to God might expect.

Willie Domingo decided his cable TV programs needed a little boost and he knew that in the world of televangelism there was only one show for holy sweeps week: Predict the end of the world and pick a date.

The Reverend knew that predicting the end of the world was a slippery slope and to pick a specific day or even suggest a particular month would break the first rule of apocalyptic fire-and-brimstone sermonizing. His old mentor, the now grizzled and somewhat demented Pastor Ron, who was wiling away the last of his years and millions in Palm Desert playing golf and wearing Depends, had explained it long ago. "The end of the world is our bread and butter," Pastor Ron told him that hot steamy summer day in Alabama so many years gone by, "but you can only bring them so close. The public, they're like a mob, don't you see. A stupid, violent mob that is easily led by promise and fear, and the end of the world, well, it's got both of those things in spades, but you can only take them to the brink. The trick is leaning them over the edge of the abyss and then pulling them back. Once you take the plunge, well, if it isn't the end of the world then it's the end of you. Course, you can always pick up and move to another town. Even change your name and dye your hair if you have to. There's always another flock,

Willie. That's the beauty of our business. There's always more people hungry for that fear and promise."

The Reverend Willie Domingo gazed at the arid desolation surrounding him. He felt the utter dryness of the air deep within his lungs. The landscape he viewed as hellish stood harsh but burgeoning in the sweet days of coming spring, the most delicate and beautiful flowers blooming miniaturely amid the creosote- and rock-strewn land. *I had no other choice. It was the only way. What have I got to lose? Even if, for argument's sake, the world doesn't end . . . well, I'll just be in Costa Rica, lying on a white sand beach, sipping a freshly squeezed tropical fruit drink.*

Willie decided he'd had enough of God's natural beauty for one day. His job was clear, and with more grim determination than eagerness, the Reverend Willie Domingo shook it off on the cholla, zipped it up and headed to the car. Back over the hill. To Valley. To continue his work. To deliver his message. To tell his flock of the end of the world.

The periwinkle 1959 Cadillac Fleetwood sped back onto the ribbon of blacktop that ran through the desert east of Valley. Willie tugged at his pant leg, waiting . . . for the inevitable drop of urine that he just couldn't get rid of on that cactus at the side of the road.

Damn! he thought and was then immediately distracted by a skinny, funny-looking coyote that suddenly appeared in the speeding Caddy's path. The Reverend swerved, barely missing the beast. *Shit!* The beast raced across the road and disappeared into the brush. The Reverend tugged at his sharp lapels and then gunned it up the grade leading out of the desert and back to Miracle Mountain.

The animal that slipped out of sight behind a giant ocotillo, cloaked in its camouflaged nature, pointed its nose in the direction of the speeding Cadillac, bared its teeth and let out a snake-like hiss.

bea's candies

wilbur bea peered through the giant plate glass wall of his office, which opened upon the interior of Building #5, the flagship production center of Bea's Candies. He watched as the giant kettles of molten chocolate were maneuvered by hard-hatted workers and poured into the hopper. He was mesmerized by the endless bags of Wad Gompers heading down the conveyor belt. *Thank God for Wad Gompers,* Mr. Bea often might be caught thinking.

Mr. Bea swiveled around in his chair behind the splendid mahogany desk that Mrs. Bea had given him so many years before when (in a move that, it could be said, was the very definition of the word *nepotism*) she put her only son in charge of the company—sort of.

Now, no one ever said Wilbur Bea didn't *like* chocolate, but beyond liking it he was distinctly unqualified in all remaining aspects of the Chocolate Industry or, for that matter, in *anything* that involved running a business. (In fact, his mother remembered Wilbur as unable to run even his own bedroom.) Really, the main obstacle to the smashingly successful operating of the fairly-easy-to-run Bea's Candies was . . . Wilbur Bea, who had a stunning, for-the-record-books case of attention deficit disorder that, had it been known to the general medical community, would have come to represent the most extreme case of this confusing mental condition. Luckily for Mr. Bea, while most places won't pay you to run a business into the ground, this, like I said, was Family.

Wilbur looked up to the huge, smiling, grandmotherly portrait of his dear old mother—founder, president and revered icon of Bea's Candies—and he shuddered inadvertently at the thought that she was, *still,* somehow alive.

He got up out of his chair and gazed lovingly at all the bustling activity down in Building #5. A small smile crept over his face as he watched another forklift full of candies heading toward the loading docks. He thought of all that tasty chocolate, all the money it provided him, the lavish lifestyle he'd come to not only enjoy, but expect. He thought how nice it was to have a fat salary, a fat wallet, a big car, a huge house, no family—but there *was* mother, still, somehow alive, and he *did* have that rather massive expense account that would pay for his weekly hooker binges. Mr. Bea smiled at the thought. Little Sasha, that hot Filipina in the tight blue miniskirt. The girl with the big mouth and full lips. And only twenty-two years old. Twenty-two!

Wilbur's hand unconsciously reached over to the bowl on his desk filled with mixed butter creams (raspberry, orange, maple and chocolate) and dropped one into his mouth. He held it there for a moment, allowing it to warm slightly as he stared out the window and thought again of Sasha's tight little ass, about the $500 he'd paid her, about the Frito-Lay buyout offer that Mother kept nixing. "Over my dead body," Wilbur could hear her rasp. *I wish.* He looked again at the portrait looming down at him from the wall, and a wave of fear ran through him like an underwater electrical charge.

Mr. Bea racked his brain for a plan as he crushed that maple butter cream in his mouth, but thinking had never been his strong suit. *How can I convince her? Sometimes I think she just says no to bug me.* He looked down at his desk, at the latest offer from Frito-Lay—$150 million—and began to fantasize what a man such as himself might do with such money. *Why won't she just listen?!*

Mr. Bea checked his wristwatch. It was time. *God, I hate these tours.* He simply dreaded the next hour or two. He felt practically nauseous. Every Friday afternoon, Mrs. Bea, founder and revered icon of Bea's Candies, insisted on being wheeled through the factory and then chairing a meeting on company policy.

And Wilbur hated it. Mother would upbraid him in front of the staff, she would let everyone know who was *really* in charge, she'd make her own-off-the-cuff policy decisions. If it weren't for his own bungling track record, Mr. Bea might have appealed for the reins of the family business on the basis of his top-notch running of it, but, alas, Mr. Bea had no stomach for work and let it go at that. *How much fucking work can there be to running a chocolate factory anyway?* As little as possible, had been Mr. Bea's conclusion.

But there were certain responsibilities, if not in one's work, then in life, and as the clock struck two Wilbur Bea arose from his grand mahogany desk to fulfill his role as reluctantly caring son and second-in-charge of Bea's Candies, and headed toward Building #2, down the longest corridor, to the end of the most deserted hallway, past even Scrimshaw's nook in Letters, to the room of Mrs. Bea, revered icon and founder of Bea's Candies. A folkloric matriarch, but to Mr. Bea the primordial mummy monster. Dearest Mummy. She was all the family Mr. Bea—father dead, sibling-free—had ever known, and even that was too much.

Mrs. Bea sat in her darkened room awaiting her son. The nurse had dressed the feisty old lady in her Sunday best and cinched the ancient candy maker into her wheelchair with a demur restraint of light cotton. Mrs. Bea, who looked something like a really old Bette Davis on a bad acid trip, peeked through the curtains of her lone window, toward the open land that rose to the east. It was still rough and tumble out that way, undulating with mountains, hills, canyons, ravines, mesas and mountains until the final drop to the vast desert floor.

Mrs. Bea remembered the crossing from Yuma to Borrego Springs nearly sixty years earlier. It was a death-defying journey back then, carrying water, hoping the jalopy wouldn't break down. Just another young pregnant Okie widow, but when they finally left the desert? And made their way past the pine and oak forests in the mountains and she got her first look at the vast orange groves that then covered Valley? It was so beautiful once. Mrs. Bea became excited.

Today was Friday—the day of her tour. *How will I make Wilbur squirm today?*

Outside of Friday's tour, Mrs. Bea spent seemingly every other second of her life (save for occasional wheelchair breakouts) in the Last Room at Bea's Candies, kept in the sort of state that Walt Disney might have hoped for had he lived long enough. The old woman employed every bit of modern medical machinery, alternative herbal medicine and anti-aging technique known to man at that point to keep her alive and well as long as humanly possible. She'd been pumped full of and hooked up to everything short of the cryogenics machinery that sat off in a corner under a plastic sheet, waiting for the moment when *it* might be pressed into action. Wilbur secretly looked forward to the day when they would freeze Mother. Mrs. Bea's secret dream was to outlive her less-than-beloved son.

Mrs. Bea sat quietly in her dark room awaiting the arrival of this son. A son she could hardly believe had somehow sprung from her loins. *He's been trouble from the start. Had to drag his prenatal ass all the way from Oklahoma. And such a big baby. What, near ten pounds! I'd like to see Schwarzenegger pass something like that! Men think they're so strong.* The shock of it all, the sixteen hours of labor followed by the problematic proud-moment free offspring that resulted, forever soured Mrs. Bea on motherhood, and so she turned to business instead.

It was back in the Depression days, when dry winds whipped across the nation's heartland, when the skies became thick with black dirt, till the sun was nearly blotted out. Back in the day when no brother could spare a dime, when the only fear was fear itself, back when Mrs. Bea, home, family and dreams buried in the Oklahoma dust, loaded up the family jalopy and headed out to the golden promise of California.

They ended up in a tiny bungalow in the then-tiny town of Valley, land of orange groves and chicken farmers, endless open country, endless blue-skied sunny days. Mrs. Bea, who'd always baked a mean pie and tasty treat, began making candies and cookies in the bungalow's tiny kitchen, and sold them to friends around the neighborhood, traded them for eggs from old man Mikkelson, for oranges from Sanchez, or some fryers from crusty Mr. Krebs.

It wasn't much of a business at first, just Mrs. Bea trying to make ends meet, trying to put food on the table during the fabled troubled times of the Depression, trying to keep the family together after losing Mr. Bea suddenly and unexpectedly in the horrible rennet catastrophe at the Cheese Mills back in Tulsa.

Mrs. Bea thought fondly of Pearl Harbor again. It really had made her. The war. WW2. *What a stroke of good fortune, the Japs bombing Pearl Harbor,* she thought and smiled. War was declared and the boys were sent overseas and the girls were sent into the factories and all was bustling again amid the killing and opportunity. But while our boys saved the world for democracy, as they slogged through their Guadalcanal marches and their Okinawa melees, they missed their sweet comfort from home, and Mrs. Bea was nothing if not shrewd and industrious. Soon small boxes of Bea's Candies were making their way overseas to our fighting boys, and by 1946 the Forces of Evil had been defeated and Bea's had become the biggest candy maker on the entire West Coast, shipping its product throughout the continental (and in Mrs. Bea's opinion the only *real*) United States.

But now, in her old age, having got tired of carrying on the life of the tough businesswoman she had led for a lifetime (earning a reputation her son, Wilbur, dreamed of having), after settling into quiet days of sitting in her room at the end of the long quiet hall—listening to music, taking lots of antioxidants, reading books, occasionally having complete blood transfusions from vegetarian, high-altitude-dwelling teenaged Swiss girls, sitting in the garden out back—all that was really left was Family. It so often is in the end, except that in this family, where the mother–son relationship best captured the spirit of the L word—loathing—

all that remained for Mrs. Bea was tormenting such an unfortunate son. The Wad Gomper took care of everything else.

Wilbur dismissed the twenty-four-hour nurse, who sat silently outside the door, and turned the knob. It was always the smell that struck him first. A smell of sourness and mothballs, of mustiness, sickness and old ladies, an acrid punch to the wasabi regions of the sinuses, a carpet ride back to childhood, and as Wilbur stepped into the room, into the dim light, he couldn't help but become again the bad little boy hoping not to be caught.

"Wilbur? Is that you, boy?" a frog's voice buzzed from the back of the darkened room. "Where have you been? Why have you kept me waiting?!"

The voice sawed into Wilbur's consciousness like a rasping, out-of-tune violin. It probably didn't help that Mrs. Bea could only speak with the aid of a handheld voice amplifier, having lost a lot of her larynx to Philip Morris some years back.

"Wilbur?!" she buzzed loudly. "Come to the mother that loves you."

"Mother!" Mr. Bea, who liked to pass himself off (and nowhere more strongly than in his own mind) as a Powerful Man of Business, but who was really much more like a kid with a very large paper route, protested. He instinctively looked over to the cryogenics machine and thought longingly of the twenty-four-hour Kevorkian hot-line number he had stashed deep within his wallet.

"I'm not dead yet, boy!" Mrs. Bea's voice was a talking electric shaver to Wilbur. "Now, turn down that oxygen tank for a minute and hand me a Virginia Slim."

"Yes, Mother." Wilbur sprang into action as though he'd accidentally stuck his finger in a light socket. He rolled his eyes as he held out a cigarette. "Here you go."

"I saw that, Wilbur." A skeletal hand snatched the cigarette from Wilbur. "Don't disrespect me. I'm still your mother and it's still *my* company. Until they lower me into the ground, it's still mine."

At that thought Mr. Bea became a tad despondent. *She's going to live forever. Gramma only died ten years ago. The last living woman who could claim to have dated one of the Wright Brothers. I really am the Prince Charles of Candy,* he thought sadly.

"Thank you, Wilbur." Mrs. Bea leaned forward as he lit her cigarette, and Wilbur was struck by the full effect of the bright red circles of rouge that were painted clownishly on her cheeks. She took a long, satisfied drag off a Virginia Slim, smacked the voice box to her throat and in her *Twilight Zone* electronica voice said, "Now, give your dear mother a kiss."

As Wilbur leaned in, she puckered her mouth into a tight lamprey-like sucker, her Cindy Crawford–placed mole and the three hairs that sprouted from it filling Mr. Bea's entire universe until his brain let out a silent bloodcurdling scream: *Mother!*

Wilbur leaned toward her, trying to make his lips (so tightly formed into a kiss that his jaw was starting to cramp) stretch out as far in front of the rest of his body as possible, and laid the fastest, lightest kiss on the soft, deep folds of her wrinkled check.

"Such a good boy." Wilbur almost imagined a bit of sarcasm in Mother's voice. "Now, let's take that tour. I want to see what you've fucked up with my company this week."

———

Mrs. Bea rolled down the catwalk above Building #5 at full wheelchair speed, a nurse on her right, manning her mobile IV nutrient station, and a doctor on her left. Scrimshaw, the near-deaf-but-in-denial head of Letters, manned the wheelchair (for some unknown reason, Scrimshaw, who might not hear a major explosion in the next room, could always understand Mrs. Bea) for the old lady, who had a Virginia Slim in one hand and a perfectly mixed Tom Collins in the other.

The tour was Mrs. Bea's opportunity to get some fresh air. To let all know who was still in complete control of every aspect of the candy factory. To make Wilbur squirm. She would have the entourage head directly to Plant #5 and then the Conference Room, where she might execute company policy new and strange at an alarming rate. One year, just to see the look on his face, she halted the lucrative production of Halloween chocolate cats, telling Wilbur about a *Dateline* program linking felines with the dreaded hunta virus.

"Now, what's that contraption over there?" Mrs. Bea rapped her cane against the safety glass that enclosed the catwalk running through the upper reaches of vast Plant #5.

"Hmm?" Mr. Bea was near swooning from his perceived embarrassment of it all. Unable to blast forth with his usual insults, anger and aphorisms, his brain was swimming with the diarrhea of it all. "The . . . that machine . . . the one that . . . wraps?!"

"The Mikroverk 1250 Depositor," Professor Theodore Broma interrupted.

"When did we buy that, Theo?" Mrs. Bea asked.

"I believe in the fall of 1989," Broma answered. "A top-flight piece of machinery. From Stuttgart."

Mrs. Bea smiled warmly at Professor Broma. He was one of the first Germans she had staffed the factory with in the fifties after breaking the infamous Brotherhood of Candy Makers, Local 23, strike. "We don't want our chocolate red," Mrs. Bea, who back in the day had the charm of Susan B. Anthony, told the papers (while secretly telling her friends, "Hey! If they're Nazis, then they sure as hell aren't Commies").

Professor Theodore Broma was now head chocolatologist and cocoa scientist at Bea's, a candy man from the Old Country. He had come to the U.S. aboard a boat many years before. Before the war. The Big One. WW2. Back when the Germans weren't real fashionable and the Broma family had to deny their Germanness, or at least tone it down a hell of a lot, in certain circles. Little Theo even had the shit kicked out of him a few times in the schoolyard (1942 being a watershed year, when the wearing of lederhosen outside of the house was no longer worth it). Broma learned how to deny himself. His Germanic Genes. He hated his culture, in fact. Loathed Porsches, drove a Saturn. Refused to eat his mother's lentils and Spætzle. Learned to love Oscar Meyer wieners and Budweiser, not even *thinking* of the existence of a fine bockwürst and bock. But he could not, *would* not, was not in any way, shape or form *able* to deny the fact that he had chocolate in his blood. It was an impossibility. His father had been a chocolatier back in Bavaria (in fact Vater had been working on a rather crude prototype of the Wad Gomper before the Hitler Thing got everything crazy), und Grössvatti had been one of the great chocolatiers of his era in Southern Germany, presenting confections to the leading Prussians of the day. *Otto Von Bismarck had slipped Opa's chocolates into his mouth, sheisskopf!* Broma's German accent often surfaced when he got excited. Chocolate just got him all worked up. He *loved* chocolate. *Choclatle. Schokoladen. Cioccolata.* Food of the Gods.

"Hmm." Mrs. Bea seemed suspicious. "I've seen enough of the plant. Let's go to the Conference Room. I want to hear what we've got coming up for the spring."

The members of the Bea's Candies management team were all present. There was Mr. Bea's personal secretary, Irene Peatmos; Professor Broma; Scrimshaw from Letters and Fretwell from Numbers, who'd been downing Freeb's Cola-Nated beverages all day and had just finished a bag of Jax Pounders from Jack Anvil's and was trying his best to belch silently through his nose. Luckily, no one had asked him to speak. Mr. Bea was fiddling with a cigar, working on a very dry martini. Mrs. Bea sat at the head of the table, alternating hits off a Virginia Slim and a very well-made old-fashioned.

Both Mr. and Mrs. Bea, like mother like son, liked to drink, not to mention smoke. Their pro-smoking policy had, in fact, caused their main run-in with the authorities. But over the years, through attrition and a sort of microsocial process, the entire staff had evolved into 87 percent smokers and 12 percent who didn't care. And Fretwell.

And they liked to drink. And as a result? Virtually any sort of alcoholic beverage or cocktail could be delivered at any time of the day or night to any part of the entire Bea's Candy Works grounds. In fact, a full 7 percent of the entire operating budget went into the maintaining of the liquor stocks (their cellar of vintage wines, champagnes, English old ales, ports, Madeiras, Scotch and single-barrel bourbons had been visited by the likes of Martha Stewart and CNN) and the twenty-four-hour two-man cocktail-making crew could serve up a world-class fresh mint julep or fully authentic pisco sour at a moment's notice. Such alcoholic beverages were available to upper management at all times and to all factory workers upon the end of a shift. It was this simple benefit, the daily grog delivered with the whistle at five, that kept the Bea's grunts in a relatively happy toiling state.

Broma had his usual full liter of southern German lager (being composed of entirely Bavarian genes, he absorbed this amount of beer as you and I would a loaf of bread). Scrimshaw had long ago settled into complete abstinence, highlighted by binges every other Thursday when he would infuriate everyone by removing his hearing aids entirely. Fretwell's family had come over with the Pilgrims, so he looked down on fun in any of its forms. Irene, opting for the "to go" route, had over the years built an amazing cellar of vintage champagnes and old French reds from Bordeaux and Provence that in value rivaled other company's retirement programs.

"Now, where were we?" Mr. Bea asked, momentarily distracted by his slow and intricate preparation of a cigar. A fine Nat Sherman Dispatch. The room was silent.

"What do I PAY you people for!?" Mr. Bea blasted. Mr. Bea had a bit of a temper. Combined with his A.D.D., this made for a management style that was a confusing (for all the other employees) mix of massive periods of goofing off punctuated by face-shaking fits of terror-reign temper tantruming that required brief periods of senseless frantic activity until his cracked attention moved on and everyone could resume the much more beloved (and technically more profitable, Fretwell argued according to the calculations he did during a company Christmas party, after Mr. Bea had passed out under the Christmas tree) goofing off.

"Screaming at your people won't accomplish anything, boy," Mrs. Bea buzzed. "Ideas. I came here to hear some new ideas, Wilbur."

"Oh yeah! Ideas. We need some ideas." Mr. Bea took a long puff. *New* ideas. We're getting stale. Scrimshaw . . . SCRIMSHAW!"

Scrimshaw looked up from his hearing aid amplifier, which unfortunately had begun to pick up the hum of the air-conditioning loud and clear. "Are you *saying* something? Is it *me* you're talking to?"

"YES! I want some fucking ideas. What have your search engines found on the World Wide Web?"

"What is it exactly that these 'engines' you speak of are looking for, sir?" Scrimshaw asked.

"Looking for? Haven't we been through this? Ideas, man! Ideas!"

"Leave Orville alone," Mrs. Bea buzzed. "You don't *find* ideas, boy. You develop them."

"That's the problem, Mother. Except for the Wad Gomper . . ." Wilbur began.

"Yes, the Wad Gomper . . ." Broma interrupted.

"Forget the fucking Wad Gomper, Theo," Mr. Bea barked. "We all know about it. Two candies in one. We got it. It's old. We need something new, okay? Let me clue all of you in. There are three kinds of people in the business world. Those who make things happen, those who things happen to and those who ask, 'What happened?' "

Everyone at the table looked around and then hung his or her head. As usual, no one knew what to make of Mr. Bea's latest nonsequitur aphorism.

"Do I have to spell it out for you? You sell the sizzle, not the steak." Mr. Bea put down his Nat Sherman. "You know, Milton Hershey once told me . . ."

Oh, Jesus, not the Hershey story again. Irene didn't think she could bear to hear it for the thousandth time. *The Prince Charles of Chocolate.*

"Heh-heh-heh-hemm." Professor Broma cleared his throat as Mr. Bea reached the part of the story where Hershey gives the young Mr. Bea a great bit of wisdom in the form of yet another aphorism, something about stopping the drilling once you've struck the oil. The Professor was almost ready to reveal his secret. It was nearly a plan. Broma was working on something most people didn't believe in anyway. The Professor had hidden away in the hills above Oaxaca private holdings of what he had archaeologically determined were the offspring of the oldest known cocoa trees. Descendants of the original cocoa plantations of the Aztecs. The trees that supplied Montezuma's pappy with the bitter elixir. "I'm working on . . ."

"You were about five years old when you met Hershey." Mrs. Bea's voice vibrated through Broma's response. "Cried like a baby, too."

"Mother . . ." Mr. Bea was sure he was blushing. "Theo, tell Mother what you were telling me about those assholes at Hershey's."

"Well"—Broma got up from his seat—"my intelligence contacts inform me that Special Forces chocolatiers working round the clock at Hershey's are on the verge of perfecting an emulsifying flavoring agent that could revolutionize the industry. It works like a mood ring. The flavor depends on how you feel when you bite into it."

"And what do we have?" Mr. Bea looked about the table.

Scrimshaw was finally happy with his hearing aid settings. "Okay, so! Are we ready to start?" he asked.

Broma got up out of his seat and adjusted the tiny thick glasses he always wore, the lenses like an old pair of photo-grays had forever stalled in mid-change long ago. "Well, I've been working out in the very fringes, if you will, of the known cocoa galaxy and am on the verge of perfecting a chocolate that is so fine, that is so utterly wonderful, a choc-olate the ancient Aztecs . . ."

Oh no, here he goes. Once he starts on the Aztecs that means he doesn't have anything. I can't believe she won't let me fire him. Mr. Bea rubbed his temples. *I don't feel like golfing, too much trouble. Ahh, I just want to hide out in the Billiard Room* (known as the Boardroom to everyone else, but seeing as Mr. Bea was the one and only board member—well, two if you counted Mrs. Bea, who was, still, somehow alive and going for her third century—it was more like an elegant after-hours boys club). *Today maybe I'll start with a sidecar.*

". . . Of course, nowadays in the Third World markets and with the rather lax controls in the former Communist Bloc nations, I mean, do you have any idea," Broma contin-ued, raising his voice, "how the use of a tiny—tiny, mind you—amount of acetone increases the stretching properties of your typical caramel? And some chocolatiers, they don't care, but in ancient Mexico, zay had integrity. Zay under-stood za schokoladen. It's za Food of za Gods, you know. A livink zing, a, a . . ."

"HEY!" Mr. Bea's thought blew forth from his brain to his voice and across the room at a deafening volume. "What about my idea with the cheese? How's that progressing, Theo? Have we made *any* headway there?"

Everyone looked down in shame.

"Well, it's no problem putting the cheese into the can-dies," Broma explained. Broma hated the cheese idea. Actually, he hated all of Mr. Bea's ideas and wished he would just finally stop with getting any more, even though it did camouflage the fact that Broma hadn't come up with a single one since Reagan could think. "But the shelf life isn't the greatest and Fretwell's numbers, well, you tell him, Fretwell."

"Hmmm?" Fretwell looked up from his internal struggle with the day's lunch and made a go at it, flipping through the giant sheaf of papers he had with him at all times. *Flippity-flip-flip*. "Well, market surveys indicate that . . . ," *flip, flip, flip*, "Here we are! Approximately—*Eeurp!*—excuse me— 76 percent of the general population and 94 percent of the crucial six- to-twelve-year-old market, well, sir, they don't seem to want cheese in their chocolates."

"You science and number guys are all alike," Mr. Bea stated with a wave of his hand. "That's why you drive Aspires and wear clothes from The Gap. With naysayers like you we wouldn't even have a fucking Reese's Cup. Just swathe those cheese-filled candies in some exciting colors and the little bastards won't be able to buy enough of them. And I don't want just any colors. Get me some of those bright Mexican food dyes. Those, those reds. And blues. Blues are good. Eye-catching."

Fretwell, sensing a gap in his indigestion, busted out with a question. "Are they legal?"

"Legal?!" Mr. Bea barked. "What the hell does that have to do with anything? How many times do I have to tell you people? It's easier to ask for forgiveness than permission."

"Cheese?!" Mrs. Bea rasped through her voice box, after removing her latest in a chain of Virginia Slims. "That's almost as bad as your idea for the Neapolitan butter cream. Remember that one? What'd we lose on that idea? Half a million?"

Everyone in the room plunged their tongues into their cheeks. She was referring to Wilbur's idea to make a butter cream filled with coconut-, raspberry- and blueberry-flavored creams and release it to coincide with Independence Day, despite both Broma's constant and dire warnings as to the mechanical impracticality of such butter cream dynamics, as well as Fretwell's report on the traditionally soft summer chocolate market.

"No, this is just no goddamned good, boy," Mrs. Bea yelled at her son, her anger displayed for the enjoyment of all, as though dogs had been loosed. "When was the last time anyone has come up with a decent idea here?"

"Hmm-hmm." Wilbur cleared his throat. "That's why I think we need to consider the Frito-Lay offer. I mean, sales . . . well, tell them, George."

"Hmmm?" Fretwell looked up and tried to swallow back a giant bubble of burger and soda gas as Mr. Bea sat down behind his desk. "Gross—*mmmh!*—sales are off 13 percent for the last quarter . . ."

"And that covered fucking Christmas!" Mr. Bea yelled as he shoved a butter cream into his mouth. "The little bastards just don't buy fucking candy for Christmas anymore!"

"Ummm . . ." Fretwell looked at Mr. Bea out of the corner of his eye, trying to gauge whether or not it was time to speak again. "Projections for the first quarter of this year are even weaker."

"That's why I think the Frito-Lay offer . . . I mean, $150 million . . . ," Mr. Bea began.

"We're not fucking selling Bea's Candies to those cocksuckers over at Frito-Lay," Mrs. Bea said so loudly her voice box began to emit feedback. "No. Screw Frito-Lay! They should be happy with chips. Chips aren't enough for those greedy bastards? No, unh-uh. We're not selling. Over my dead body. This is a goddamned family-run business. Can't you understand that, Wilbur?!

"We don't need to sell," Mrs. Bea continued, and stared hard at her son. "You just need to get your lazy ass off that chair and get your people working. A complete idiot off the street could come up with a better candy idea than that cheese thing," she stated disgustedly. "I've seen enough. Cancel all work on the cheese candy. And get that Frito-Lay offer out of your head once and for all, Wilbur. Orville, wheel me back to my room, please."

"Yes, ma'am." Scrimshaw tucked his hearing aid amp into his pocket and the two left.

That night Wilbur Bea sat in the Billiard Room, sipping on his fourth sidecar, taking a thick rich puff off a Partagas 898. Mr. Bea came up with his half-assed, half-baked plan because he was simply too tired of waiting for Mother to die already and it was now obvious she would never let him have complete control of the company that he so craved. *Won't sell to Frito-Lay? Make fun of me in front of everyone? Won't let me run the company? We'll see about that. We'll see who gets the last laugh.*

Mr. Bea's plan was to bring down the company to the point of bankruptcy. There were many who might say that he was already doing exactly that, but Mr. Bea was thinking of something a little quicker than the slow piling up of debts that was taking a lifetime to kill the company. *His* lifetime.

Mr. Bea was smart enough to know that in business, bankruptcy was no moral dilemma. There was no shame. *It'll be more like a good spring cleaning. A shaking out of the* carpet. *I'll send us straight into chapter 11 and then I'll reform it. Reform it as the Wilbur Candy Company.* A company where Wilbur Bea would be sole CEO, President, Owner and Decider of All Things.

Mr. Bea looked again at the various logos he'd had secretly submitted by a topflight team of graphic designers. *The Wilbur Candy Company. We'll keep the Wad Gomper, of course. Fire Scrimshaw, he's out! And Broma, too. Get some new blood in here. Some candy makers who were kids after they invented rock and roll. That's the ticket. And Mother?*

Wilbur polished off his fourth sidecar and took a satisfying draw off his fine cigar. "Ha-ha . . . Ah-ha-ha-ha . . . AHH-HA-HA HA-HA! All I need is . . . a plan. That and a patsy."

the patsy

sydney corbet nervously checked his wristwatch as he headed down the sidewalk. 9:45! He quickly picked up the pace as he walked the six blocks to work. He only had fifteen minutes to report to work at his already loathsome new job at Jack Anvil's Charbroiled Burgers (Home of the Jax Pounders). He tried to walk faster, but it was hard to do while rereading a letter he had composed the night before.

Dear Mr. Rather:

Your smugness on last night's *48 Hours* Special Edition was not just appalling, but distressing as well. I don't understand how you can sit there, just barely concealing your glee as the self-appointed Keeper of the Facts concerning the tragic assassination of our young nation's most beloved President, when, in fact, Muddler of the Facts is a more apt title for you.

Yes, we all know you were there that tragic November 22, you will never let us forget and yet you've been working tirelessly ever since to try and dupe the gullible public into believing the hapless Lee Harvey Oswald somehow displayed shooting skills that would put Natty Bumppo to shame and then, I assume crazed with blood lust, killed a Dallas police officer on his way to a Van Heflin movie! All I have to say to you, sir, is get a city map of Dallas. They're available at most any AAA office. From Oswald's boardinghouse to the theater was over two miles. The usher distinctly remembered Oswald purchasing a ticket at 1:04 and yet witnesses put the Tippit slaying at between 12:45 and 1:00. No wonder more and more people are turning to Peter Jennings.

Sydney tucked the letter back into his pocket and continued his quick-walk to work, his pants sliding off his scrawny hips. He made a mental note to fill out a requisition form for a smaller belt, although he feared that even this legitimate request would be greeted by a shower of abuse from his arch-nemesis, Miles McPhearson.

Sydney Corbet was tall and skinny. His arms were thin, little more than buggy whips, and his feet were very tiny indeed, save for the fact that they were always loaded into a clumsy design of orthopedic footwear. The left shoe, sporting a T-bone-thick sole, might have come from the Donna Summer collection. Because his left leg was shorter and rather weak, Sydney's walk had a distinct hitch. His right leg would march forward smoothly, effortlessly, but each left step was accompanied by a forward thrust of his hip as he consciously swung his leg to the side and then forward, before tentatively setting down his orthopedic-shoe-clad left foot onto the sidewalk, as though checking a tub that usually proved too hot.

During the special years of childhood, from about four to twenty, this walk had been the source of endless jokes and laughter from the sandlot pals, so that now, at thirty-one, Sydney had ingrained deep within his mind, wired throughout his entire consciousness, a hypersensitivity to and awareness of his handicap that was a far greater problem than the handicap itself. It was the reason why no woman would ever want him. Why he thought himself most singularly unattractive. Sometimes it made him sad and lonely.

Sydney made his way past one quiet house after another happily chomping away on some Wad Gompers. He walked past one rock garden after another, a patch of succulents here, fifty-foot palm trees reaching gracefully into the particulate-laden skies there. White plastic bleach bottles sat on lawns in their invisible and mysterious anti-dogshit force-field formations. His black, grease-coated orthopedic shoes squeaked on the dry concrete sidewalk. Some sweat beaded on his forehead and he licked his lips once. It was almost hot out.

Money, Sydney thought ruefully. *Money is why I'm walking to the local Jack Anvil's when I should be continuing my research!*

He could hardly believe it. Ever since his release from the Koala Center (a Positivistic Care Facility for the Mildly Neurotic), money had become a driving force in his life. Sydney tried to think about money, to care about it, but he had no interest in it. He wanted nothing to do with money, but his brother, Martin, obviously desperate for the stuff, kept saying how the "real world" completely revolves around it. It was the lubricant of all human interactions, all the things Sydney was used to having: food, shelter, books, paper, pens, stamps. He needed money for all of that now. *It wasn't like that at Koala.*

Sydney remembered back to the Koala Center, the tender care of the greatly esteemed Dr. Jenkins, the rock garden outside the sliding glass door, the mad desert heat that pounded at the windowpane. In Tempe, Arizona, the heat was symphonic. Sydney would almost hold his breath as he made his way across the patio to the computer that sat in the mostly ignored library, other Koala Center guests content to remain in the TV/game room.

He looked at his watch. *Oh, I'm going to be late again!*

miles mcphearson, burger manager

miles mcphearson pulled his fully restored purple 1975 Gremlin into the parking spot he liked to think of as his alone. He shut down the powerful "straight 6" engine, cranked up one of the last fully-operational eight-track tape players in all of Valley, leaned back for a moment and listened to the final bars of BTO's "Takin' Care of Business," rocking his head back and forth to the beat. Miles quickly surveyed the lot, saw no one in sight and then sang the final refrain along with Randy Bachman, while playing air drums with brother Robbie.

The song played on in Miles's head as he unlocked the service entrance door to the Jack Anvil's franchise #7571114. He felt a kinship to the portly Canadian rockers that morning. *We're both underrated*, Miles thought and imagined sharing a beer and some burgers with the Bachman Brothers. He spied the now beloved and industrious Norbert readying the all-important fryer. Cornerstone of the entire Jack Anvil operation.

"Norbert!" Miles came up behind the unaware form. "We're takin' care of business, eh?"

"Huh!?!" Norbert spun around, for a flash of an instant imagining he was about to be bound and gagged by minority robbers looking for quick drug-fix money. The slaughtering of innocents. "Oh! Mr. McPhearson . . . sir. Good morning . . . sir."

"Fryer's looking good, Norbert." McPhearson put on a curious smile and then shot a wink. "How's it goin' . . . 'dude'? Heh-heh." Miles chuckled uncomfortably. "Everything . . . 'cool'? . . . 'chill'? Hch-heh."

"Umm, fine . . . sir." Norbert was now completely confused. You could never figure McPhearson. Usually he was kind of a dick, but every once in a while he'd act all weird and friendly. Kinda catch you off guard.

"How 'bout fetching me a nice cup of Jack Anvil's coffee, son?" Miles asked. "Hope it's not too hot. Heh-heh. Wouldn't wanna haveta sue ya. Heh-heh."

Norbert went to fetch the coffee—one sugar, *two* creams—as Miles entered the women's room and surveyed the small bathroom. It gleamed all shiny and white, porcelain and tile. He threw back a stall door and noted the toilet paper dispenser loaded and ready to roll. Toilet seat down and spotless. That fine scent of pine-fresh disinfectant in the air. Miles McPhearson knew the importance of a clean bathroom. *That lesson wasn't lost on* this *student back in the college days at Hamburger U.* Clean rest rooms and impossibly long and slender french fries were what had *made* Jack Anvil's in Miles's humble opinion.

Miles walked over to the mirror and looked himself in the early morning's eye. He smoothed his thin black mustache, adjusted his paper Jack Anvil's hat, retucked his starched white shirt into his store manager's dark blue slacks (the regulars wore black or brown), checked the shine on his

Jack Anvil's belt buckle and patted the set of keys that hung from his right hip. The ones attached to the retractable cord.

Miles McPhearson had carved something of a niche for himself as a Jack Anvil's manager. Jack Anvil's was something Miles understood, something he'd grown up with. He'd spent many a childhood afternoon at "the Anvil," spent plenty of his paper route money on double cheeseburgers and large fries. He'd eagerly tried the Big Jax on the day of its unveiling, as well as the, in Miles's humble opinion, superior Jax Pounders with cheese, the hockey puck–sized burgers that came by the half dozen, burgers the surgeon general himself had declared a menace to public health.

Miles patted his paunch as he remembered the days of milk shakes and burgers, the big open fields behind the school, and then evil high school and pimples and . . . the hair thing.

Miles took off his paper hat and combed back the few fine wispy hairs that remained on top of his head. He shook the hairs from his comb into the trash and then smoothed his hair back with his palm and shook the hairs out of it, deeply lost in the mirror's reflection.

Miles was entirely convinced that had it not been for the tragically hasty loss of most of the hair on the top of his head the month before graduating from high school, things might have turned out quite differently. Quite differently indeed.

Miles pulled out his wallet and took a peek at the photograph he kept stashed in the depths of the tooled leather wallet he'd bought in Tijuana. It was his graduation picture. The one taken the fall before the hair disaster, the one so expertly touched up to remove the stunning acne that had forever scarred much of Miles's lower cheeks and throat.

Boy, what a looker, huh? Miles smiled. *Ahh, if it hadn't been for the hair thing I bet I might have ended up marrying Betty Jo Zablonsky, Head Cheerleader. Too bad I never asked her out. I was gonna. I wanted to . . . Just never quite got around to it.*

It was the hair. Miles looked back into the mirror. He'd thought about transplants, but the hair doctor said the top of his head was to hair what the Mojave Desert was to plants. That even with a state-of-the-art full-blown $10,000 micro-graft session, the hair at best, *at best,* would always have a singed look to it. Until it finally fell out, that is. It just wasn't worth it.

"Ah, fuck it!" Miles said aloud as he slapped his hat back on and headed out of the bathroom. *Where are all those guys now anyway, huh? Mr. Football Star? Mr. BMOC? Rakestraw's some deadbeat dad livin' in Cajon in a ratty trailer, and Flood? Well . . . shit, he was doin' pretty good what with gettin' into computers when he did, not to mention still, I can't believe, still married to Betty Jo. Fuck 'em! I got Jack Anvil's!* And at that thought he nodded his head and jangled the set of keys on his hip. *Lotta keys. Sign of responsibility. Sign of importance! Let's have that cup of coffee.*

"Norbert!" Miles smiled broadly.

"Here's your coffee . . . uh, sir. One sugar, *two* creams." Norbert said "two" with extra reassurance, McPhearson being somewhat paranoid about his morning coffee.

"Oh, come on, son." Miles grabbed the steaming large. "Mr. McPhearson will do. The bathrooms look tip-top. Ready to . . . 'rock,' heh-heh." Miles did the finger-snap-point-with-squinty-eye-and-chuckle routine that convinced Norbert that McPhearson was a complete idiot loser.

"Yes, the bathrooms look tip-top." Miles rubbed his chin and leaned in for a tentative sip of the coffee, his brow furrowed. Norbert looked up at him with expectant resignation, but as Miles timidly lipped the brew, he seemed pleased, and then took a full sip. "Mmmm. Coffee." Miles smiled and looked straight into what Norbert felt was his very soul, causing the young part-time Jack Anvil's employee to blurt, "Tip-top."

"And how's the front looking, son?"

"I've got Sydney on that detail, Mr. McPhearson."

Miles took the news badly and sipped more coffee for strength. He reached over and put his arm around Norbert's narrow shoulders. "Son, the first rule . . ."

"The first rule is to make sure all french fries exceed Jack Anvil's Corporation minimum standards," Norbert interrupted.

Miles was taken aback by the young man's inadvertent insolence, but wrote it off to youthful exuberance. "Uh, good. That's good. Now the second, the *second* rule of business, do you know what that is?"

"Uh . . . no, sir. I mean Mr. McPhearson."

"Norbert, the second rule of a well-run Jack Anvil's is: A supervisor is only as good as his crew. Remember that." Miles, who this entire time had not released Norbert's shoulders, gave them a firm, manly squeeze and liberated the boy, much to the relief of Norbert, who now rubbed his shoulders as though he were freezing or badly infected with cooties.

"It's like a chain, son." Miles linked his fingers together. "It's called a chain of command and it's only as strong as its weakest link. Do you follow me? Are you digging my . . . 'rap'? Do they call it a 'rap'?"

"Um, okay." Norbert had by now come to terms with the fact that today wasn't going to be classified as a "good" day at work.

"Well, all right then. Now, c'mere." The two employees, now only minutes from opening the doors for a day's business, strolled across the room that for some reason—Miles McPhearson still couldn't understand why—wasn't referred to as a dining room. "Now, look out there and tell me what you see."

Norbert scanned the mostly deserted blacktop in front of the restaurant. It was starting to heat up again after last week's storm, and already the asphalt parking lot was hungrily sucking up the sun's warmth, which it would release late into a night where the stars above were drowned out by the city's light and smog.

A lone figure, Sydney Corbet, Koala Center refugee, JFK Assassination Scholar/Detective, Media Watchdog and now marketing and advertising freelancer, was sweeping furiously in a far corner of the parking lot, having particular difficulty with one of yesterday's dropped burgers that had cooked onto the asphalt, the soft fibers of the broom unable to budge the dried, mudlike patty.

"Now, you see Sydney over there?" Miles asked Norbert.

Norbert sighed deeply, yet discreetly. "Yes! Yessir, Mr. McPhearson, sir!"

"You gotta keep your eye on that man. The weak link? Like we were . . . 'rapping' about?"

"More coffee?" Norbert looked at McPhearson quizzically. He wondered why, now that he'd been accepted to USC, he had to work in this burger hell, but Dad kept bringing up his Peace Corps days like he'd saved the world or something.

"Don't you see? It's called the 'big picture.'" Miles looked up to the heavens and down at Norbert, who was stifling a yawn. *Kids today.* "This could one day be yours. I won't be here forever. The reins will be handed over. The torch will be passed on. Can you . . . 'dig' where I'm . . . 'coming from'?"

Norbert looked at his watch. Twenty-seven minutes down, only 363 to go until he could breathe the fresh smog outside. "You can count on me . . . sir. I mean Mr. McPhearson."

"Well, okay then. Let's get busy. It's almost time to open. Gonna be a busy day. I can feel it. Oh, and tell Sydney I want to see him in the office first thing after he finishes with the parking lot."

marty

in the warm rays of the setting sun, Marty and his
buddy Ellray were sitting at the edge of the loading dock of
the Stromboli Poultry Company, the workday over, each
sipping a bottle of Freeb's Cola-Nated beverage.

"Ya know, there ain't nuthin' like a Freeb's," Ellray said
with true heartfelt conviction.

"Taste of the times. Join the Cola-Nation," Marty said
with a sarcasm lost on the country boy.

"Marty, let's take a ride up into the hills," Ellray suggested.

"What for? It's Thursday." Marty's mind was fussy on
the two latest great tragedies in his life (three if you count
the lack of available-on-demand sex): his gambling debt,
which was beginning to take on TBS-late-night-Italian-
gangster-movie proportions, and life with his special new
roommate, his brother, which was pretty bad.

"So?" Ellray asked.

"What would we do up there?"

"Just take a drive. Get some fresh air." Ellray still liked
to go out to the hills, to the last bits of open space. Marty

had lived in Valley long enough, had drank enough, had gotten old enough, had lived his life always connected enough to the gray concrete of the sidewalk or the black asphalt, to forget there still was an outside left, which was easy to do in Valley. They wanted you to forget.

"Let's get a beer," Marty suggested, as though this were a novel thing.

"Well, sure," Ellray agreed and the two men headed to Marty's home away from home.

As they drove the twenty minutes to Dutchman's, Ellray began a long story about hunting for coons with his greatly beloved bloodhound, Chester.

"Ya know, sometimes I think I miss that dog more'n anythin'. Well, not like I miss Maw, but *you* know. D'ja ever have a dog, Marty?"

"Huh? Naw, I had these pet turtles once. Kept 'em in an aquarium. They had a little pond with a fake palm tree. They kept crawlin' outta the thing while I was in school. I don't know *how* they got out, but I'd come home every day and find them under my bed nearly dried to death."

"Little turtle's not much of a pet."

"Excuse me." Marty looked bitter. He remembered the time he came home and it was too late. The turtles were dried up for good. "I don't know how they climbed out."

Marty rubbed his chin and then felt angry. He was pissed at Ellray for bringing it up. *He ain't such a good buddy. Only reason I hang out with him is, well, the guy has a car.* Marty was one of about two thousand adults in Valley that didn't. He was one of the few carless white men. It was another world, a different caste. It made sex virtually an impossibility. If you didn't have a fucking car by the time your face cleared up, there was something seriously wrong with your whole trip.

Ellray and Marty sat at their usual stools at Dutchman's. Marty was workin' his grip on his bottle of beer a little hard, workin' his grip on his life along with it, suckin' air, thinkin' things weren't lookin' too good. Marty's brain again persevered on The Call and The Debt. In fact, both items now seemed to be permanently seared into his gray matter and apparently looped through his consciousness on a regular basis.

The Call had come in three weeks earlier, just as Marty had given up any hope of Dick Trickle coming back and taking the checkered flag for the Pep Boy's Manny Moe and Jack 500. Especially with the way Dick's car came apart after saying hello to the retaining wall at 187 mph. And so Marty said good-bye to another $250 and could hardly believe how huge The Debt had become, and wondered if now wasn't a good time to move to an entirely new town.

Marty looked up to the final minutes of an NBA game on the TV, his neck cocked back. "Can't you lower that damn TV, Ben? It's killin' my neck!"

"It only seems to bother your neck when you're losing." Ben the Barkeep walked over. "'Nother?"

"Fuck! Come on!" Marty yelled at yet another turnover, and ran his fingers through his jet-black hair. His normally tense, wiry frame tensed some more. Marty had recently reached the blood-sweating level of sports gambling debt. The shitting-bricks stage. The money he was already hopelessly behind on (a sum the mere thought of which could raise the temperature of Marty's entire head) now instantly colored all bets placed with a lung-filling wave of energizing euphoria, splashed across a background of curdling desperation.

The Debt Marty had gotten himself into had lain in his

mind the past few weeks like a shallowly buried corpse that was well on the way to ripening, and Marty simply couldn't avoid getting a little whiff, taking a quick peek now and again.

And at that combination whiff/near-lingering gaze, Marty exhaled quickly and tensely, and drew the glass to his lips. *$3,476.45. Yeah, only with Poplotnick can you get a gambling debt involving pennies. His special bet-now-pay-later-let-me-tack-on-interest-immediately scheme. It's like a fucking credit card company.*

The Debt was fucking up Marty's very luck. He figured it was what was making him lose all the time in the first place. He was on a bad streak. A *real* bad streak. Now, at the very moment his team fell behind, a great wave of tense ill blushed over him. He was just getting deeper and deeper in, and now his brother?

"Ya know," Ellray said as he drained his glass, "I really like yella beer. Doan like that fancy-assed macrow-brewed shit. It's beer, dammit. Am I raht, buddy?"

Ellray wasn't from these parts. He'd up and hopped into his Ford F-150 one fine fall afternoon back in Gobbler's Hollow, where he was from. *Not gonna sit through another Tennessee winter, not with California just sittin' right on out there. You can drive there,* he'd realized one night while settin' a spell with the boys. And so he did. *Left Maw a note so 'in she wouldn't worry and such, stuff about a man havin' ta find his fortune. Left Betty Sue behind. Not sure if'n she was pregnant or not.* Not if you believe what Maw told him months later over the line at that pay phone near Temecula, Ellray's fortune not found, what little he'd had lost in the wasteland of LA. *Even had to perform in a coupla male homo films for that Hungarian freak, couldn't even get hired on to the straight ones.*

Tried. Homos like a country boy better, I guess. Hope nobody ever sees them movies. Haveta deny it was even me. Ol' boys back home pretty much'll kill me if'n they ever seen that shit. Boy!

But Ellray made $500, enough to fix up that Ford and drive as far as the next big town, Valley, where he got a job, then an apartment and then TV and then cable and what more was there? It was okay. And the weather was nice. So he stuck. There's lots of human tumbleweeds like Ellray all over the Southland.

"How 'bout another round, buddy?" Ellray offered.

Marty looked up from the game and shook his head in the sickening realization that he'd lost again. Was another $200 in the hole. "Fuck it! Who cares? Yeah. More beer! Ben, my man, Ben! Beer!"

Marty and Ben had been friends since they were boys, back when chaparral covered most of the canyons and mesas, and Marty and Ben, and sometimes Sydney taggin' along, used to march about the landscape, scaring up tarantulas and jacks, rattlesnakes and the rare roadrunner. But over the years, like the chaparral, Ben had faded away. He became one of those context guys. One of those people who only populate a certain world, a particular address, a distinct set of hours. Marty now only ever seemed to see Ben at the bar. It was like they locked him up after hours, stashed him behind the bar with his Bushmills, or that once the bar was closed Ben ceased to exist. Turned out like the lights.

"Marty." Ben was screwing back the top to his secret stash of Bushmills. He normally didn't sip much while working, but Marty was one of those people that inspired alcoholism. "You should bring your brother in sometime now that he's back."

"What, Sydney? He doesn't drink, Ben."

"He can just hang out. I haven't seen him in years."

"Maybe he could move in with you. Then you could see him all the time."

"So how is he?"

"Crazy?" Marty shrugged. "How the fuck do I know? He just fucking got here, okay?! Now you got me thinkin' about Sydney! I came here specifically *not* to think about all sorts of shit."

"Sorry."

"You need sumpin' packs a li'l more punch, buddy," Ellray said consolingly. "Ben, get ma buddy here a nice shot a some a that Turkey. A *nice* shot."

As Marty brought the glass to his lips and slammed back the shot of smoky sweet, burning bourbon, he was for all intents and purposes back home receiving The Call.

The Call always began with the serious yet gentle voice of Dr. Jenkins, kind and caring director of the Koala Center, a Positivistic Care Facility for the Mildly Neurotic.

"Sydney's being released," The Voice said.

"Released? Why? I mean, is he cured?"

"Well, the money has run out." The Voice lulled.

"Run out?! What about the old man?"

"Your grandfather? He died last week. Didn't you know?"

"He's dead?" Marty's first reaction was a loud cheer from the bleacher section of his brain (which so shocked him with its enthusiasm that he promised himself some tears for dear old Grampa . . . later) followed by an excitable urge to lay lots of money on the upcoming World Championships of Figure Skating. "Dead?"

"Yes, I'm very sorry. I thought you knew, and unfortunately, there was nothing left in the will to provide for your brother's care, and he is, after all, only here on a voluntary basis.''

Marty could hardly believe his luck. *The family Fortune. All that money. I've been practically waiting my entire life. I'm goin' ta Vegas, baby! This is when my luck finally changes.* ''What about me? I mean, what is the, uh, status of our grandfather's estate?''

''Well, he left you with his baseball card collection. I hear they're rather valuable.''

''And . . . ?''

''Well, that's it.''

''That's it?! The guy was worth like over a million. Grampa was rich. He's been strip mining most of Arizona for the last fifty years.''

''Well, Mr. Billings left the bulk of his estate to provide for the flowers and salmon dinner at this year's Arizona Young Republicans Convention,'' Dr. Jenkins said, as though it were a good thing. ''As well as funding the construction of a Jonathan Billings Wing on Biosphere 2 in Oracle. I think they're going to try and grow bananas.''

''What?! Bananas?''

''The will was quite specific.''

''The Biosphere? And I get baseball cards? Are you shitting me?''

''No, I can't say that I am.''

''The Biosphere?''

''Mmm-hmm.''

''What about my brother? Grampa liked Syd. Did *he* get anything?''

''Well, Sydney was given some books, Mr. Corbet's stationery and pens and a one-way ticket to Valley.''

''That's it?! You get more for losing on *Jeopardy*.''

"I wouldn't know; I don't watch much TV."

"Wait a minute." Marty began rubbing his forehead; the new parade of facts had him reeling. "Sydney's coming *here*?!"

"He's being provided with a job. A way to reintroduce him to the outside world. At one of your many fast-food outlets."

"But, I mean, is he cured?"

"Sydney suffers from a mild mixed-type delusional disorder. It's an extremely rare combination of various mental disorders amalgamated in their mildness into a general neurotic field of consciousness that many trained therapists misdiagnose as Ansparger's Syndrome, but which is, really, more closely allied to an internal Tourette's Syndrome."

"Huh?"

"Unfortunately, social skills are a weakness of patients such as Sydney, but it's nothing very serious. He *was* here on a voluntary basis. Let's just say that Sydney will always be . . . eccentric, but then, who isn't?" The Voice began to chuckle quietly in a manner Marty took to be the exact opposite of reassuring.

Let's say nuts. Marty really didn't know what to make of it. He hadn't seen Sydney in years. Had hardly ever visited him out in Tempe, it was so far away. "He's coming *here*?"

"Yes. He likes to watch TV and write letters. Sydney's at his best when he has a pen and paper to . . . keep himself occupied."

"Mmmm," Marty grumbled, still unable to process the rapid turn of events that had transpired over the phone in the last two minutes: *Grampa's dead, I'm goin' to Vegas, baby! I don't get shit. Sydney's coming back. Make sure he has paper . . .* "I don't get *any* money?"

"No."

"You're sure?"

"Positive."

"And my brother's coming?"

"He'll be there on the four-forty-five."

Marty gripped the receiver as though he were trying to get the last bit out of a tube of toothpaste, and in the ensuing silence, in one flashing moment of decisiveness and false enthusiasm, he decided to take in his long-lost brother. He decided to embrace with open arms his brother, Sydney. He decided, as he hung up the phone, that life with his crazy younger brother wouldn't be so bad. He then immediately headed to the corner store for a 1½-pound can of Dinty Moore and a twelver of Rocko's DryIceLite beer.

oasis

at last, another workday done. Sydney labored up the stairs home. And home? Home was now Apartment 17 on the second floor of the dilapidated Oasis Apartments, which he shared with his brother, Martin. The Oasis came complete with algaed swimming pool, laundry room, candy and soda machine and a green and blue neon sign of a palm tree and the name "Oasis" with the O burned out.

Sydney bemoaned his wretched fate living on the second floor as he labored up the stairs, imagining for a frightened moment his desperate attempt at escape during the inevitable fire caused when the chain-smoking, drunken Mrs. Bilge finally fell asleep in apartment 1, with her millionth Marlboro dangling from her mouth, and proceeded to burn the entire place to the ground. *In the panic and confusion, can Martin be relied on to carry out all of my important documents? Probably not.*

He checked the door. It was locked. Sydney smiled and fished out his single key, the one Marty had given him along with a stern lecture about losing it. It was tied to a leather thong with a two-ounce fishing weight on the other end.

Martin was probably getting drunk, Sydney thought happily. Peter Jennings was now only a few minutes away.

At exactly six o'clock, with a satisfying half hour of national network news fresh in his mind, Sydney closed the door to his room, carefully slid the small bolt to secure it and sat down at his desk.

He positioned his chair, loosened his shoulders with a couple of moves he'd surreptitiously learned from the Yoga Channel, cracked open his thirty-two-ounce plastic bottle of Freeb's decaffeinated Cola-Nated beverage and a 'Cono bag of Wad Gompers.

He immediately fired off a letter of concern prompted by a rather disturbing segment he'd seen on the *ABC Evening News*.

Dear Sirs:

As a longtime fan of the fine line of Mrs. Paul's seafood products (I especially enjoy your delectable fishsticks) it is with great resignation and heavy heart that I pick up my trusty Mont Blanc pen. Let me get right to the point: I have just finished watching my usual half hour of national network news, and while the Chicken Little quotient of prime time news is undeniable, I could not dismiss out of hand a rather alarming report that our fine nation's seafood catch is plagued with every known carcinogen ever produced by the people at Dupont. PCBs, dioxin hexchlorobenzenes, aromatic something or others, even DDT, which Peter Jennings and his establishment clan have led the gullible public into believing is no longer in use. My question to you, sirs: Could I receive a printout of the toxin levels found in your typical Mrs. Paul's fishstick? Is there need for concern? Would the clam strips be a more healthful choice? Thank you for your time and concern.

Sincerely,
Sydney Corbet

Next, Sydney fired off a letter he was sure would make piles of money for the Corbet household, not that Sydney cared much for money, a serious scholar like himself being driven by higher ideals, but Marty had hammered home the importance of the stuff the week of Sydney's return, when, after watching a video of *Rain Man,* Marty bitterly complained, "Why can't you be more like Rainman? At least then I could take your ass to Vegas and make some money for us."

"What possible purpose would someone like myself have in Las Vegas?" Sydney had protested.

"Shit, Syd, it's not like your paycheck from Jack Anvil's is exactly covering expenses, huh?"

"Your incessant gambling has obviously affected your mental health. I'm sure Dr. Jenkins might have just the man for you."

"Syd, you're the . . . guy. I mean, shit."

"What are you saying?"

"I just wish you could be like Rainman is all. Make some money for us. Make our life a little easier, you know?"

"Hmmm, well, if it's money you're after, I'll see if I can fit it into my already rather full schedule of research."

"Oh, that'll be great, Syd. I can hardly wait."

Sydney again wielded his trusty Mont Blanc and sent off his latest idea.

Dear Rocko's:
While in no way endorsing your product (in fact, my somewhat tender system precludes any actual consumption of alcohol, though my brother more than makes up for this as he slides head-long into a life of alcoholic oblivion), I have come up with a surefire

method to foist even more of your beverages upon the drunken sports- and sex-crazed masses.

While your scantily clad "Rocko-ettes" and your somewhat inspired "live" footage of debauched "college students" on spring break in Florida (a state that we might all benefit from if it were possible to saw it off and float it out into the mid-Atlantic), extolling the "party-ability" of Rocko's DryIceLite, seem to contain the proper pablum recipe of sloganism and sexual innuendo, I have something that, as they say, cuts right to the chase.

I call it the "Hooker in a Bottle Cap" campaign. Here's how it works: Winners get an all-expenses-paid trip from their nearest airport to one of those somehow state-sanctioned brothels they keep out in the farthest desert reaches of Nevada like the scourge that they are. The winner gets one free act or thing or hour or however it is they classify the activities that take place there. My own academically inclined mind can, thankfully, not even begin to comprehend the utter depravity of such a milieu.

The contest is run along the lines of a lottery. Toss out about eight or ten instant winners throughout the continental United States, add a few mail-ins for an insanely long-shotted non-chance and there you have it! Can you imagine how many alcoholics and sex addicts will be scurrying to their nearest liquor purveyor to buy your beer?! You'll barely be able to produce the swill quickly enough to meet the demand.

For use of this idea, I require only that my name is never associated in any way with the aforementioned contest (like Peter Graves's faceless bosses, I will disavow any knowledge, etc., etc.) and a check for $5,000.

Remember: "Hooker in a Bottle Cap." Thank you for your time and consideration.

Sincerely,
Sydney Corbet

With the money worries of his brother now taken care of, Sydney set about his more important work. He opened the folder marked "Recovery Journal" and put Mont Blanc to paper.

2/9/9–

As per Dr. Jenkins's request, I continue, despite all manner of setbacks and relentless distraction, my most valiant attempt at keeping the daily journal that the good doctor has assured me will prove to be the key to my continued and complete recovery.

While I neither question the proud Dr. Jenkins's qualifications or his prescription, I still cannot see how my job at Jack Anvil's Charbroiled Burgers will have any sort of favorable effect on my recovery. Were it not for my continued trust and confidence in this kind and worthy physician, I would almost suspect my stint at our local burger emporium was some sort of ruse to distract me at the crucial moment when I am beginning to formulate the solution to the most vexing murder of our young nation's entire history. But I shall trust in the good doctor.

My chief problem at work lies with my immediate supervisor. He's a petty tyrant who swaggers about the place in his paper hat and polyester slacks like some sort of a Hamburgerland Adonis. Just the other morning he called me into his office (actually, it was his acne-ridden flunky, Norbert, who was summoned to fetch me). I was in the middle of some rather serious parking lot sweeping and thought it a good opportunity to mention to management that the brooms the Powers That Be at Burger Control provide have little effect on the sun-baked fries and partially eaten burgers dropped by the unfortunate youngsters in the course of the day. Of course, Mr. McPhearson (or "Sir" as he so often enjoys to be called) immediately launched into some vague complaint regarding the quality of my work. He seems hell-bent on some mad personal vendetta against me! I'm sure that all of the innovative suggestions I put in the official suggestion box are passed on to Burger Control as his own. He never misses a chance at pointing out the tiniest slipup I might make, making a good many of them up, I might add. The man is in serious need of psychiatric help. In fact, as he raged on this morning I was good enough to recommend the names of some highly regarded experts. This only seemed to madden him further. I don't understand it. I guess some people just can't be satisfied *or* helped.

The other problem area at work is the utter isolation I feel amidst my coworkers. It goes beyond the usual degree a learned scholar of my qualifications would feel when confronted with a group of GED holders and semi-literates. The fact is that besides the evil tandem of McPhearson and his oily toady, Norbert, every other worker seems to be Hispanic in origin. The kitchen In the height of the lunch rush sounds like a Mexico City bus station. I'm surprised that the Great White Fathers at Jack Anvil's haven't acquiesced with the unveiling of the Jax Taco. Unfortunately, I spent my school years in the tireless study of French and, as such, am unable to converse with these industrious and happy cocoa-skinned workers or, as they explained to me they are called in their homeland, hamburgereros.

There was a knock at the door that startled Sydney. Marty was home. "What is it?"

"Hey, Syd, it's me, I'm home. I got us some dinner. Hungry Mans. Turkey. Four of 'em."

"That sounds fine," Sydney said. "I'd love to chat about it or baseball for that matter, but I'm in the middle of some important work."

"Well, I'm hungry as shit. You want me to put yours in the oven or not?"

"All right, I'll be out in twenty minutes. Perhaps we might watch PBS while dining? Give the sports a rest for a minute, so to speak."

"Yeah, whatever, Syd."

Sydney listened as Marty made his way down the hall. He closed the Recovery folder and opened the one marked "Autobiography." He flexed his fingers in anticipation and picked up the trusty Mont Blanc—*Thank God Martin doesn't know its value, or he'd have pawned it to help pay for his cheap beer-fueled gambling excesses*—and began again on the crucial Page One.

MY LIFE

Sydney pondered the assignment, all the while dreaming of the two Hungry Man turkey dinners that Marty was now placing into an oven Sydney was certain his brother lacked the foresight to preheat.

Sydney thought fondly of the Swanson's Hungry Man Turkey Dinner, soon to have its foil top peeled back, releasing the wondrous aroma, revealing the fine slices of turkey breast, gravy, peas and mashed potatoes, the little dessert saved for last. It dawned on Sydney that Hungry Man Turkey Dinners were nearly the only frozen meal that even approached the quality of the venerated Mrs. Paul's line of frozen seafood delights. That and the ever dependable chicken pot pie.

Perhaps I'll fire off a letter thanking them for a job well done.

Stop thinking about food! Sydney scolded himself. *There remains much work to be done.* He thought about the title—

My Life—as he walked up to the podium to accept his Pulitzer (the Nobel Prize would be a few more years in the making) and decided that, while concise, *My Life* did not possess the necessary weight to carry it down through the ages.

Sydney crumpled up the piece of paper and tossed it into the fifteen-gallon trash can three-quarters filled with crumpled balls of yellow paper, empty Wad Gomper bags and boxes and two-quart bottles of Freeb's decaffeinated Cola-Nated beverage.

Hmm . . .

Ahh! Sydney wrote feverishly:

The Struggle of Genius

Sydney smiled and nodded, taking a long, satisfied drink of the sweet, burning black beverage. *What a title!* Sydney enjoyed the romantic notion of having Scotch or Canadian whiskey by his side as he composed his opus, or even a Balzacian espresso rig for long night bouts of creative frenzy, but his delicate system seemed only able to tolerate sweets and fats. Anything else might throw him right out of kilter and Dr. Jenkins was so far away. Yes, *The Struggle of Genius*. Sydney turned the page and wrote in the top middle of the next page:

Chapter One
Childhood, The Testosterone-Free Years

Sydney wondered why it was that he couldn't remember back to his sweet mother. He opened the top drawer of his desk and pulled out the small dog-eared black and white. There she was, preserved forever, young and smiling, standing at the water's edge, but not at the beach, which Sydney did remember, with Aunt Sally. No, this was a lakeshore with thick woods, her mousy brown hair in her eyes as she smiled broadly into the camera, holding the upstretched arms of a young boy (in actuality, a young Marty, but Sydney had cut out a baby picture of himself and pasted it over Marty's face so that it could be he, Sydney, held so lovingly at water's lapping edge on that grand summer day in which he never took part).

Another knock at the door.

"Yes, what is it?!" Sydney quickly returned the photograph to the drawer and slammed it shut.

"Dinner's ready if you want it."

"All right, is it possible that we might watch something intellectually uplifting while we dine tonight?"

"Syd, you know the game's on. When it's over, huh?"

"All right, I'm coming right out." Sydney shook his head in disappointment. He was almost ready to give up on his sincere attempt at raising his brother's station in life. "The Game." Sydney scoffed. They make it sound like there's only one when, in fact, it's endless. "The Game" goes on forever. One season after another, one sport hot upon the heels of the next. The day he caught Martin watching the NHL draft on ESPN2 had clinched it in Sydney's mind. There was little hope.

Marty and Sydney were all set up and properly positioned in their living room dining seats, both strategically placed eight feet from the sixteen-inch color television. Their TV trays, so often in use that they were never folded up and stowed away, sat locked and loaded: two Hungry Mans each, stacked one atop the other, Jack Anvil's napkins Marty had brazenly stolen in front of the aghast Sydney, Sydney with his thirty-two-ounce Hunchback of Notre Dame SlushyD cup filled with Freeb's, Marty working on the fourth of a twelve-pack of Rocko's DryIceLite.

Click!

"At Jack Anvil's we charbroil our beef at temperatures no strains of e. coli known to science can survive, creating the kind of burger you remember from—"

Click!

"Here at the beautiful resort of Isla Basura off the coast of Costa Rica you'll be pampered to your heart's content, and speaking of the heart, Romance with a capital R is numero uno on the list of attractions at this world-class seaside resort."

"Oh, man . . ." Marty began to drool over the tanned beauties sipping tropical cocktails.

Click!

"*. . . Rocko's. Drink Rocko's. It packs a punch, it's got the gusto. Clean, crisp flavor. The beer with party-ability . . .*"

Click!

"Included in *Thurston Howell's Insider Trading Tips* is a seasonal guide to the commodity futures market filled with dozens of no-brainer tips on when to buy and sell your favorite agricultural products.

" 'I made fifteen hundred dollars on soybeans!'

" 'Well, I was kind of skeptical, but George finally convinced me and we made three thousand dollars in Sulawesian coffee futures.'

"Learn the secrets of Wall Street. And if you order now, Thurston will throw in this yearly exotic-fruit market flow chart portfolio tracking the stock movements of kiwi, cherimoya, guava and many other exotic fruits as far back as World War One!"

Click!

"The female termite lies deep within the colony's nest.

An egg-laying machine, she must be constantly tended by the workers."

Click!

"Hitler's mountain retreat, deep in the Black Forest, was tremendous in scope, and yet, mysteriously, Hitler's own bedroom shared a common wall with the kitchen. He left strict orders that no strudel or kuchen production was to commence until after he had risen. To this day, military historians cannot explain—"

Click!

"... *Freeb's. It's Freeb's.* Taste of the Times. Join the Cola-Nation now! *Get Freeb's. That's Freeb's . . .*"

Click!

"The Miracle Ab machine keeps your body in a perfectly upright, *holy* workout position. It's lightweight and easy to store. Don't be fooled by workout machines manufactured in Third World countries under appalling conditions by idolater-owned corporations that sell for two hundred, even three hundred dollars. The Miracle Ab is made by vegetarian Christians of Reverend Domingo's own flock here in America and it can be yours for only three easy payments of $49.95 plus shipping and handling, and if you act now, we'll throw in the Reverend's famous *Sweatin' with the Lord* workout and prayer video that, used in conjunction with the Miracle Ab, is guaranteed to increase your Faith *and* your fat-burning potential. So call now! And remember, your money is helping in the continuation of KGOD, a holy voice in the media wilderness for over five years. Now back to our workout."

Click!

"Sydney, if you don't stop flippin' around like a fuckin' maniac I'm gonna take that remote from you and we're gonna watch the game."

"I'm merely trying to find some sort of suitable dining viewing. Unlike yourself, I cannot enjoy my turkey dinner while being subjected to shameless sex and gratuitous violence."

"Well, what was wrong with that one show? The nature one. You like those."

"Surely the egg-laying proclivity of the African termite is enough to put a crimp in even *your* gluttony. It was thoroughly repulsive."

"Well then just put on that war documentary. With Hitler. Hitler's always good."

"What is it with you and 'Der Führer' anyway? Need I remind you that we're of French descent?"

"They was all livin' upstate. Our family's friggin' been here for like a hundred years. Oh, wait! Turn it back to that! That's *Club Jailbait!*"

"May I guess? The channel where the underaged girl's derriere filled the screen?" Sydney shook his head in shame.

"Oh, forget it," Marty said disgustedly and thought back to a now-wondrous time when his brother was this person who existed in a far away place. Like the president. Except his brother was never on TV. "Just put it on *something,* huh?"

By now Sydney was engrossed in an Underdog cartoon, methodically shoveling forkfuls into his mouth. First a scoop of stuffing, followed by a stab of turkey, a smearing of gravy, a trip to the mouth and then the ensuing pea-studded load of mashed potatoes.

After dinner, Sydney decided it was time again to gather source material for his newly titled autobiography, *The Struggle of Genius.*

"Now, I'll need an anecdote concerning our dear mother," Sydney stated seriously. "Tell me about the time at the lake again."

"I'm not really in the mood, Syd, huh? I told you about a hundred times already. You know it better than me by now."

"I was too young. You were there. Let me get the photo album to help jog your memory loose from the beer's grip. I'll be right back."

"Syd . . ." Marty sighed and drained #7. He didn't love these moments of family nostalgia, as they huddled around the hearth, which consisted of a Krups portable heater that had the annoying tendency to suddenly break out into a high whine, quickly followed by a blown fuse that plunged the apartment into darkness. Sydney had even written an inspired letter to the manufacturers, but was only able to drum up a $5 rebate coupon for their next Krups purchase. This response, combined with the disturbing association with the infamous arms manufacturer, made Sydney vow to never again purchase another product made by what he called "those goose-stepping makers of minor kitchen appliances."

"Well," Marty began, "I guess you was about two, and the three of us—Mom, me and you—went down to the park where they had that little lake. It was fall. I remember the leaves were changing and some of them had fallen. I had that little boat I wanted to use. A little model powerboat, it had these two batteries. Anyway, Mom had you in the stroller maybe, I don't remember, you were real little."

"Too little to remember," Sydney said sadly.

"Yeah . . ."

"And what was she wearing?"

"You see the picture, Syd. It's always the same." Marty

64

thought back to the days. She seemed so young. Younger than he was now, and it was now, almost thirty years later, that Marty wished he could look out for her. That he hadn't let her down. He took a big swig off his Rocko's. "You were real interested in the swans. You kept wantin' to chase them along the shore. I guess they were geese probably."

"No, they were swans."

"Okay, they were swans. Whatever. I wanted to try out my new boat and we knelt by the water and I flipped the switch and watched that little propeller spin and Mom was telling me something, but I was too excited to listen and I put the boat in the water and let it go and it sailed straight into the middle of the damn lake. Slammed right into one of those damn geese."

"Swans," Sydney corrected.

"Okay, Syd, swans. Slammed right into one of 'em and sank right then and there. Like it was the *Titanic*." Marty let slip a corner smile and slight chuckle.

Sydney was scribbling furiously in his notebook, a big grin on his face. Marty looked at his brother and got thick in his throat for the flash of an instant before he furrowed his brow and reached for his empty can of beer.

miracle mountain

jesús sat in the booth at the gate that guarded the end of the road at the top of Miracle Mountain. He had on his official gatekeeper uniform, which made him look more or less like a Mexican Maytag repairman packin' heat for the Baby Jesus (though the Reverend never let him have any bullets).

Winter was easy for Jesús. There was little yard work in February, no cutting back of the thick, encroaching chaparral that wanted to consume the entire place most of the year. The rains had at last come in their near torrents, big muddy rivers of water cutting deep gullies down the mountain's slopes and into the canyons that snaked toward the mesa where the town sat. Jesús would laugh to himself. Only *los Gabachos* would name a mesa "Valley." Valle, he called it.

"Jesus. How are things today?" The Reverend pulled up to the gate in his Cadillac. The Reverend like to call Jesús "Jesus." It made him feel good to be Jesus' boss.

"Oh," Jesús began his English bluff, "how are you I am fine." He smiled at the Reverend and concluded, "Ease okay."

"Close the gate, son. It's time to start the show." The Reverend pointed to his wristwatch and performed an eyebrow semaphore indicating: Come inside and man the controls. It's time for another episode.

"Ohh . . . thaz fine." Jesús smiled broadly. Jesús had a truly heartfelt smile and he used it whenever he didn't quite understand, which was quite often.

The Reverend managed a smile back and then pulled into the parking spot marked "Reverend Domingo," amid crunching gravel, clouds of dust and the pounding of a *Pat Boone's Greatest Hits* CD. The Reverend turned off the engine and sat in the car for a moment, slowly rubbing his eyes with the heels of his hands.

As the Reverend waited for his cue to begin the program he began to pray. He prayed long and hard to God. He prayed that God would give him courage.

"You're tuned to KGOD, Channel 77 on your cable system. Your All-God, All-the-Time Holy Cable Network broadcasting from high atop Miracle Mountain located right outside Valley, California, God's own suburb. And now, the Reverend Willie Domingo." Jesús switched off the recorded introduction to the show and gave the cue to Reverend Willie Domingo.

"Hello and welcome to another edition of *Sweatin' with the Lord*. I'm Reverend Domingo and I'll be your host today for this program, which celebrates the Lord Jesus in exercise. Now, we all know Jesus is coming back and, as I promised, in the coming weeks I'll be outlining his return. It's sooner than any of us imagined, but first I'd like to talk about the Sweet Lord. I was at my local supermarket buying some fresh vegetables and fruits, bounty provided by our Lord and master, Jesus Christ, and as I waited in the checkout line I noticed one of those magazines, I'm sure you've all seen them. Profane, titillating, showing pictures of wanton women, headlines screaming supernatural blasphemy. Well, this one in particular claimed there's a new monster afoot in our land. A blood-sucking hairy beast, some pet dropped off by aliens centuries ago. A chupacabra they called it. Well, it got me to thinking, all this belief in the supernatural, in aliens coming down to save or enslave us, crop circles, Bigfoots, the Roswell UFO crash sight—it's all part of the Devil's plan to distract us from the sweet love of Jesus. These fairy tales require you to believe in them, that's what gives them life, but God doesn't need such attention. God doesn't need a PR department. God is like physics. God *is* physics. Jesus is gravity. You don't have to believe in gravity, you can be blissfully ignorant, and yet anywhere on this planet if you step off that twelfth-floor ledge, you *will* fall, and after the fall, when you hit the concrete, your body *will be broken*. Whether you believe in gravity or not. And that's what Jesus is like. He doesn't require your belief for his power. He doesn't require your worship for his omnipotence, and let me tell you listeners, we're all on that ledge right now. Our entire society is on a narrow ledge twelve floors up, and all those fairy worshipers, Chupacabra lovers, flesh-crazed infidels, sugar- and meat-deranged sinners—their very existence is yelling at us to jump.

"But worry not—for the Chosen Few, sweet redemption is right around the corner. The End Times are upon us. I have studied the Bible, I have examined the facts. He is coming back, and in the coming episodes I'll pinpoint exactly when! Jesus is coming because the time is nigh. He sees what's happening to our world and let me tell you, He is not very happy.

"Are you having a little trouble leading a pure and holy spiritual life? Well, it's not real likely you're living life as Jesus intended if you're smoking cigarettes and drinking coffee. Craving dainties, lusting for the blood-red flesh of cattle. FOR IT IS WRITTEN!

"Proverbs 23:2 and 3: 'Put a knife to thy throat, if thou be a man given to appetite.' 'Be not desirous of his dainties: for they are deceitful meat.'

"You're not just sacrificing your health in the here and now, but any hope of Heaven. You think they're lighting up in Heaven? It's No Smoking. Think there's an espresso machine or a Starbuck's? Doesn't work that way. Jesus is not going to need a cup of coffee to get going on Judgment Morning. FOR THE SCRIPTURE COMMANDS:

"Acts 15:20: '. . . that they abstain from pollution of idol, and from fornication, and from things strangled and from blood.'

"But go ahead, don't listen to me. Have another burger, another cup of coffee with lots of sugar. Here, have a candy bar. The price? Oh, just the Eternal Peace of Heaven!

"You think Jesus is coming back after nearly two thousand years with a beer belly? You think Jesus gets winded going up a flight of stairs? You think His arteries are clogged with cholesterol? He's not coming back for an angioplasty, He's coming back to save our souls, to vanquish Satan once and for all. How can I put this? The Battle Royale for dominion of all the Earth and our very souls is scheduled. You won't need pay-per-view. It's coming right into your living room within the year!"

The Reverend was glowing with the excitement of his

sermon. Lots of power. There has to be power. Power and fear.

"All right, everybody. It's time to get up. Time to put down that coffee, put down that candy, put down that vile burger, and pick up the Lord. I want you all to climb aboard your StairMaster to Heaven and I want you to turn the adjustment knob all the way up. All the way to Rapture. Forget about all the temptations, forget about all your appetites. Forget the flesh, and the soul will appear. Remember, The Path to Heaven is littered with the weak. Let's start with the Exerciser's Hymn. FOR IT IS WRITTEN!

"Isaiah 10:11, read it with me people: 'Therefore shall the Lord send among his fat ones leanness and under his glory he shall kindle a burning like the burning of a fire.'

"Come on. Gimme twenty minutes. I want it to burn. Burn for Jesus. It's like a heat—God's Love—it's like a fire. A fire burning in your muscles, burning in your bones! Feel it! Hallelujah!"

After the Reverend had driven down Miracle Mountain in his fine Cadillac, Jesús locked the gate, went inside his tiny bungalow and heated up his small can of beans while his pot of rice finished steaming. He made the rice just the way Santa Madre had taught him—the grated tomato and onion, the pinch of oregano and salt, water to the second knuckle— "Fry it slowly, *mijo*," she would say. Jesús crossed himself at the thought.

He could hardly wait for the weather to start warming up. Even Southern California seemed cold to him. Cold compared to Michoacán, compared to Uruapan, his hometown. He thought again of sweet Reyna, the wife he left behind a year earlier when he came to El Norte.

And after that year Jesús still could not understand the Norte Americanos, *Los Gabachos*. Jesús would listen to the broadcast sometimes, to try and receive some of the Lord's sweet comfort, but since Jesús spoke very little English, it was just a bunch of gibberish to him. He certainly didn't understand the Reverend. Padre Ewilly, Jesús called him. *All those funny juice drinks he wants me to share with him. And no meat! Muy estraño, los Gabachos.*

But Jesús did understand that he had it pretty good up there on Miracle Mountain. If he had been brought up in another culture, he might have termed his new existence "chill" even. Jesús had stumbled upon the job on his third day in *los Estados Unidos*, when the Reverend drove up in his gigantic Cadillac and, upon learning that his name was Jesús, hired him on the spot and even offered him a place to stay, atop Miracle Mountain.

Jesús liked his job. Manning both the gate and the sound equipment, tending the grounds on Miracle Mountain, keeping back the brush as much as possible, watering all the funny, thirsty plants the *Gabachos* liked to grow. *They don't believe how dry it is in their land. How hot and dry it gets in the summer.* All summer long Jesús would listen to the sprinklers clattering and hissing in the early morning heat of another hot and dry day.

Jesús finished his simple meal and kneeled before his makeshift altar. He lit his Mexican candles in their waxy paper containers and crossed himself, honoring the dog-eared photograph of his dear mother, Santa Madre. Then he crossed himself before the framed picture of the Virgin Guadalupe and thought for a moment only the pure, sad thoughts of great languishing Love that he felt for sweet Reyna, his wife so far away. It was with such longing and loneliness in his heart that he opened a page to his Bible, the one that could fit in his shirt pocket, the one dear Santa Madre had placed in his hand as he boarded the bus in Morelia.

Galatians 3:4: "Have ye suffered so many things in vain? If it be yet in vain."

And the words brought him some small comfort as he stepped outside to light one of the three contraband cigarettes he allowed himself each and every day. The ones he kept hidden from Padre Ewilly.

It would be up atop the mountain, alone, well after the Reverend had left, looking down at the twinkling lights of the city, watching Valley flicker and blink in the warm summer night air, or in the cold winds that would howl in the winter, that Jesús would wait for the arrival. To see if it would come again.

He'd turn the lights off in his bungalow, leaving the transmitting tower blinking sleepily into the night air the only light on the mountain, light his cigarette and silently wait. For the little beast. For the Chupacabra.

He'd seen a picture of it, in a magazine. That one with the bloody death photos of traffic accidents, flayed corpses lying facedown in dry fields, *brujas* who could curse a man's family for generations, but the beast Jesús saw that day last fall was leaner, more sinewy and longer in the waist— though it was hard to tell. He'd only seen it once, after all, in the dead middle of a hot, still October day. A small, skinny beast, a red flash of its eyes. It had appeared and disappeared behind the brush so quickly that to this day Jesús almost doubted it. Almost. But he was sure he heard it now and then late at night and smelled it outside his window, a scent thick of animal and matches. He was sure it was *el Diablo*'s pet, yet he couldn't help but want to get another look. And not the usual flash, the shadow quickly disappearing. Jesús wanted a photograph, a photograph he would sell to the magazines and get enough money to bring his wife, Reyna, and maybe dearest Santa Madre up to *el Norte*. He knew it was true, that such a beast existed, but he wondered, why would it come to Miracle Mountain, so close to the electronic voice of God? *La Phantasma.*

chaim poplotnick,
hebrew scholar

marty walked up the twenty-three steps to the upstairs office of Chaim Poplotnick, Hebrew Scholar, carrying
a small box. As per instructions, Marty had donned his yarmulke a minimum four blocks away. Actually, it was the
yarmulke that almost pushed Marty toward a life free of
gambling, but Poplotnick would have it no other way. The
only saving grace was that after placing a minimum of $500
in bets (a total Marty Corbet had passed, and lost, a long,
long time ago) Poplotnick even provided a yarmulke he
claimed was sewn by virginal Hudson Valley Jewesses sum-
mering on northern Israeli kibbutzim prior to entering Bran-
deis. Marty liked to picture these girls with long, lean legs,
that soft, downy blond hair on their thighs. He'd had a Jewish girlfriend once. She like to give head, so Marty assumed
this came with the culture, and he wondered where she was
now and how things taken for granted had so long ago evaporated.

Marty opened the door to the office that passed itself off
as a rabbi's. Chaim Poplotnick *had,* in fact, briefly studied
the Talmud, and possessed a passing interest in the religion,

and, at least in Chaim's mind, these facts had evolved over the years into the somewhat bogus truth—yet a truth nonetheless!—of his being a rabbi. But to most people, Chaim Poplotnick was merely the town's bookie and not a rabbi at all. In fact, some people weren't even sure he was Jewish; maybe he was just a guy with a beard.

Behind the desk, as usual, sat Little Johnnie Lydell, the latest in Poplotnick's long line of ever-changing bootlickers and brownnosers. "What can I do for you, sir?"

"Come on, Little, do we have to go through this every time?"

"That's Lie-DELL. Lie-DELL!" Little Johnnie had the demonic look of a crack fiend pasted on his fat face.

"Yeah, whatever. Poplotnick here?"

"Do you have an appointment with the"—Little Johnnie cleared his throat—"uh . . . rabbi?"

"Why don't you give it a rest, Little?"

"Lie-DELL." Little Johnnie Lydell, for reasons only clear to himself and his whatever God, would not give up on his mission to convert all into calling him by his given last name, Lydell, even though since third grade—when it became undeniably obvious that Lydell was very, very little—the pronunciation of his name had been cast in stone for all time, surviving even the fact that the four-foot-ten Lydell had by his twenty-second birthday permanently ballooned to a remarkable two hundred and forty pounds. While this didn't make people stop calling him Little, it did dash his secret desire to become the greatest jockey in history, one day riding the winner at the Greeder's Cup. "Come on, Corbet, let's hear it. You know the routine."

Marty had slipped momentarily into his pounding-Little Johnnie's-fat-face-into-a-bloody-mess reverie, and emerged disappointed in the fact that, despite Little's diminutive stature, his awesome girth precluded any hurling-of-his-body-against-the-wall scenarios. Marty made a sour face. "Is the rabbi in today?"

"Do you have . . . uh, an appointment?" Little Johnnie actually licked his lips and twitched his nose like the Devil's own fat little Easter bunny.

"Yeah, umm, I need help with some . . . shit! What is it? The . . . the thing. *That thing!* The b-baptism!" Marty smiled proudly.

"The what?!"

"No! The beer, the . . . like beer, where you get beer, the bar . . . the bar mitzvah!"

Little Johnnie was trumped. He disgustedly flipped the switch on the static-laden intercom. "Uh, Mr., I mean, Rabbi Poplotnick, I have an, uh, Marty Corbet to see you . . . about an, uh, bar mitzvah." Little Johnnie's voice practically winked over the intercom. The device emitted an unintelligible crackling sound that somehow instructed Lydell to say, "He says go right in."

"Marty, Marty, what a pleasant surprise. I was hoping to see you." Poplotnick sat behind his desk, bits of glazed donut icing glistening in his long, gray beard.

"Uh, yeah," Marty said uncomfortably. "Probably not for long."

"Hmm? Why don't we go inside?"

"Yeah, sure. Inside." Marty answered.

With tremendous sighs and lamentations, the "rabbi"— who on many levels was a sort of human Jaba the Hut, slightly more mobile, but granting no ground in the areas of repulsiveness and greed—got up from his seat and moved aside the life-sized poster of Charlton Heston as Moses on the wall behind the desk, exposing a short stairway that led to the secret back-room gaming headquarters. The room was done up as a cross between a suburban enclosed-patio addition and a second-rate, county-where-prostitution-is-legal casino.

There were two tables off to the side for the Friday and Saturday poker games. And a craps and roulette table for the quarterly casino nights Poplotnick would rig when he was cash strapped. And, of course, there was the pièce de résistance, the center of Chaim Poplotnick's book empire: The Board.

Upon the Board Chaim had scrawled his slightly worse than Vegas odds, and points on various major sporting events held throughout the land, and, in some cases, throughout the world, though Chaim had no taste for the too-obscure Ping Pong or European Cycling.

He had the usual shit—the baseball games and football games, basketball, hockey, whatever was in season—but the most exciting part of Chaim's Board was the daily specials. This was where Chaim's true genius flowered.

There were two types of bets. There were Today's Hot Picks. Long odds on the possible but unlikely: Nomo gets 11 strikeouts, 5–1. Braves win the Series, 4–1. NBA star making more than 2.4 mil a year gets involved this month in a scuffle involving strip joints/nightclubs/or the striking of fans, 15–1.

And then there were the Futures. This was Poplotnick's bread and butter. Specials of long-term proportions. Yesterday: 3–1 odds that the Tigers wouldn't finish in last next season, $100 minimum. To Poplotnick's thinking it was seven months until you had to pay up for those few who won, and odds were that 34 percent of them (Chaim had determined this to within a few percentage points) would lose the betting stub, and as at the laundry, at Chaim's—no betting slip, no payoff.

That morning, as he did each and every morning, Chaim Poplotnick had locked himself into his gaming room, broken out his small laptop hookah and packed into its brass bowl some broken bits of pungent chronic he'd collected from the hapless Cree who simply couldn't stop betting on the Magic.

Chaim loved his hookah and kept it shiny clean. He kept it locked in the big bottom left drawer of his massive desk. *Only goddamned worthwhile thing the stinkin' Arabs ever made,* Chaim thought as angrily as any Zionist. *Well, that and their hashish, not to mention couscous—I think that's Arab. And pastilla. Oh, how I'd love a steaming chicken and almond pastilla the size of a child's lunch box. And some mint tea! Could there be anything sweeter in all the world? I think not,* thought Chaim as he took match to bowl and filled his lungs deeply, reverently.

He held it there in that *supreme* moment of use before the effect that all Jonesers know so well. A savory delight of salvation proved false, but before all that, Chaim took his monster hit and then another for good measure. It was time to get to work. Chaim had all the tools before him: *Sporting News,* racing form, *Valley Times* morning sports page, his computer World Wide Webbed straight into the heart of the matter. Little Johnnie was down at the track, and if he could stay away from the phone sex and hookers for just *one* morning, he might be counted on for some big tips. Inside dope. Always go for the groomers, Chaim thought, and Little Johnnie had even been a jockey back in high school or something, actually gotten on a horse once way back. Though now Chaim laughed at the thought of the kind of horse necessary to bear Lydell. They'd have to use one of those monster beer horses Rocko's wheeled out every holiday, those big white ones whose coats seemed to have yellowed under the smog, blinkered and oatbagged in some sun-beaten back lot.

Also on Chaim's desk sat, to his right, a steaming cup of coffee and his trusty mouse, and to his left, a stack of three raised glazed donuts (one maple, one chocolate and one iced) and a cinnamon roll the size of a Frisbee. The portable phone sat at the ready, Chaim expectantly awaiting the first morning's call from Johnnie, *but, really,* Chaim thought satisfyingly, *it all sat up here.* All up in that amazing numbers-crunching brain of his. *I was the reigning Math Challenge Champion from sixth grade on, for cryin' out loud.*

Chaim reached for the donuts, made a tentative move toward the chocolate and then grabbed the glistening maple-coated delight instead and in two quick chomps removed a good third of the yeast-raised toroid.

In a leap of faith and blood-sugar level, with the fervor of the true believer and the assuredness of Dionne Warwick's pals, Chaim made his first post: Monarchs to win the division, 5–2, $100 minimum. Always play on a fan's loyalty when their team has more hope than skill. Chaim smiled and stroked his gray beard.

"So, do you have good news for me today, Marty?" Poplotnick had sat himself down at a near-replica of the desk in his office and begun twiddling his thumbs as he allowed Marty to squirm for a moment.

"Yeah, well, I don't exactly have the money." Marty was defiant.

Poplotnick began to go through facial contortions rivaling Brando's. "Marty, this is beginning to get serious."

"Yeah, well . . ."

"I'm not a bank," Poplotnick interrupted. His voice took on that air of aggrieved righteousness he'd perfected over time. "You know how it is."

"Yeah, well, I get paid next Thursday and—"

"Let's see . . ." Poplotnick flipped through his desktop calendar. "Looks like that falls on the twenty-second. I'd wager, heh-heh, excuse the pun, that most of that check is going to the landlord. Now, why is it that the landlord gets preference over me? A rabbi!"

Marty tilted his head and began to puff up with air. *Oh, how I'd like to bash in Poplotnick's face. Just grab him by those gigantic ears and smack his face repeatedly onto the desk, steal some money while I'm at it and then go and kick fuckin' Little's ass, pummel him until his nose is mashed and he's cryin' for mercy. Rabbi, my ass.*

Chaim had by now pulled out his famous book. The one that stated who'd bet what, who owed him how much and when he could hope to collect. His ledger domain. He licked his thumb and fluttered through the phone book–sized notebook. "C, C, Cameron, Carruthers—here it is, Corbet. It says here, with interest of course, can't forget the interest, that you now, as of today"—Poplotnick pecked at a calculator with amazing speed—"you owe me . . . $4,136.74."

"Forty-one hundred bucks?! No fucking way!" Marty sprung out of his chair. "It ain't more than three. Three G's, something like that."

"Interest, Marty. Interest."

"What kinda fuckin' interest are we talkin' here?" Marty grabbed a half-eaten glazed raised and hurled it across the room.

"Calm down," Poplotnick said unconvincingly and hit the intercom. "Johnnie, would you come in here please?"

"That's fucking bullshit!" Marty ranted.

"You knew the deal coming in. We have to make *some* sort of arrangement. Surely you knew I would want to collect at some point. I mean, why did you come in today?"

"I wanted to place a bet."

"More bets on credit? I'm a bookie, Marty, not a bank."

"I'm gonna win it back. I can just feel it. And I got some real old baseball cards here, maybe we can work a deal."

"Hmmm . . ." Poplotnick was just curious. That's all. "What'd you have in mind?"

"Well, I was looking at that one with Jason Kidd and the car accident or nightclub fracas."

"Mmmm, you *are* a betting man, Marty. Let's see these cards."

irene peatmos

irene peatmos drove her eight-year-old Japanese tiny car down the freeway after another endless day of work. It wasn't the work itself that was endless so much as the way Mr. Bea could make a single hour seem to drag on forever. The glacial pace at which he comprehended things that sat right before his eyes (and then blasted forth his anger to hide his slowness), the infinite repetitions of the same old stories. She really didn't think she could take another rerun of the Milton Hershey story.

What's the use? Irene nearly cried as the lurching traffic came to its latest complete stop on the packed freeway. *There's not even a good song on the radio,* though lately all Irene seemed to like were the sad ones. The ones about love lost. All the songs were about love lost, either that or love found. *Like that's likely to happen. What am I supposed to do, date Fretwell?*

What was bothering Irene, besides the slow wearing down Mr. Bea was unwittingly performing on her, was that she was deep in the middle of neither love lost nor love found. She was lost in the much more common, tepid pool of love lame.

It was Wednesday, time for the biweekly, midweek visit to her "boyfriend," whom Irene even *thought* of in quotes—nameless, interchangeable, generic. Her feet flopped leadenly up each step to his apartment. Irene stood a good five-foot-ten, but despite her lithe frame and lean limbs, she moved with a clumsy, tentative air. Mostly because her feet were really huge. You might not notice their size in dress shoes or sneakers, but Irene liked to wear clunky sandals, their soles beefy and wood-reinforced (exposing her often garishly painted megatoes to an unsuspecting and unready world). These shoes merely made her already-not-tiny feet appear near gigantic.

She headed to number 317 as though by rote. Out of habit, like some sick swallow returning to Capistrano. A thing she automatically did after every other Wednesday shift and each Saturday or Friday, depending. *I should've just gone home,* she thought as "he" opened the door to the apartment.

After letting Irene in, giving her a perfunctory peck on the cheek and a near silent three hours of TV, the man, a few years older, sank his tired body back into the cool comfort of his bed, pulled the thin blanket over his shoulder, turned away from Irene and began his long-anticipated dreamy slipping away from this realm, with visions of those three chicks in the tiny bikinis in that new Rocko's beer ad dancing through his head. *Where do they find bitches like that?* he wondered. *And why won't I ever get to fuck one? . . . Rocko's, the beer with party-ability. Rocko's. It's Rocko's . . .*

"Guy? Would you . . . Guy!" Irene nudged his shoulder with the pointiest of forefingers.

"Wha?! I was just fallin' asleep. Jeez!"

"No, you weren't."

"What, how do you know if I was fallin' asleep or not?"

"I could tell by your breathing. What were you thinking about?"

Guy released a big, overly dramatic sigh and turned onto his back.

"Were you thinking about me, Guy? Huh?"

"I don't know. I was tryin' to fall asleep, that's all."

"Well, you had to be thinking about something. What was it?"

"I don't know!"

"You were thinking about some other girl I bet, huh?"

As soon as Irene mentioned "other girl" the "Rocko-ettes" appeared again in his mind in the most juicy of rein-carnations: big tits, big hair, big smiles, offering up big glasses of ice-cold beer. *Grab yourself a piece of the Rock. Rocko's packs a punch, it's got the gusto. Clean, crisp flavor. Rocko's the beer with party-ability.* "I was just trying to fall asleep."

"Yeah, right." Irene again shook his shoulder. "Guy?"

"Yes?" His voice was now calm and resigned

"Would you still love me if I were a quadriplegic?"

"What?!"

"Like, say I was in an accident, heaven forbid, knock on wood." Irene knocked on the headboard of the bed, which was actually compressed fiberboard and probably only par-tially covered her bet. "And say, you know, like I couldn't walk anymore and was in a wheelchair."

"Are you fucking serious?"

"Would you still love me? Huh, wouldya?"

"I don't know. I mean, I guess."

"No, you wouldn't. You'd be outta here so fast."

"If you're so sure what I'd do, then why the hell did you ask?"

"I'd stay by you, you know. If *you* were in a wheelchair. I would, you know." Irene was almost crying, and Guy knew there was only one thing left to do, the best he could do: The *next* time they got together, he'd have to get drunk enough to reach the point where he kinda sorta, in the right light, with his eyes squinted, loved Irene and was able to tell her so. Typically, this amounted to between 84 and 120 ounces of Rocko's Draft or two Rocko's ML40 malt liquors. Enough to create a blood alcohol level sufficient to realize that warm, squishy moment where his feelings could slip out of the maximum security prison of his heart and he might, however fleetingly, feel the release of love's abandon.

Meanwhile, Irene lay in that bed, her brow furrowed and her sweet little bowtie mouth screwed up in a late night's lament. Guy had now gone to sleep, lying on his side, his back to her, his body rising and falling with sleep's gentle breath. She watched him as he slept in the dim light that filtered through the blinds from the street below. It had been a long time since Irene had watched him as he slept and felt good, excited and warm. There was a time when her entire being would flood, her skin almost tingling. A time when she could hardly wipe a smile from her face. It's only love, but it's so hard . . .

That was hardly ever the case anymore, and tonight Irene missed again the troubling wonderment of new love, missed the excitement of nights spent in a bed new and wonderful, telling her friends about the *new guy,* disappearing from their lives for a bit as she dove in without hesitation. A thing to have. Finally complete.

Irene missed those fresh, lively days that slid deliciously

into the comfortable favorite clothes period (she was now deep into the mental slide show of her two-year "vacation" with Guy), the bags of groceries carried into the kitchen and plopped on the Formica counter, cookin' dinner and watchin' movies at his apartment, goin' out for a drink, the county fair with that big momma pig and the squealing-bloody-murder piglets all shrieks and corkscrew tails. The days when his room was their little love nest, snug from the rest of the world. It was summer.

Irene was now back in the room, intensely aware of her presence lying in the bed. Her eyes wandered around the room in a quick breather from her yawning midnight brain-work. She could make out all the familiar shapes in his room. That pile of laundry, how many days—weeks?!—had it been lying there?

She listened to the world outside, the occasional car whooshing by, the crickets that'd been creaking all night, but was drawn back into her reverie like a person fighting the anesthesiologist's art. She missed now even the routine days, when seeing him was like going to work every day and always the same, when it became like some married couple. It was almost like a married couple. But they weren't. There was no ring, no home and no dreams for a future together. *Everything's just taken for granted. Like life. It's too fucking much like life.*

Irene watched Guy as he slept and she filled with a . . . *a loathing. Yes,* she nodded, *a loathing. I just can't stand him anymore. In a nutshell, he's bringing me down.* Any good feelings, anything positive she might have once felt in her heart, had been transformed into loathing. It was Love's Anti-Alchemist Trick. Gold into lead.

What's the use? she thought. She ran her hands along the

length of her body, which at thirty-two was still ripe and desirable. *I'm not so bad. There'd be plenty of guys who'd appreciate a woman like me. Ahh, I'm not getting any younger and look at the fish in my pond. There's that Mexican forklift guy, but his breath! And that paunch. Great. How 'bout Guy's friend, Danny?* Irene was secretly kinda hot for Danny. *I'd show that Midwest boy a good California girl fuck,* she thought and nodded, *but, I don't know, there's something funny about him. I think he's gay.* She remembered when she asked Guy about it and he got all bent outta shape, like if Danny *was* gay that meant that the two of them had secret side-bys and circle jerkings or naked ass snappings with wet towels in the imagined locker room of things male that Irene had in her head. Shit.

Irene could hardly take it anymore. Her eyes welled up again with tears at the thought, and then she swallowed once and it made her sick and lost. Then strong.

post office

sydney headed to the post office on his way home after work to peer with great anticipation into the long, narrow Box 10014 and see how the world was responding to his letters, protests, ideas, suggestions and contest entries. There were many people to be heard from: Campbell's regarding the fish stick toxin levels, his ongoing dispute with Pea Soup Bergeson's, who still refused to make amends for the desperate morning when Marty was unable to order pea soup for his breakfast. How could a place with pea soup in their very name be out of pea soup? Sydney had demanded to know. They had passed a wall full of the canned stuff on the way in! And still, all he had to show for his efforts was two coupons and an unsigned form letter of apology.

But most importantly Sydney was hoping to receive either Rocko's response to his "Hooker in a Bottle Cap" campaign, or from Bea's Candies. *The Chocolate Jesus . . . for Easter.* Sydney smiled, his brother's money worries could well be solved that very afternoon.

Sydney leaned with anticipation toward the small glass window and peered inside. *Nothing!? This cannot be!* He marched over to the dispenser and took a number. About forty minutes later, just before nodding off in the strange atmosphere of the Valley Post Office, he was granted the privilege of walking up to the window.

"I would like to lodge a complaint regarding tampering with the United States mail," Sydney announced in a loud voice.

"What?! Mail tampering?! Who's been tampering with the mail?" exclaimed the thin, wrinkly woman seated behind the fully enclosed *Andromeda Strain* security level plastic bulletproof window/walled fortress with tiny money/stamp/letter slots and full-lockdown, spin-around package receiver/dispenser.

"Surely *I* don't know. *You're* the mailman!" Sydney protested.

"Well, how do you know the mail's been tampered with?"

"First of all, I haven't received a single letter this week and it's already Thursday!"

"How do you know anyone's written you? Are you expecting something?" the sun-shriveled woman countered, ticking off the minutes until her next cigarette break. *Damn! These Nico-patches just don't have any kick.*

"I assure you, madam, I'm not waiting at home for an occasional letter from a long-lost grandparent, or correspondence from a lonely prisoner in a maximum security prison. I'm an esteemed scholar who conducts very important research and I rely on the security of properly delivered mail."

"How about a form? You can fill out a form with a specific complaint. Would you like a form?"

"I don't want a form. I don't need a form. I'm telling you directly."

"There are people waiting, sir. How about a nice form to fill out?"

A sizable crowd had formed behind Sydney. As per government instructions, after a sufficient number of people had entered the building, a silent alarm had gone off instructing all but the most sluggish and belligerent clerks to close their windows for a break until business slowed down again. Luckily, a chair had been found for the little old lady whose cane was no longer enough to keep her upright during the endless wait.

"I would like to speak to your supervisor!" Sydney demanded.

"She's on break."

"Hey, come on, buddy, I ain't got all day here!" a man yelled angrily from the line.

"Is there anything *else* I can help you with?" the clerk asked with an insincerely helpful tone.

"Just your full name and badge number should suffice," Sydney said. "After I speak with the postmaster general, I'm certain that if the mail ever *does* arrive, your termination papers will be included in the day's post. Good day."

scrimshaw

orville scrimshaw was sitting at his desk in Letters, the near-forgotten department that sat toward the end of the long hall in Building #2, just past the thirty-fourth of sixty-two portraits of Mrs. Bea, tributes to the revered icon and founder of Bea's Candies, that hung in various places throughout the factory.

Scrimshaw was in the middle of sorting through the regular mail, which consisted of just three letters, having once again been thwarted in his attempt at gaining access to the IBM computer, Bea's Candies Web Page and e-mail. "The PC," Scrimshaw might be heard muttering in his office if anyone ever made their way over to that end of the factory. "One big electronic glitch if you ask me. E-mail. Fax."

Oh, how the fax made Scrimshaw pine for the days when the words Western Union *meant* something! How that computer made him think longingly back to his Remington manual typewriter. The day Mr. Bea had burst into Scrimshaw's office and yelled, "Can you man a mouse?" had been a black day indeed.

Scrimshaw hadn't been dragged into the Information Society kicking and screaming so much as he'd been slowly and inexorably pushed in that general direction over the past few decades, through forces similar to those governing plate tectonics.

Scrimshaw had worked in Letters since before there were computers. In fact, he had been there from the start. From before the start. No one knew it anymore. Anyone from back in that day was long dead or packed away in a rest home or carefully trimmed trailer park placed amid rock gardens of white, gray and black. Only two people still remembered that it was Scrimshaw who had once owned the candy factory that had become Bea's so long ago.

He was Fezziwig on the details, but after the sale, Mrs. Bea hired him on as a consultant, later paid him as an accountant and finally moved him to Letters, since no one ever wrote anymore and Scrimshaw was tired of working anyway. He felt he'd earned his soon-to-be pension and $320-a-week paycheck.

Mr. Bea walked in looking for . . . something.

"What have you found today?" Mr. Bea asked, rubbing his hands together excitedly. "Any good ideas come in on our web page today?"

"What? Are you *saying* something?" Scrimshaw looked up from his pile of letters. "Do you *have* to speak so quietly?" He began fumbling with the complicated control panel of the Sony Walkman–sized device that operated his gigantic hearing aids, as though he were dialing in a distant radio station.

"The web page!"

"Oh, *that.* Well, I did finally get the thing to turn on and there were a hundred some messages and then—that damned contraption—I got locked out again," Scrimshaw complained

"Locked out?!" Mr. Bea could hardly stand it. "There are no LOCKS. You don't need keys for a computer! You don't *need* them!"

"Well, it's about time," Scrimshaw answered. "Can I fire up the telegraph again, sir?"

"What?! Hell no! Is that thing still here?!"

"Wait. I'm losing you. Hold on one dolgarn minute." Scrimshaw began some very delicate twisting of the volume, bass and balance knobs of his hearing aid. Mr. Bea simply didn't have the time—he never had the time—and so he grabbed one of the large devices wrapped around Scrimshaw's ear, held it to his mouth like a microphone and screamed, "FORGET IT!"

"All right, all right. You don't have to yell. It's not like I'm deaf!" Scrimshaw winced painfully.

A few hours later, a bit after five, after everyone had gone home, Scrimshaw closed his book and got up from his chair. He carefully locked the door to his office and took a bite out of the single raspberry-cream dark chocolate confection he allowed himself each and every night upon closing.

Tonight he turned left and was soon sitting in the darkened room back at the *end* of the hall, sitting beside the large four-poster bed that dwarfed the napping Mrs. Bea. Scrimshaw gazed at her thin form under the light white cotton sheet that veiled her still body.

Scrimshaw had removed his hearing aids and was wiping clear the thick lenses of his glasses with a cloth handkerchief, the monogram *HB* embroidered in delicate red letters in one corner. He had something he thought Mrs. Bea might be interested in and decided to help himself to the oxygen tank while he waited.

Mrs. Bea made small noises as she roamed the atmosphere just beneath wakefulness, myriad surreal images of a life and time gone by montaging past her soon-to-be-wiped-clean dream consciousness. Her bony hand twitched and so did her fine feet under the thin white sheet.

She had such fine feet and hands, and a well-turned ankle back in her day, and that day Scrimshaw now admired as he sat silently in the chair. It was 1949 and the war had been won, Bea's fortune made. The year she bought the factory. Scrimshaw could see and hear. He was young. He could get up out of a chair without preparation. He looked upon an attractive women with the eagerness a man should. That woman was Helen.

"Wilbur? That's not you . . ."

"Helen . . . ," Scrimshaw said in a quiet, beautiful voice that no one else ever heard, the crotchety old-man rawness smoothed away.

"Orville?"

"Mmmm," he agreed.

"How nice."

"Can I get you anything?"

"A cigarette would be good. Would you?" Mrs. Bea near whispered in a soft falsetto without her contraption.

They were smoking cigarettes together, sipping on Lime Rickeys in the soft, filtered, singularly golden and doomed sunlight peculiar to Southern California. The two of them sat silently, thinking of the good times, small smiles creeping onto both their faces as Orville stroked her hand.

"I received a very interesting letter today," Orville said, smiling.

"Mmm? Read it to me, would you, Orville?"

Scrimshaw let go her hand, pulled the letter from his breast pocket and adjusted his glasses.

Dear Venerable Candy Makers:

It has recently come to my attention (from no less an authority than Bernard Shaw of CNN) that your company has fallen on somewhat hard times. I am not only a lifelong fan of your great butter creams (your famous Wad Gomper is the greatest candy ever devised in modern times, by the way) but also freelance in the areas of product development and marketing. I currently have proposals under consideration by the Rocko's Brewing Company among others.

Let me get to the point. I have a candy bar design that I think will put your company right back on top. The Chocolate Jesus. For Easter. Can you think of two more beloved things? Brought together for the first time. Everyone loves Jesus. Everyone loves chocolate. What a combo! It can be marketed for Easter, Christmas, even Halloween for parents not comfortable with the overt Satanic imagery found in other candies (I refer, of course, to the candy corn).

For use of this idea I require a check for $5,000.

I anxiously await your reply,

Sydney Corbet
Respected Scholar

"What do you think of that?" Orville chuckled as he folded the letter and put it back in its envelope.

"Mmm, yes." Mrs. Bea nodded. "This could be fun. Put it into a new envelope and address it directly to Wilbur."

"To Wilbur?"

"Yes. I want this to cross his desk *first*." A devilish smile grew out of the corner of the candy icon's mouth. "You wouldn't deny an old woman her fun, would you, Orville? Besides, seeing that sickly look on his face when I make him kiss me is getting a little old. I need a new game."

Orville was quite pleased by the possibilities. "Another Lime Rickey?"

"Why not? I can feel the life surging in my veins. Ring 'em up and let's go to the garden," Mrs. Bea ordered.

fryer detail

sydney walked from the bus stop to Jack Anvil's, his mind filled with, for no apparent reason, the theme song to *Underdog*. It wasn't even the entire song, only a single verse concerning lightning, thunder and the endless repetition of the name Underdog. Sydney often had problems with things looping constantly in his brain to a degree where he had a far better grasp of the term "ad nauseum" than most. Dr. Jenkins told him that he suffered from a rare form of *silent* Tourette's syndrome, but that he should consider himself lucky because he would never suffer the shame nor have to brave the threats as did the unfortunates who helplessly yell out "Let's fuck!" to the biker dude's girl or "Tool rules!" at a Yanni concert.

Yet still, this was small comfort after the twenty-seventh verse of *Speed of lightning*. So Sydney tried to get at the root of the song, the source. Get to the source, Sydney, Dr. Jenkins would always say. Sydney always rooted for the underdog and his work as Media Watchdog and Kennedy Assassination Scholar made him a fighter of those that robbed and plundered.

The speed of lightning would have to be viewed meta-phorically, Sydney decided as he stepped into the back en-trance of Jack Anvil's. *Shoeshine boy!* Sydney recalled. *Underdog's cover. Clark Kent. Bruce Wayne. Sydney Corbet, Jack Anvil's part-time employee . . . or so it seemed, but in the dark of night? The man who cracked the Kennedy Assassination.*

Sydney was quite completely pleased as he placed his paper hat on his head and straightened his Big Jack buckle and then wondered whether Oliver Stone would honor him with a film biography or shun him out of jealousy for having solved the crime of the century. *Only time will tell. Only time will tell.*

"Now, you must remember, Jack Anvil's is famous for our french fries. Are you listening?" Norbert asked Sydney. The usually disgruntled and listless Norbert always sprang to life whenever he was in any sort of supervisory role. "No one, and I mean *no one* makes french fries like the 'Big J.'"

"Norbert!" It was McPhearson slipping unseen from be-hind like he did a lot. "How many times have I told you not to refer to Jack Anvil's as the 'Big J'?"

"Sorry, Mr. McPhearson. Sir." Norbert readjusted his glasses and tightened the strap on the back of his neck. He was never without his eyeglass neck mount with nonslip rubber grippers, since the day when McPhearson was show-ing him the very important fryer ropes and his glasses slid off his oil- and steam-covered face straight into the deep fryer, melting over a fresh batch of Cowboy Fries. They had to shut the entire machine down and call in a special Jack Anvil's oil changing/delivery/repair team (known among management as the Char Crew and among the Latinos as

"Los Babosos") well-versed in the latest deep- and hot-oil frying procedures. The day was a complete disaster. The normally docile and overweight Jack Anvil's crowd, deprived of their potatoes, nearly erupted into a riot upon word of the eighty-sixing of the apparently *very* cherished Cowboy Fries. McPhearson was only able to defuse the tense situation with a free round of Apache Shakes. It had taken Norbert the entire winter to work off all the demerits McPhearson had tacked on.

Sydney looked carefully into the deep fryer as Norbert said something *he* seemed to think important about some of the various knobs.

"Now, you have to make sure the fries match up against the Jack Anvil official templates. Fries must always, and I mean always, exceed minimum corporation lengths. Do you got that?"

Sydney looked at him blankly, wondering, *Why has no one looked into Tippit? Officer Tippit was supposed to arrest Oswald. Of course! That's why he was in the neighborhood. Met with the two men from the grassy knoll. Tippit was in on the conspiracy. Of course! He got cold feet right at the end and they had to shut him up.*

"And whatever you do," Norbert continued, "don't leave the delphan knob on override if the timer's got less than twelve on it. Unless you want McPhearson calling in the Char Crew again, and believe me, you don't want that."

And they even pin Tippit's murder on Oswald. That's it! Sydney peered into the roiling 375-degree oil and then up at Norbert and had a sudden panic. *Delphan? Timer 12? Char Crew . . . ? What if the fry station results in a case of acne along the lines of the one Norbert's sporting today? That one in particular. That big one. In the center of his forehead. It looks like a candy corn has been embedded in the poor lad's skull by wind forces found only on Neptune, leaving just the white tip visible.*

"What are you looking at?" Norbert asked. "Are you even listening? The fry station is serious business. Frying is the cornerstone of Jack Anvil's. McPhearson'll have you back out in that parking lot if you can't cut it."

click!

"**the reverend domingo's team** of crack Christian Biblical Researchers are working round the clock to get you the most accurate dates for all of the exciting End Times Events. In this exciting new video are included specific times and windows of opportunity for all of the following:

The Rapture

The Tribulation

The long awaited second advent of Jesus Christ himself!

All the information you'll need regarding Armageddon. And that's not all. Call now and the Reverend will include, at absolutely no extra charge, details of the coming Millennium for the Chosen Few. And now, back to the program."

"Hello, viewers and fellow Vegans for Christ. Along with this evening's workout I'd like to read some passages from the Bible and take a few calls. Now, we all know that Jesus is coming. My calculations put his return sometime between Labor Day and Yom Kippur. The *real* question is, Are you ready to face Jesus? Can you look him in the eye when He returns? Now many people have come out against me for predicting the return of Christ. Mostly sinners who aren't very comfortable with the Tribulation, with Damnation. They don't want to face the facts. They want to make you forget. That's their plan, to make you forget and turn away from our Savior. With their tawdry sex, their wanton temptresses, they spoon feed you their alcohols, their tobaccos, their hamburgers and candies. Why do most people act like machines? Because they've lost touch, lost touch with their souls, with their bodies, with Jesus Christ. They wallow, godless, souls asleep, in the blue glow of their televisions, having fallen prey to acts vile and sordid, drunk on their greed lust, controlled by the vast invisible machinery of Satan. FOR IT IS WRITTEN!

"Proverbs 19:15: 'Slothfulness casteth into a deep sleep; and an idle soul shall suffer hunger.'

"Hungry, hungry for all of Satan's little dainties. Now, some people ask, they say, 'Hey, Reverend Domingo, how do you know Jesus wants us to be fit, to abstain from candies and meat?' Well, it's all in the Bible, I tell them. Read the good book. FOR IT IS WRITTEN!

"Ezekiel 44:31: 'The priest shall not eat of anything that is dead of itself or torn whether it be fowl or beast.'

"Seems clear to me. Need some more?

"Ezekiel 47:12, speaking of the river flowing from the temple: ' . . . upon the bank thereof, on this side and on that side, shall grow all the trees for meat . . . the fruit thereof shall be for meat.'

"See, Jesus is looking out for us. He knows that meat is bad, packed with antibiotics and hormones, making us fat and listless. Jesus wants us to eat nuts and fruits, things from those trees growing alongside the river flowing out of God's temple back there.

"Now, I know it's hard. The temptations offered by Satan seem sweet indeed, but God is testing our faith and the time is nigh. Let's not fail Jesus now. Not now when he needs all the help he can get to vanquish Satan once and for all. FOR IT IS WRITTEN!

"Revelations 22:2-3: '. . . bound Satan for a thousand years, and cast him into the bottomless pit and shut him up!'

"And it's going to take some strong Christians when Armageddon comes, to bound Satan and throw him in that bottomless pit. And not just strong of spirit, but strong of back. Well, why don't we take some callers before we start on the lats?"

C: Hi, Reverend. Love your show, well, I guess you might call me a backslidden Christian. I've been having trouble with Christianity, well, all the rules mostly, and I just can't seem to quit the burgers or the beer!

R: Numbers 21:16: "And from thence they went to Beer, that is the well whereof the Lord spake upon Moses, Gather the people together, and I will give them water." Don't you see?

C: Uhh . . .

R: It's a parable. A parable for nonalcoholic beer. Nonalcoholic beer is a very healthful exercise beverage, but do they ever advertise that on the TV? No! They have instead promiscuous harlots, scantily clad, offering Rocko's, tempting you with Satanic alcoholic malt abominations, teasing you away from the cradle of Christ . . . but thanks for calling and let's take our next caller. Hello and welcome to the show.

C: Repent, Reverend Domingo. Repent before it is too

late. For it is written! No man can know the hour or the season . . .

R: Yes, and thanks for calling. Let's take one more call.

C: Hello?

R: Yes, how can I help you?

C: Reverend Domingo?

R: Yes.

C: Oh, well, I'm just a guy who works at a Wal-Mart . . .

R: The Good Lord honors all work, my friend.

C: Um, I just called to tell you after listening to your show that I've not only been saved, but I've lost fifteen pounds and have a lot more energy. I've taken the vegetarian Jesus into my heart and I'm just one happy boy.

R: Why, I am so happy for you. Thank you for calling and may you continue to work out with Jesus. Now, let's work on those lats.

my blood pressure?!

marly was clutching a can of beer in one hand and the telephone receiver with the other, listening to some of the latest at Chaim's.

L: We got some pretty tasty stuff on the board today.
M: Oh yeah?
L: Oh yeah. Cricket Championships from London.
M: Cricket?! Fuck that!
L: Okay, Weekly Special?
M: What's 'e got?
L: How 'bout Tiger Woods whines to the media in the next two weeks?
M: What's Poplotnick callin' whinin'?
L: Anything where he's miffed about something or feels he's not treated fairly.
M: Nah.
L: Shit, there's a tournament coming up. I'd take that, Corbet. He'll be cryin' like a baby before the week's out.
M: What else ya got?

L: Figure skating.

M: Championships?

L: We ain't talkin' NC2A Division 2 shit.

M: Who do ya got?

L: How 'bout Kwan?

M: What's the odds?

L: Seven to five.

M: Seven to five?! I can't make any money on that.

L: Whaddaya want? She's defending champ, Corbet.

M: Mmm, put me down for five.

L: Five hundy?

M: No, five cents. What do *you* think?

L: You're gonna have to grovel to Poplotnick for that kinda dough. He's not feeling real generous on credit for you. You're in deep, buddy. Deep.

M: Is that right, Little?

L: That's Lie-DELL! You want a hot tip, Corbet? I'd start watchin' my back if I was you.

M: Yeah, well you're not.

While Marty continued with the frantic ditch-digging period of his life, Sydney was busy again taking pen to paper. He began with a quick entry into his journal.

3/06/9—

I am not sure how much longer I can hold out at Jack Anvil's. I stand on the verge of vegetarianism as a result of having to deal with pork and beef products for thirty hours a week. Just yesterday a senior citizen found what I believe might have been a hoof fragment in her burger. And then today the ominous sight of a gigantic semi bearing Baja California plates pulling into the lot filled with the week's pork, potato, beef and nondairy shake emulsificants.

La Frontera! It was manned by two men, whom I took to be Brazilians, obviously shipping rain-forest-eradicating sub-grade beef from the Amazon. That televised image of the deranged English bovine in the final throws of Mad Cow Disease does not comfort me in any way. I'm certainly not willing to be left holding the broom so to speak at Ground Zero of a Continental United States outbreak. One can only hope that they'll send someone taller than Dustin Hoffman to investigate.

On the home front, it turns out my brother, Martin, suffers from a dangerous gambling addiction. The dilemma is compounded by the fact that he's completely allergic to the placing of a winning bet. In the six weeks since my return I have only seen him gloat once over a winner. When some basketball hooligan was arrested for putting a full court press on some stripper's bottom. It's become so desperate that all his beer cans bear the crumpled marks of a man who's been clutching them with a death grip for twenty minutes as the Lakers once again fail to make the spread.

Sydney shook his head in disgust, closed the journal, took a sip of Freeb's and popped two Wad Gompers. With that out of the way, he started in on his "Health" folder.

Today I received the most troubling news from the blood pressure machine at our local pharmacy. It seems that since my release from the Koala Center this public device has become my "doctor" so to speak. Burger Management has decided that the obscene profits they realize from the tons of ground beef products they sell are somehow insufficient to afford the toiling workers any sort of health plan, let alone a retirement program. Why, just this week I inquired as to the existence of a 401(k) plan and was greeted with McPhearson's usual brow knitting followed by a shower of scornful laughter. If only I could speak Spanish, perhaps

I might be able to organize a general strike and alert the media and public-at-large to the pre–New Deal conditions we work under. Sadly, perhaps there is no time for this or the many other projects I have upon my desk at this very moment. I am afraid that my time in this world is short, indeed. Oh, cursed mortal coil!

I stopped in at the pharmacy on my way home from work to check on my vital signs as well as talk medicine with the pharmacist. He seemed a bit put off when I inquired as to his opinion on the ever-loosening FDA restrictions on once-prescription drugs, barking out a "You got a prescription to fill or not?!" I believe he knows his pill-counting days may be numbered and the strain is beginning to take its toll on the poor white-haired near doctor.

It was then that I decided to take my seat at the blood pressure machine. Imagine my shock when the appropriately red-colored numbers flashed a near death sentence: 147/97! Of course my immediate conclusion was that the machine was malfunctioning, that possibly it wasn't being regularly serviced. Perhaps the poor pharmacist, faced with career extinction, had let upkeep slide. I decided to try it again as soon as an overly belligerent for her size and age, grandmotherly woman was finally done with it. She was unimpressed when I informed her that I was in a bit of a hurry, and actually became upset when I asked if she shouldn't be back home baking cookies or updating her brandied fruit. She glared at me not once, but twice, before she slowly headed off in the general direction of the laxative aisle. I sat down and saw there was no denying. The fault lay not in the machine, Horatio. The tiny old woman's score read: 128/84. This woman was old enough to have breast-fed Joe DiMaggio, the Yankee Clipper!

"Syd, we're not gettin' a blood pressure machine," Marty calmly explained as he took another huge bite out of the XL Leaning Tower Pizza topped with every known version and form of pork products, both cured and noncured, allowed by the FDA.

"You don't seem to grasp the enormity of the problem," Sydney insisted. "We've reached the Crisis Point here. How can I explain it so you might comprehend? It's the Two Minute Warning. The game is on the line. Time is running out." Sydney looked at his brother imploringly.

Marty drained some more Rocko's and gave his brother the Jack Benny . . . "Your blood pressure's fine. You're not fat, you're not old . . ."

"What did Mother die of?" Sydney asked.

Marty froze for a flash the instant he heard the question. His breath stopped, then he blinked twice and drew a shallow breath. "Not blood pressure. She was too young for that."

"I simply must have further information." Sydney was again hot on the trail of his autobiography. "Wait here. Perhaps you might have some more of your beer. Make yourself comfortable. I'm going to get my paper and pen, uh, pencil."

Sydney ran to his room and Marty sat there, clutching his can of beer, staring at the space his brother had vacated. *My life is the biggest piece of shit in the entire fucking miserable world. I just wanna be left alone. That's all. Just everybody leave me the fuck alone already.* Marty often felt like this. Almost all the time in fact. Except maybe with men while watching sports, or better yet sitting in a bar watching sports. With women he, in a way, always wanted to be left alone. Women kinda freaked Marty out. He didn't know what to make of them unless they were well on their way down the Road to Sex. You might say Marty was always ill at ease with any woman if either of them was standing up.

Marty tried to imagine having a wife instead of an insane brother. Not in the sense of Love or Romance, but more as an accessory, a sort of home improvement. In this line of thinking, he imagined this wife as a mail-order bride of sorts. From the Third World or, better yet, Eastern Europe. The kind of a woman for whom a roof over her head, plenty of food, nice supermarkets without all those post-Fall-of-the-Soviet-Union lines would constitute a veritable paradise. Marty could continue in the behavior that had already soured all the women in North America. *That'd be all right. Beat the hell out of waiting to get your arm broken living with your nut brother. Thank God the folks are gone. Can't move back with them at least. Come on, Kwan. COME ON!*

the two dudes

"**uh, yeah, uh, like,** I'd like a Jax Burger with cheese and, uh, like a Geronimo Egg'wich with Buffalo Bill Bacon, dude."

Norbert surveyed the two cretins swathed in thick stocking caps even though the thermometer was already inching toward the eighty-degree mark and thought to himself, *Just wait. One day guys like this will be doing my lawn or cleaning my pool. Wait until then, boy.* Norbert knew that Jack Anvil's Charbroiler was just a dues-paying section of his long and soon-to-be-respected life. That a career, esteemed and high paying, was on the way, and then, even, one day, a woman. Norbert would get to have sex, and he smiled at that thought and wondered what it would be like. "We stop selling Indian breakfasts at eleven o'clock, okay?"

The two dudes looked at him blankly.

"And then," Norbert continued, "we begin the selling of Jax Burgers and their related potato and beef products. Make sense?"

The two dudes looked at each other and then back at Norbert. Blankly.

"Look, it works like this: Before eleven o'clock, Geronimo Egg'wiches, Navajo Short Stacks with Jack's own New Hampshire imitation maple syrup, Sitting Bull Sausages for all. Then, when the big hand hits twelve and the little one hits eleven, it's the Jack Anvil's of old: Jax Burgers, Jax Pounders, Cowboy Fries, Apache Shakes . . ."

"Uh . . . like, you don't have any Geronimos left from ten minutes ago, dude?"

"Yeah." Dude #2 began to feed off the Abbott and Costello/Dr. Dre and Snoop Doggy Dogg energy that was their friendship. "Like you made the exact number of Geronimos and Sitting Bull Sausages you needed?"

"Chyeah," Dude #1 agreed.

"Not likely."

"Indeed. Hey," Dude #1 began a slow realization, "aren't you that dude? Yeah!"

"What dude, dude?"

"He's that dude, the dude that messed up the fries that day!"

Dude #2 looked at Norbert and began to laugh. "Yeah, you're, like . . . that dude."

Norbert felt the blood rise in his face and wondered if the Fry Incident would ever stop haunting him. "It could have happened to anyone."

"Anyone like you, dude."

"Yeah, totally."

"Indeed."

"Is there any problem here, gentlemen?" McPhearson appeared suddenly from the back and leaned over the counter toward the two dudes, his eyebrows arched in a facade of helpful concern. "Anything I can help you with? I heard your question from before and, yes, we do make the exact number of Indian breakfasts needed. It's planning like that that makes this one of the best-run Jack Anvil's franchises in the entire state."

"Like, there's not one Indian breakfast in the entire place leftover?" one of the dudes asked.

"It's like Wounded Knee back there," Miles said. "There's not an Indian in sight. I'd love to take you on a tour of the entire kitchen to put your mind at ease, but state health regulations, as well as the rather more exacting Jack Anvil's Corporation Bylaws, just don't allow that type of activity. Can you 'dig' my 'rap,' 'dudes'?"

"Let's go, dude."

"Yeah, this place bites."

"Let's go to McDonald's."

"Yeah, at least McDonald's doesn't, like, suck."

"Totally."

McPhearson watched the two dudes walk out and looked over to Norbert, who that morning sincerely didn't believe he could last the summer. "Don't take it so hard, son. They always like to rub McDonald's in our face, don't they? But we know, huh?" He gave Norbert a playful nudge. "Huh? Yeah? 'Word' . . . to your 'mother'?"

Miles nodded with satisfaction. He'd defused yet another potential situation and bolstered Norbert's shaky morale in one fell swoop. "I'm going to my office for a moment. Send in Sydney, I need to talk to him again."

Chaim Poplotnick sat behind the oversized desk in his office drumming the tips of his stubby fingers together as was his wont. He'd fired up the hookah back in the Gaming Room before the two gentlemen arrived and was now primed and ready for his favorite activity in the entire world: Planning.

"So, what's the game plan?" Chaim's fingers picked up the tempo of their roll.

The two dudes looked at each other, shrugged and shook their heads.

"Uh . . . game plan?" said Dude #2.

"Yes, whatcha got in store?"

"A store . . . ? Like?"

"What the hell is your plan?!" Poplotnick yelled. He was still pissed off about the baseball cards Marty had dealt him. They were barely worth half what he claimed.

"Oh, the Plan? Well . . . ," Dude #1 began. "Oh, uh . . . go ahead, dude."

"No, go on, dude."

"All right, heh." Dude #1 laughed self-consciously. "Well . . . we could . . . like . . . fuck him up."

"Yeah," Dude #2 agreed, grinding his fist into the palm of his hand. "Fuck him up and shit."

Chaim stroked his gray beard. At that moment he was barely listening to the two young men. He was going over in his mind that morning's call to the synagogue. Passover was a troubling time for Chaim and his enormous dietary requirements, and after lighting up the morning's first bowl of endo, he'd had that brilliant brain wave: Burritos! Of course, tortillas, the *other* unleavened bread. Obviously he'd have to stay away from the al Pastor and the carnitas, but why not a nice carne asada burrito? He quickly called the *real* rabbi, who, sadly, didn't share Chaim's enthusiasm and felt, in fact, that the entire idea was not in keeping with the Passover spirit.

"Ahem." Chaim cleared his throat and stroked his beard. "Let's hear the details."

"Uh, details?"

"Yes, what is it, exactly, that you propose to do?"

"Propose . . . ?"

"The plan!"

"Uh, why don't you . . ." Dude #1 turned to Dude #2.

"No, go ahead, dude."

"No, you."

"No, you, dude."

"Well." Dude #1 readjusted his navy blue watch cap. "Uh, we just go and find out where this dude lives and, like, well, then we just fuck him up."

"Yeah, like we get him on his way to work and shit," Dude #2 agreed.

"Yeah, and then we, like, totally fuck him up."

Chaim liked these boys. They were stupid, and that made Chaim feel, well, smart. He smiled his Grand Benefactor smile. "No, no, no. I want the money. What I'm after is the money."

"Oh, yeah . . . well," Dude #1 said, "like we, like, threaten him first."

"Yeah, tell him we're *gonna*, like, fuck him up and shit," Dude #2 added

"Totally. We, like, tell him that if he like doesn't pay and shit? Then we're gonna fuck him up."

"Yeah, like, 'Listen, dude, if you don't pay, POW! We're gonna, like, fuck you up and shit.' "

Chaim smiled and nodded. "Sounds like a plan, gentlemen."

little johnnie
goes online

little johnnie lydell, within minutes of Chaim Poplotnick bidding him adieu and heading to the Steambaths for activities even Little Johnnie didn't care to imagine, was logged on to Poplotnick's AOL account under his brilliant disguise of Brooke, the nineteen-year-old hot Bi-Fem. Innocent, fresh and curious. Little Johnnie had even recently downloaded an obscure and completely convincing amateur photo of a hot young girl spreading it wide on some chintzy bedspread in some cheap motel room: hot little Brooke.

Little Johnnie was armed and ready in a flash. Out came the big 'Cono box of Wad Gompers, the fresh ML40 and he was soon stripped down to his tentlike boxers and stretched-to-straining, slightly yellowed tank T-shirt. Why someone exhibiting such exceptional rotundity would choose to wear a tank top, only Little Johnnie might explain.

Little Johnnie threw a handful of Wad Gompers into his mouth and began enthusiastically chomping away as he scratched at his hairy and swo' gut and moused down the rooms list:

Bored and Lonely Housewife
Married and at the Office
Barely Legal Girls
The Simpsons
Men in Uniform
Swinging Couples in NJ
The USS Enterprise

And there it was: **Hot Bi-Fem Teens**. Little Johnnie double clicked and took another long shlook off his ML40. Brooke was online!

Little Johnnie knew the game. He'd quickly realized that even with the benefit of no one actually being able to see his repulsive form or whiff his peculiar brand of body odor, a single guy got no action online. He'd even tried a new male persona for a while: Lance, six-two, blond, blue-eyed surfer from Doheny. Nothing. More action from guys than anything else. Little Johnnie had learned the first rule of the Internet adult chat room food/sex chain: Single guys were the bottom feeders. It went: single hetero men, bi-guys, couples, Big and Beautiful women, married women, young single women and, at the top, the Queens of the Internet: the Bi-Fems.

They got it from all sides. They were getting it from women. They were getting it from men. They were as prized as black truffles by couples. They could fit into nearly any sexual permutation or combination thrown at them, except, of course, in Gay Men World. But Little Johnnie, while not exactly admiring, was—way in the back and off to the side of his mind where Little Johnnie kept Gay Men World—at least jealous of the all-out feeding frenzy of sex he imagined took place over there.

And since Bi-Fems kicked such sexual ass in cyberspace,

one day Little Johnnie, as the result of a rare idea, was struck with the genius of passing himself off as a hot Bi-Fem. And so was Little Brooke, young and bi-curious, born, and she would be his ticket into realms well beyond the limits of his 59-inch, 240-pound craft.

Oh, it wasn't easy, Little Johnnie'd be the first to tell you, if he had the nerve to admit to *anyone* what he was doing in the first place. No, the Internet was littered with fat, sweaty guys passing themselves off as either young, muscular and handsome, or possessing entirely different genitalia. And the savy Bi-Fems were on to the subterfuge. They patrolled the Bi-Fem and women-only rooms with the thoroughness of the KGB, regularly issuing general announcements of "I think there are some men in this room" or "This is a woman-only room!"

That was good to blast out a good half of all the fakes, but Little Johnnie one night weathered the storm, sitting off to the side, reading all the smutty talk among the women, all of whom he pictured as young, built and impossibly hot. And then the night came where he joined the fray and was soon pulled into a private chat room and licked his lips in anticipation, listening to the women bustin' out with dirty-assed shit that he'd never imagined. But soon Little Johnnie realized he had to learn the code. There existed a password. He had to know the answer to the secret question that virtually no known single heterosexual man in the entire Americas knew: What size panty hose do you wear?

A, B, or S. *S?! Where'd they come up with shit like that?* Little Johnnie wondered the next day down at the panty hose section of his local pharmacy, after getting eighty-sixed the night before during some furious bra peeling, with promises of a good tongue lashing to follow, when he made the mistake of answering, "Sheer."

But now he had it down. The panty hose sizes, bra brands, favorite cosmetics, PMS medicines. Really, once you knew the basic facts and threw in some light men bashing for good measure, you were in like Flynn. And when Little Johnnie came up with the genius of the innocent bi-curious nineteen year old, he had Bi-Fems beggin' him. Brooke was practically the fuckin' Bi-Fem of the ball and Little Johnnie Lydell was soon surfin' the Web, speeding along an information superhighway that headed straight for the folds of his ample and slightly musty boxers.

aunt sally

sydney was again hard at work in his room.

Dear Chief of Police:

It has recently come to my attention that crime is on a dangerous upswing and running more or less unchecked throughout every major metropolitan area of this once-great democracy of ours. As we speak, Master Locksmiths are turning to crime to supplement their declining earning power. I recently viewed a television program with Robert Stack (now retired from his days leading the Untouchables but, thankfully, still eager and willing to fight crime into his old age) and this show illustrated how easy it is for even a dropout from the Mississippi elementary school system to quickly and unnoticed break into virtually any home! On Channel 20 I've seen numerous examples of people who can get into a locked car and drive it away faster than the rightful owner. Thank God I'm limited to public transportation. In fact, Channel 20 seems to specialize in the sort of programming that leaves your typical suburban dweller in a state of unbridled terror. I refer to *The*

Streets of San Francisco, Mannix, Jake and the Fatman and *The Rockford Files.*

My request? Let's get tough on crime already! If you need any assistance in this matter please feel free to contact me, though if you stop by my apartment I would appreciate it if you didn't examine the possessions of my less anti-crime brother, Martin, too closely. He doesn't need any more trouble at work than he already easily gets himself into.

Thank you very much,
Sydney Corbet
Chief Officer, Citizens Against Crime

Sydney reached into the drawer and pulled out the photograph again. *The* photograph. One of three in the entire apartment (at Aunt Sally's existed the treasure trove, a couple of albums' worth). Sydney looked again at his photograph, smiled and loved her so and closed his eyes and tried to conjure her, the mental image he was sure existed somewhere in his brain. He willed it again for naught, for he had no picture. He was too young when she died and Marty wasn't talking.

Sydney put down the photograph and opened up his Journal.

The all-important autobiography is going much slower than anticipated. My brother, Martin, acts as though he were Göbbels at the Nuremberg Trial whenever I ask the hard questions concerning our family. Especially concerning the chapter on Mother. He has yet come to terms with her tragic loss and seeks comfort in his alcoholic malted beverages.

Sydney sat for a moment sipping his Freeb's. He could make no sense of himself. He might scan the horizon of his family and see no signs of life. At least not the signs that might point to the existence of such a serious scholar as himself. *Marty's a poster boy for beer-drinking blue-collardom. Aunt Sally, while sweet, never attended college and rarely reads anything outside the* TV Guide. *Father, so the story goes, was a boozing, ill-tempered man, and Grandfather, while rich and successful, did not possess either my refinement or intellect.* At times Sydney imagined there had been some sort of mix-up at the hospital, or perhaps he was the result of some ungodly alien artificial insemination. *Perhaps that is what killed dear Mother.*

No, anywhere Sydney looked he saw a cultural wasteland. It was obvious that the Family Tree was firmly planted in white trash soil.

It's only through some mysterious accident of Fate that I don't aspire to be a demolition derby driver, but then Darwin has already noted how the mutant, the spontaneous arrival of a form strange and different, is the lynchpin of evolutionary theory. I am obviously the forerunner of a new and vastly improved Corbet.

The drawback? In a flush of blood to his face, his neck hot and prickly, he realized this meant he would have to . . . breed!

"We must visit Aunt Sally," Sydney announced.

"How the hell did Kwan lose?" Marty asked, as though they'd been Charlie Roseing the subject for the past fifteen minutes.

"I beg your pardon?" Sydney asked.

"I mean, who ever heard of this fuckin' Lipinski? Huh?"

"Surely not I, but there are far more important matters at hand."

"Come on, Syd. It's Saturday. It's my day off."

"Aunt Sally will have the answers I need to finish my autobiography."

"Aunt Sally isn't going to know anything. She was the old man's sister, not Mom's."

"Well, I have no other option. Whenever I ask you anything, you act as nervously as a man made to testify before a Senate subcommittee on Organized Crime."

"Man . . ."

The two boys walked the ten suburban blocks to Aunt Sally's place. Marty was deeply lost in THE DEBT. THE DEBT held him captive right then like a serial-killer clown. Zabiglione, the insane murderous clown. It began to dominate all his waking hours. He tried to imagine escape. But there he was: Zabiglione. Angry and with painted face. Scary clown, the worst kind of scary there is. *I don't even have a fucking car. Poplotnick's gonna send the goons over.* Marty'd seen the shows, all the movies. He knew what happened when it was past time to collect and the guy didn't have the money, and he knew that Poplotnick would have some second-rate version of it. Throat slashing with a nicked, dull blade. *Some dumb speed freak biker shit! It's gonna be trouble all the same. Big Trouble. Fuck! How the fuck did that little bitch Kwan lose to Lipinski? What kind of fucking luck.*

Aunt Sally lived at the end of what was called a cul-de-sac rather than a dead end. Near the outskirts of town. It was a street like all the other streets in Valley. Wide streets with few trees, mostly palms, but nice curbs and wide side-walks. Rock and cactus gardens adorning the fronts of all the two- and three-bedroom homes, with curving driveways and added-on enclosed patios. The gleaming kitchens devoid of any smells or signs of life from cooking food and simmering pots.

Somehow, beyond Aunt Sally's house, lay open land. Some of the last open space in the county. Land that headed east, toward the desert, along crooked wild canyons, through impenetrable chaparral, past a few tough oaks and tall sycamores that had established themselves in the dry washes and intermittent creek beds that turned into raging torrents now and again each winter.

Marty and Sydney had lived with Aunt Sally when they were kids. After what happened. They lived in the little house at the end of the cul-de-sac with Aunt Sally and Uncle Karl, who was no longer around because he had smoked cigarettes all the time. Marty would remember Uncle Karl each time he stepped inside, remember when Marty was in high school and Uncle Karl was getting thinner and thinner with the emphysema, those last few agonizing years. Every day he became a little weaker and shorter of breath. Finally he parked himself almost permanently on the La-Z-Boy with the remote control in his liver-splotched hand and then it got to where he always had to have the tank by his side. The tank of pure O_2. The man was once huge. He stood a good six feet tall, with big forearms and meaty hands with sausage fingers, and there he was in the end like a wraith fading before their eyes, fumbling for the mask, fiddling with the knobs as he took short, whistling breaths in anticipation of the release of pure oxygen.

"I don't know what happened to Pierre," Aunt Sally said as she greeted them at the door, as though they were in the middle of an important conversation. As though Marty and Sydney showed up at her door each and every day, when, in reality, they hadn't stopped by since Christmas, when Aunt Sally had inadvertently immobilized everyone at breakfast by serving a ludicrous amount of pork products. "Hi, Sydney," Aunt Sally said warmly as she patted him on the back. "How's your new job going?"

"Well, as I'm sure you can imagine, it's proving to be a very damaging obstacle to my important research."

"I'm sure he'll be back," Marty said as he opened the refrigerator and began peeling open Tupperware containers, peeking under foil wraps. "How long's he been gone?"

"There's some ham in there if you want. Want me to make you a nice sandwich? Would you like a sandwich, Sydney?"

"I believe I've already reached this week's quota of pork products and must limit myself to fish and chicken for the next few days."

"You want I should make you some tuna fish then? Huh? Or would you like a soda?" Aunt Sally asked. "Get your brother a soda," she told Marty.

"Only if you have something decaffeinated," Sydney stated. "I've recently received some very alarming news regarding my blood pressure."

"How 'bout some juice then?" Aunt Sally asked. "Marty, get your brother some juice."

"I refuse to add to the coffers of that maniac Anita Bryant," Sydney declared.

"I don't think she works for the orange people anymore," Aunt Sally told him. "Two weeks, Marty."

"Huh?" Marty cracked open a can of Rocko's.

"Pierre. He's been gone almost two weeks. I saw a coyote in the back, you know. The next-door neighbor, Mrs. Cummings? Remember her husband . . ." Aunt Sally performed the *glug-glug* thumb sign for Problem Drinker, making Marty look guiltily down at his can of beer. "They're not together anymore, but her little Siamese? Cynthia? You know, the cat she got after Mr. Boots died? Mr. Boots had that rare case of cat hip dysplasia? And Dr. Green, we both go to the same vet, he's so good . . ."

Marty was crumpling under the weight of facts and details; he was lost in a crowd of people he didn't know. Finally, Sydney couldn't wait any longer as Aunt Sally went on about the vet's sister being in the same class as Marty, the short, stocky blond girl?

"Aunt Sally," Sydney interrupted. "I'm sure this woman is of no great importance to any of us right now. She's probably become some sort of unwed mother who spends her days cashing government checks and smoking generic cigarettes while watching *Cops* and wondering if she might muster the nerve to call up about being on *The Jerry Springer Show*. The true reason for our visit is that I need to interview you for my autobiography."

"Oh, you want to see the photo album again," Aunt Sally said and smiled. "Why don't *you* take more interest in the family, Marty?"

"I . . . ," Marty protested.

"When am I gonna see some grandkids, huh?"

"Who's gonna marry me?" Marty answered. "I'm thirty-eight and work for a meat-packing plant. I smell like bacon most of the time . . ."

"That's good honest work, Marty. And remember all that beautiful meat you brought over for Christmas? Remember the big breakfast?"

Each boy grabbed his stomach, the aftermath still raw in their systems some three months later.

"So what's with Pierre?" Marty said, eager to change the subject. Pierre was a tiny Pomeranian that Aunt Sally had got soon after Uncle Karl died, to fill up a vacuum in the house that threatened to swallow her up whole. And Pierre wasn't tiny just because he *was* a Pomeranian. Pierre was tiny *for* a Pomeranian. Pierre would be the runt of your basic Pomeranian litter. Pierre was the size of dog that kittens might imagine kicking ass on. Yet, despite weighing in at grams, Pierre was as feisty as Little Johnnie Lydell, and he had a very large bark considering his size. A *grrr-yipe-yipe-yipe* that he used on anyone who came anywhere near him, save for the tenderhearted Aunt Sally. As soon as someone stepped inside her house, Pierre would run up to within six feet and commence with the *grrr-yipe-yipe yipe! Grrr-yipe-yipe-yipe! Grrr-yipe-yipe-yipe!*

"I'm worried about him," Aunt Sally said.

"When'dja last see 'im?" Marty asked.

"Two days ago."

"That's not so long. Maybe he's just runnin' around. I don't know!" Marty was basically a failure at reassurance in any form.

"But he only had on his light sweater," Aunt Sally protested.

The two brothers looked at each other and nodded in silence. Tragically, six months earlier Aunt Sally had seen a program on dog grooming and decided that for Pierre to get the fashion kick-start needed for a ten-year-old dog, the best bet would be to shave him bald and start from scratch. From then on Aunt Sally had visions of the tender and constant grooming she would bestow upon the minuscule, bitter-natured dog and dreamed that one day, perhaps, she would even enter him in the great Valley Dog Show, Senior Division.

This great wave of tender tending was still on hold because for some reason tiny Pierre's subatomic internal system seemed unable to grow the hair back. Three months had gone and Pierre still could not shake his resemblance to a newborn piglet. Two months later and only Aunt Sally, with the use of a powerful magnifying glass in conjunction with the brightest of light bulbs, was able to see the growth of fine, wispy hairs, but Marty knew it wasn't true.

"Maybe you could dip him in Rogaine twice a day" was Marty's idea, but Aunt Sally wasn't amused and instead knit Pierre an entire wardrobe of sweaters (in crew, V and turtlenecks), bought him thermals, flannel pajamas and even a tiny tam-o'-shanter for his wee head. Marty, who had never liked Pierre, would quietly, when Aunt Sally was out of the room, taunt the poor dog. "You look like a fuckin' idiot, you know? Other dogs are laughing their asses off at you. Look at you in those silly pajamas." Pierre responded with a baring of his pencil-point fangs. *Grrr-yipe-yipe-yipe. Grrr-yipe-yipe-yipe.* "Marty, are you bothering Pierre again?" Aunt Sally would ask from the other room.

After the photo albums had been brought out Aunt Sally had answered Sydney's questions about her sister-in-law. Aunt Sally let Sydney operate under the fantasy that their dearly departed mother had died some sort of American Movie Classics death: lying in bed, the sheets tucked under her arms, her head propped up on a fluffy white down-filled pillow, the family gathered about the bed holding her weak, slight hand, people outside the bedroom door murmuring in deathbed's quiet tones, a doctor at her side, his medical bag open, his stethoscope at the ready, later shaking his head slowly to the grieving family. It looked bad, she might not make the night.

Marty wished he could remember it like that, that he could pull the tapes from his head, hit Play and get that same soft-focus vision, but it could never be. He was there that night. The night when it was so cold and the snow lay thick on the ground. It was when they still lived upstate. The ground was frozen so they couldn't even bury her for four weeks.

But Marty had an altogether different reason for stopping by Aunt Sally's, and it was killing him. He didn't like to ask for favors, he hated asking for favors, but he had no choice. If he didn't get some money fast . . .

"Marty! I don't have that kind of money," Aunt Sally told him. "I just have Social Security. Thank God the house is paid for. What kind of trouble are you in?"

"What's the difference?!"

"Is it drugs? Are you hooked on crack? I saw this show and it was just terrible—"

"I'm not hooked on crack."

"It was horrible. They were selling their belongings, stealing from their families, remember Eunice's boy, Charlie . . . ?"

"Aunt Sally . . . Let's forget I ever asked, huh?"

"No, that was Emily's boy. John! That's it, John. Oh, it was terrible, Marty. The stuff is dangerous." Aunt Sally looked troubled. "You wouldn't steal from your auntie, would you, Marty? I know you're a good boy, but you gotta get off it now! You can't keep smoking that crack!"

"I'm not on crack!" Marty yelled. "Jeez! I just need some money, I thought maybe Grampa left you something in the will. Let's just forget it, huh?"

"That rat bastard?!" Aunt Sally scoffed at the memory of her newly departed father. "Not likely."

high chaparral

jesús again waited for the night, after Padre Ewilly left, when the sun began to sink fat and red into the Pacific, after he had heated up the *comal* for the tortillas and cooked up the thin slice of beef he'd sometimes smuggle deep into the center of Saturday's shopping bag, along with some eggs with chile and tomato and onion and potato. A small pot of beans or some rice.

After Jesús washed the dishes and said his prayer in front of his altar of the Virgin of Guadalupe, next to Jesús Cristo lamenting on the cross that hung from a silver chain burnished the dull white color of plata, and the little black-and-white photos of Santa Madre and his sweet darling Reyna, he stepped outside for that third and last cigarette and waited for the Arrival.

Jesús stood against the wall of his tiny bungalow in the quiet and still compound atop Miracle Mountain. He looked down and saw the city twinkle and blink in the warm night air. The lights looked different from those back home, in Mexico. Like it was a different form of electricity and, he was sure, the *gabachos* had the better kind.

Jesús lit his third and last cigarette of the night, his face momentarily lit up yellow and red in the match's flame, and walked out to the edge of the landscaped grounds that he would toil on all summer. He sat down under some scrub brush, his legs stretched out in the still-warm sand. He hoped tonight would be the night the little beast would show itself.

As he sat quietly under the bush waiting for the little beast, Jesús would, inevitably, be swept away with sweet thoughts of dearest Reyna. As night fell, he could picture her thick black hair, so rich and long, to the middle of her back when she had it down, which was how Jesús would remember it. He could almost smell her out there so far away. He could almost feel her beautiful skin, sweet *moreno,* that wonderful little mouth, *boca dulce,* her small, bright teeth, her full lips, the surprise of her pink, moist mouth against the brownness of her skin as she opened for a kiss. And sometimes Jesús would remember it all so well that his head flooded with the thought. The Missing. The Separation. He'd keep silently still through it all, not a peep, maybe dragging a little twig aimlessly through the sand in a design that could only mean: her!

Every evening at dusk the sweet smell of the chaparral emerged as though it hid from the heat of midday, from all the cars and the pavement, from the exhaust fumes and the smog. The chaparral would awaken and the animals would come to life in the hazy yellow light, in the sweet dusk, out at the edge of Valley, where the houses finally stopped and the dry, crunchy ground reappeared. You might smell, again, the raw land reemerged in the rosy light under purpling skies. You might hear anew, above the distant track of freeway sounds, the cricket's sonar as the light faded, the rustling of the rabbits unseen in the brush as the sun sank, the chirping of birds come alive or see a fine hawk wheeling far above on the gentle warm caress of a fresh, dry Santa Ana wind, floating in from the lost, pure desert.

The scrawny beast made her way silently through the fresh, darkening canyons that ran for miles throughout the open land that lay east of the city, down animal paths in the east county that had existed for hundred of years. She could still feel the footsteps back four hundred years. The juice of the bald little dog's blood filling her with visions and power.

She waited for night proper under a scrub oak near one of the many cul-de-sacs that marked the eastern edge of town, and as she crouched, nearly invisible, under the short, gnarled tree, she slipped back, back to when the land was more vibrant. She remembered its bristling defiance, the air crystal clear in a way it never could be again once the first smokestack had been fired up. Back when the night was dark in a way it never could be again once the first street lamps had been lit.

She sniffed the air, smelled a distant scent of rabbit near the mountain and, as night grew, centuries-old wafts from the first Spaniards, smelly and foul, their armor shiny, with the glint of worked metal. And their beasts. An acrid sour aroma of goat and horse. She smiled at the banquet's excess.

They came with their Jesus back then. They came to conquer a land, they came to save the souls, to subjugate the flesh, to exploit the back, employing the whip and shackle and the word of Jesus slipped through their bearded lips carrying smallpox. In their saving of the souls of these heathens, the heathens dropped before them, racked with disease, and the Bearded Ones took this as a sign that God was not pleased with the heathen natives of California, who did not have Jesus in their hearts, who spoke of coyote, performed ghost dances, painted the sand, performed the jimsonweed rituals in the dead of a moonless night. But Chupe remembered it differently: From the first dust rising on the far southern horizon, like a bad storm brewing, the barometer on a way of life was plunging.

When darkness proper covered the land, El Chupe braved her way down the back streets quietly, near invisible, relying greatly on her cloak of disbelief, climbing over fences, looking for small dogs or, better yet, cats.

Chupe slipped over a fence and made her way down the steep hill into yet another wild canyon that ran toward the ocean. She sniffed and blinked, again lost in her past, the last of her kind. The rest were all gone—friend, foe, family alike. Gone to the smokestacks and the pavement. Dead from a disbelief, from a computer virus, from a machined malaise, from a broken heart over a world long gone. But El Chupe refused to let go. And on a quiet night like tonight, a deep whiff of the heady vespertine chaparral was enough to make her linger, to wait for just one more rare yellow sunset after a rain washed the sky momentarily clean, so you could near smell the life left in the land once again. That was enough. As long as someone believed, as long as there was even just a glimmer of fading hope. A patch of raw earth. It was enough. She slipped into the night wilds of the canyon, eager.

Marty was again at his home away from home. Dutchman's. Marty loved it at Dutchman's. It had that darkness, no matter the time of day. That sharp tang of stale smoke and alcohol sweat, sometimes that arousing aroma from the popcorn machine at the end of the bar that Ben fired up now and again when he was feeling festive.

Dutchman's was the Bar That Time Forgot. It was a place covered in a comfy yellowed patina of wasted nights. The bar was crowded with the ghosts of empty glasses, the spirits of spilled drinks and past parades of crumpled cocktail napkins. The stools dug in by the seats of all the years' crews. The wallpaper held the most animated of conversations, last calls, affectionate good-byes and teary-eyed remembrances. Dutchman's had the look of a place that hadn't changed in ages, that had been there forever (which in Southern California amounted to "In business since 1974!").

The very bottles of liquor—the Makers Mark, the Rock and Rye, Old Overhold—had a mantle of grimy dust on their shoulders. Nobody drank that shit. The pot of coffee that sat off to the side, the coffee in the pot thick and bitter. The life-sized cardboard cutout of the "Rocko-ettes," hosed down and wearing the tiniest of bikinis (the kind of shot where some guys had to check behind to make sure there wasn't a backside view).

On certain nights, the rare nights when it got cold in Valley, when the winds blew, when the heavy winter rains pummeled the ground, Dutchman's would live up to its name. It would take on the air of a great ship making its way through some fog-lost sea's storm toward a home now mythic. The door would be closed and the smoke would hang up by the ceiling and the yellow light would be warm and the chatter of the sports on the TV comforting. And then the door unexpectedly swings open and a blast of cold air bolts in, the sudden sizzle of rain upon the sidewalk and in steps another passenger and the door slams shut and drinks are in order.

And on those nights, when the door closed behind you and Dutchman's took on the air of a snug hold on a great sailing ship, there was something vaguely doomed about the night's voyage, when it most blushed with home's security and a longing for deep love, for an unattainable moment of life slipped by at Dutchman's bar, no grill. Just that popcorn machine and Ben the Barkeep suited Marty just fine, because he'd figured a while back that he was goin' nowhere and Dutchman's was the perfect place to go and feel just fine about exactly that. That you were goin' nowhere.

Marty staggered out of Dutchman's. Ben had offered to call a cab, but Marty knew he couldn't afford no cab fare, so he acted all tough, like it was just a short jaunt home, when in reality it was nearly two miles back to the Oasis Apartments.

Marty made his way down the sidewalk through the drunk's amplified invigoration from the fresh air—moist, clean and alive—against the warm glow of his beered brain. He made his way past houses he'd known since he was a kid; they moved there back when he was eight. Marty's mind spun with the old house back east, with pictures of Mom, with all the money he owed, the treasures he was sure to soon win; his mind spun about in the quiet late-night streets shrouded in a thick ground fog.

Tule fog, Marty remembered, though tule fog can only be grown in the vast, flat moonscaped expanse of the San Joaquin. Thick as proverbial pea soup and hugging the ground in vampirish clouds, malevolent and impenetrable, but the cars keep flying up and down I-5 in some frenzied attempt to get to or flee LA. Sealed in their metallic chariots, the heat on and the radio up—it's Merle Haggard, he goes good in the San Joaquin 'cause it's sorta like Oklahoma— and then somebody stops and the mayhem begins and all the cars pile up and crumple and crush, are bent and mangled, bodies are broken, windshields spiderwebbed, and blood spills on the dead, silent road moist with the tule fog. *The record's like ninety-something cars!*

Marty was quite entertained by the car pileup and picked up his pace a bit on that street that ran along one of the canyons. He could smell the sage, the chaparral, the freshness of all the plants, and he decided to take a shortcut through the canyon.

"Dude, wake up!"

"Huh?" Dude #2 shook himself awake; the two of them were stashed behind a hedge.

"There he is!"

"A chubalabra?!"

"No, dumb ass, that guy we're supposed to fuck up."

"Cool."

scrapin' the bowl

it was friday night, and every Friday at around seven or eight, earlier in the winter (Mr. Bea always felt the setting sun the perfect send-off for the weekend's debauching), Mr. Bea would enjoy the deepest, darkest night that Valley could muster.

Like tonight. As the entire town lay asleep in their beds, or huddled in front of the godly blue glow of their televisions, the Bea's Candy Works sat near silent, all the machinery and assembly lines shut down. Only the generators purred, a catlike slumber, and a lone light shone from an upstairs window. The Boardroom.

"You know what I like about Scrimshaw being in charge of Letters?" Mr. Bea asked his guest up in the Billiard Room. "Nothing ever gets answered. If the letter writer doesn't have access to a telegraph machine? Forget it! Just as well— most people write complaining about something or wanting free shit. No, it used to be buy your candy and shut the fuck up. Pay your money and get the hell out. That's how you run a business. Not all this catering and genuflecting to the all-powerful consumer." Mr. Bea began to mime an enthusiastic genuflector.

He set down his cue, picked up his fine Por Larranaga Lonsdale and a glass of '55 Graham's. Sasha sat quietly on the couch, along with a beautiful and expensive Latvian whore by the name of Tatiana.

"You know," Mr. Bea told his guest, "I've always thought someone like Tatiana was one of the finer things about the fall of Communism. All those Soviet Bloc beauties unleashed upon the West. Care for a butter cream, Jim?"

"No thanks, Wilbur. I don't eat much candy these days. So how's business been anyway?"

"For shit. Little bastards not buying candy like they used to. It's the fucking parents. Damn yuppies all hung up on health and fitness. Government coming out with reports about fat kids. It's got 'em feeding their little bastards fruit for chrissakes!"

"Yeah, government can be a bitch."

"At least I'm not one of those poor bastards in the tobacco industry. Those fuckers are being strung up by their balls, they are. No, wouldn't want to be one of them."

"My shot?"

Mr. Bea nodded. "You wanna know our secret?"

"What's that?"

"Sugar."

"Sugar?"

"That's right. Sugar. Sugar and caffeine are the last bastions. There's a nation hooked. You like sugar don't you, Sasha?"

The juicy young girl crammed into a tight, shiny miniskirt looked up from her port wine fog. "Hmmm?"

Mr. Bea smiled. "Don't you just love 'em, Jim? Yeah,

sugar. Do you have any idea how much a 'Cono box of Wad Gompers costs to produce? Twenty-six cents. I've got the little bastards shelling out a dollar eighty-nine of their damn parent's money for the crap. No one cares. Once that sugar hits their bloodstreams, they're as happy as clams. And those anti-fat wonks in DC? They try and come after me, I peddle a low-fat version. Cut the fat and up the sugar some more. I can practically pass the shit off as health food!"

"Sounds good to me, buddy."

"Yeah, I wish the government was my only problem. I've got Mother to worry about. I've negotiated Frito-Lay up to $150 million and Mother still won't sell!" Mr. Bea licked his lips. "150 million!"

"That'd pay for some cigars and girls."

"Mmmm." Mr. Bea took a sip of his port. "But I've got something in store."

"That so?"

"Yeah, a little plan. Chapter 11."

"Huh?"

"Good old Chapter 11. You see, then I can re-form the company. The question was, How? How to bring down the company? When it comes to me and business, well, I'm like King Midas. I almost can't *not* make money, but then I got this idea. In the mail. It's perfect. Not only will it sink the company, but, and here's the part I love, I'll have someone to blame."

"That's always good. But why don't you just quit Bea's and form your own company? Why go to all that trouble?"

"What, and have Mother as competition? She'd kill me. Besides, I need that Wad Gomper. Yeah. The Wilbur Candy Company." Mr. Bea drew his hand across the air. "What do you think? Huh?"

"Hmm?" Jim was lost on Sasha, practically squirming in her seat.

"For the company's new name?" Mr. Bea smiled proudly and took a long, satisfied puff off the fine cigar.

"Sounds great, buddy. Which one do I get?"

"Jim, take your pick. Trade in the middle of the night. Whatever. You're my guest."

Later that evening, after his old buddy Jim had gone off to the guest room to debauch Sasha, Mr. Bea stumbled down the hallway, his arm hanging on the fine, creamy shoulder of Tatiana. He heard a sound behind him, coming from down the hallway.

"Why don't you make yourself comfortable, dear?" Mr. Bea pointed the girl to a room. "I'll be right back."

Wilbur headed down the hallway toward the darkness, toward the faint sound. As he slowly crept forward, toward the noise and into the darkness, he felt ever smaller, it felt ever later at night and his skin began to crawl as he could now make out the sound, very faint but becoming stronger, closer, an almost creaking of the boards.

"Wilbur, Wilbur," called the fragile, thin voice. "Wilbur? Do you have some dirty little girl with you? Is there a dirty little tramp in our house? I won't have it. I won't have it, I say!"

As he turned the corner, Mr. Bea snapped to with a momentary fear like the faint taste of blood in his mouth. It was Mother. Somehow Mother had got out of her room and was wheeling through the corridors.

"There you are, boy. I knew I heard you. Why are you up so late? Is there some filthy little slut in your room? No wonder you never get anything done."

"Mother, it's Friday night!"

"Come to your mother, Wilbur." Mrs. Bea pursed her thin, withered lips. The room began to shrink for Wilbur as Mother's mole and the three hairs that sprouted from it again filled the entire room, the entire Candy Works, Wilbur's entire world. "Come to the mother that loves you, Wilbur."

Wilbur approached as one might a skunk, leaning away as he inched forward.

"Now, tell me, what is it you're *really* up to? Hmm, boy?"

"N-nothing, Mother." Wilbur swallowed. "Heh-heh, you know me."

"Something no good, eh?"

"Why don't I take you back to your room?"

"Mmmm." A faint smile turned the corner of her thin lips as she shot him the Evil Mother Eye.

Click!

"If you're suffering, if you're arthritic, high blood pressure, overweight, no energy, God wants to heal you. He has provided all we need on this Earthly plane. Now I'd like to send you this beautiful Miracle Workout Elixir, a healthful tonic, pure, organic even, mixed to the exact biblical proportions. It's God's smart drug and, along with a good diet, regular exercise and prayer, gives you a bond with the Lord. It's reaching out with God's love. Now I have prayed over this special blend of trace elements, amino acids and herb extracts, and as you use it, you will see your Faith grow, your health, your vitality, your love of Jes—"

Click!

"*. . . Rocko's. Drink Rocko's. It packs a punch, it's got the gusto. Clean, crisp flavor. The beer with party-ability . . .*"

Marty sat once again in the sickly blue light of the TV, six beers into a rather harsh funk. The evening's beating by the two punks—which resulted in an actual broken nose, the loosening of a couple teeth and a severe blackening of most of the left side of his face—had pretty much dominated the day's events and set its tone.

"Oh, shit!" was Marty's diagnosis as he got his first glimpse of his face in the bathroom mirror and saw his bruised, broken and bloodied reflection. His eye was mostly closed and already starting to turn the many amazing shades of the ultraviolet end of the spectrum. He felt the top of his head where the hair was moist and matted and his skull incredibly tender. *Nose is broken. I'm gonna kill those two fucks. Wait till I see them again.* "Fuck! Fuck, fuck, fuck!"

The babbling of TV (*"Drink Rocko's, it's Rocko's* . . . Freeb's, the soda that sizzles, Freeb's packs the maximum phosphoric acid allowed by the FDA . . . We'll always have Paris"*) drifted unheard into Marty's consciousness, which was quite busy questioning its place in the great scheme of things. As he zombied the remote through the channels, Marty wondered again what his purpose was for living, tried to find solace in the smoking volcano glowing at him from the TV. He looked for some sort of reassurance as to the basic sense of his life, but answers were not to be found as Lucy fell behind on the chocolate conveyor line and a new sort of pizza with cheese loops was unveiled. Tonight, Marty Corbet was dark and beaten and finally convinced once and for all that Life was an evil and tiresome job that he didn't want but couldn't quit.

It just wasn't supposed to work out like this, was the conclusion Marty now and again reached in his darkest moments, when he woke up unexpectedly at 4 A.M., when the night was at its fullest, when the streets at last sat silent, absorbingly quiet, like that night at the old place.

Like tonight, when he felt that twinge of fear, that threat of sorrow like a tsunami warning broadcast from far away. He looked at the night's table littered with empty cans of beer, he touched his swollen right eye and dabbed at his numb, puffy lip. He didn't even dare to touch his nose. *Fuckin' punks. I'm gonna kill one of those fuckers.* But in an instant his anger dissipated and a lump of dread formed in his throat, the bristling of fear appeared on the back of his neck. *I still gotta come up with the money. This is fucking serious!* Marty felt sick, sick in the stomach it felt, but it was deeper than his guts. He felt it in his chest and in his now-hot, squealing brain.

Marty'd been scarred, though he'd never admit it. He didn't even know it, but Marty carried with him a mark on his soul that ran long, that cut deep, roughly healed over with a winding river of hard plastic scar tissue, his very soul like Frankenstein's monster, patched together with nuts, bolts and surgical thread. But beneath this tough, frightening cover, indeed because of the armor shell in which it was encased, lay something soft and defenseless, something afraid of the light, and because no one clued him in, Marty never imagined what he might be missing. He instead took comfort in his armor shell of anger and hardness. If no one got close, if he never cared, he would never be hurt again. Not like Mom.

Marty felt sleepy from the excitement of it all. *Sleep.* He actually smiled. It was the only escape from the cold, dark hand that reached out to him in his depths; the only solution, the only reprieve. Sleep, the thankful pardon of untroubled sleep, because, no matter what happened in the real world, no matter the tragedy or crime, no matter the misfortune or unfairness, Marty's dream world remained a safe and untroubled one.

He thought of the room upstairs. He felt himself shrink in size. With his eyes closed, he could feel himself getting smaller and smaller. The bed grew in size, the door reared up and Marty could almost feel the soft flannel of his pajamas again and hear Mom quietly shut the door. He could almost remember her smell, the comforting bouquet as she blew him a kiss and he would fall off into that safe world of untroubled dreams.

The door flew open as though set off by an explosive device and Sydney stepped into the room wiping Marty's dream world out of existence.

"What's happened to you?" Sydney stopped dead in his tracks.

"Wha'—!" Marty bounced awake on the couch.

"You look as though you're trying out for a role as Jake LaMotta in a village dinner theater production of *Raging Bull.*" He put down his papers save for an envelope he had clenched in his right hand. He sensed fear on an instinctual level. *Something very bad has happened.* The Koala Center flashed in Sydney's head. He pictured the long bus ride through the desert at night.

"What? What?!"

"Nothing." Sydney looked down at his feet.

"Look, Syd, you just don't get it. I'm in a fucking lot of trouble."

"What seems to be the problem?"

"If I don't come up with some *real* cash, *real* quick, I'm fucked." Marty stared Sydney down. "Oh, fuck it! Why the fuck am I telling you?"

It dawned on Sydney: "Perhaps I can get you out of this jam."

"What are *you* gonna do?"

"I'll loan you the amount."

"Syd, where you gonna come up with four thousand dollars?"

"Four thousand?!" Sydney spun a 360 quite gracefully on his good heel, cradling his head in the palms of his hands. "Have you *never* placed a winning bet?! Oh, for the love of God, March Madness approaches!"

"Syd, you're not helping, huh?" Marty marched into the kitchen and yanked a whipped cream canister out of the refrigerator and packed his mouth with a couple of good blasts of the nondairy wonder of emulsification. "Where you gonna come up with that kinda money? Use your fucking head. You work at a burger joint. Damn, boy!"

Sydney waved the envelope in front of Marty's face with the biggest smile. "I can assure you I've swept up my last parking lot french fry!"

"I don't got time for your games!"

"Bea's Candies has decided to go with my Chocolate Jesus idea!" Sydney waited for the praise to be heaped upon him.

Marty simply looked his brother in the eye, and his shoulders visibly slumped.

"Perhaps you need it in black and white." Sydney whipped out the contents of the envelope. "Here, a check for five thousand dollars."

It took some time. Marty looked the check over a number of times. Quizzed Sydney thoroughly, sat down with a new can of beer and reread the letter. Hoped for a 1-800 number for verification and finally decided it was the mythical Governor's Death Row reprieve call. "Yes!" Marty yelled, and actually made physical contact with his brother in the form of a clumsy sideways hug.

Later that night, Marty long gone to a delightful night's snooze, in the western wing of the apartment, Sydney sat at his desk scribbling furiously. Sydney rarely slept—four or five hours were plenty for him and he was often up late into the night. He had out his folder marked "A Day in Dallas," making notes on his most recent of shocking revelations. On a somewhat obscure NPR program—*Oh, how they hide these programs at the oddest of hours*—Sydney had learned that in 1948 a young oil equipment salesman from Midland, Texas, by the name of George Herbert Walker Bush began dealings with a certain Count de Mohrenshildt. Sydney could hardly believe it. The man who would later head the CIA and then become president of the United States having a close and personal relationship with the man who would later become a "sponsor" to Lee Harvey Oswald.

Sydney took a swig off his Freeb's Cola-Nated beverage, chowed down on three—his own personal favorite number—Wad Gompers and picked up his cherished Mont Blanc.

De Mohrenshildt was posing as some sort of "oil geologist" [Sydney could hardly keep from laughing], but in all probability had close ties to the CIA. The Count was an old OSS man and well connected in Eastern Europe. He's been tied to plots to disrupt Soviet Bloc oil production and exploration while keeping the pipes flowing to the U.S. Remember, H. L. Hunt figures into the assassination, so it's entirely possible that big-time oil businessmen wanted Kennedy liquidated so he wouldn't do to them what he'd done to U.S. Steel. And two?! Texans, Johnson and then Bush,

later become presidents? Hands were covered in oil as well as
blood.

Sydney set down his pen and felt *very* pleased, and then he
picked it up again.

It is no coincidence, that nearly every president after Kennedy has
had a connection with the assassination. Then-Senator Gerald
Ford even sat on the Warren Commission. At the time he was
known as the "CIA's best friend." And now Bush. The trail will
never lead to Reagan, Carter or Clinton. They were outsiders—a
peanut farmer, a puffy, swinging wheeler dealer and a former Bor-
ax salesman and mediocre actor.

Sydney smiled in the remembrance of when they were boys
he and Marty had loved that movie where Reagan played
the drunken baseball pitcher. He crossed out "mediocre" and
wrote down "adequate."

Sydney closed his eyes and hoped that in a single flash
of brilliance it would all unfold for him. For the last week
he'd been troubled by the recurrence in his exhausting research of two names: Richard Nixon and Gerald Ford. Two
men that would one day exchange the greatest of favors
imaginable. One would be chosen to become the only un-
elected president in U.S. history, and in return, he would
grant a pardon to his "benefactor," who might have become
the only president to serve jail time immediately upon being
ousted from office. Sydney began writing.

As if that wasn't enough, Nixon and Ford each pardoned one of
the biggest fish the Kennedy Brothers had nabbed in their noble
and zealous crackdown on organized crime: Carlos Marcello and

Jimmy Hoffa. We already know all about Marcello. The Don of New Orleans. And Nixon was actually in Dallas on November 22, 1963. On business for, of all groups, the Pepsi Corporation.

It's all too transparent. I've never liked Pepsi's insipid, overly sweet brew. It's always been a poor second cousin to Freeb's burning black fizz. He made one last entry.

Mysteriously, sales of Pepsi begin to skyrocket in the years following the murders of the Kennedys.

Sydney got up and walked over to his bedroom window. It was getting late. He drew back the blinds.

It's really not all that different. Except for all the houses. And all the cars. Otherwise it was pretty much the same. Dry and hot.

But it was different at the Oasis Apartments. The sodium-yellowed streetlight's night sky, the blue glow and sports cheer from Marty and the TV, the rushing by of cars that almost never stopped, except for maybe from three-thirty to five o'clock. It was darker and more still at the Koala Center, and the night sounds would be dominated by the desert. The Land. No longer Man. The coyote. The millions of invisible desert bugs, their very respiration into the night sky. The creosote waving in the wind still warm. A languid wind no longer racing as it did during the hot, dry days filling in the Lows and Highs on the great weather map of the southwestern United States. The desert would creak and moan as the sun disappeared. It would whisper and whimper at night. And then lie still.

there's been an idea!

professor theodore broma was up on the catwalk watching the assembly line machinery crank out countless bags of Wad Gompers. For many hours each workday Broma would pace about the catwalks that laced through the upper reaches of Building #5, thinking, thinking, thinking . . .

Professor Theodore Broma was thinking, concentrating almost, about how famous he was in chocolate circles. He stood up there on the catwalk, his arms outstretched, grasping the catwalk's railing. *Broma. The Man. The Myth*—he simply couldn't resist slipping into a deep daydream when he was supposed to be coming up with ideas. In fact, he'd been supposed to be coming up with some new ideas for ages now and, in reality, hadn't come up with a single good one since the Wad Gomper.

Professor Broma *was* a well-known player in the Chocolate Game, though many thought him washed up, past his prime, working for a candy company that was in pretty much the same state. But there was a time when Professor Theodore Broma was a veritable Cocoa Einstein, a blend of old world confection wizardry and modern Food Chemist specializing in things chocolatey. Professor Broma thought back to the young, idealistic phase of his career in chocolate, when he was hired as a young graduate chocolatier in the late sixties by Mrs. Bea. *It saved the company. They were stuck with boxed chocolate candies, Easter bunnies and chocolate Santas. They didn't see the opportunity in the mass candy bar market. But I did. My Wad Gomper.* He looked down at the infinite line of Wad Gompers bags rolling down a conveyor belt and smiled, not just at his invention, but for his foresight in demanding a percentage of the sales. It had made Broma a rich man.

And, more important than the money, Broma knew he was going to the Chocolate Hall of Fame in Hershey, Pennsylvania; they'd probably put a bust of him right next to Milton S. or Lord Cadbury. That was a lock, but Mr. Bea wanted more. He always wanted more, and kept bringing up all the young up-and-comers graduating from Cornell and Das Institution von Schokoladen in Vienna. Combination candy scientists/business managers. *Yeah, but how many of them have created a candy bar to be found at every supermarket checkout line in America? Scheisskopfen!*

For the last few years Broma's heart hadn't been in his work. He'd grown bored with coming up with this year's latest model of gimmicky candy. The market had long ago shifted toward bright and sour things anyway. Candy that made kid's teeth green, or emitted sparks when you bit down on it. *It's impossible to come up with something good and hope it will sell. The streets are lined with former hotshots from Leaf and Mars, entire chocolate research teams that tried to elbow some room at the supermarket checkout line and failed. All the greats have been installed for years. Baby Ruth. Mounds. Cracker Jacks. The candy bar world is as rigid and unchanging as the Vatican's.*

Besides, Broma had been secretly working all these years, all the years everyone else figured he was just goofing around, which is mostly what he was doing, but he was also secretly working a little. And his secret? Professor Broma had been working on a new process, a chemo-chocolate galvanism employing the latest in electro-cocoa biology.

Employing this process on my heirloom cocoa beans from my secret plantation in the hills above Oaxaca? Roasting the beans just so? Conching them gently for three full days! And then treating them with my near-perfected chemo-chocolate galvanism? Those schweinhunds at Nestlé. They know nothing! I will create a high-cocoa liquor chocolate the world has never seen! Broma smiled at the fantasy.

He thought again of the Aztecs, of the cocoa plantations stashed in the wet jungle heat of the mountains to the west of Oaxaca. The cacao trees were like none he'd ever seen. Fifty, sixty feet tall and spread about the sloping grounds in a haphazard manner. Nothing like the neat rows of trimmed fifteen-foot trees found in their other plantations. It was like discovering some unknown Grand Cru vineyard in Provence run by ancient masters of an ancient art.

And so it was in the hills between Oaxaca and Angel. The ancient Zapotecan family, working in the ancient way. It was as primitive as something out of the *National Geographic,* employing stones and wood and burros. The sugar they used was coarse and they diluted the chocolate with cinnamon and nuts. That's what threw the rest of the Cocoa World off, but in its bitter, pure form, Broma could tell. It was the greatest cocoa of them all.

As Broma again worked on his acceptance speech for his

induction into the Chocolate Hall of Fame, Scrimshaw at long last pulled himself up the stairs to the catwalk, leaned against the rail as he caught his breath, readjusted the pressurometer to his brand-new PowerAid 5000 hearing aid amplifier, walked up to Broma and yelled, "There's been an idea!"

Broma jumped, caught unaware, while Scrimshaw fiddled with his hearing aid amp as though attempting to dial in Heaven's Gate.

"An idea?!" Broma yelled back. He liked getting visits from Scrimshaw because it offered the chance to scream. Which he liked to do now and then.

"Yes. A new candy design idea." Scrimshaw was looking down at his PowerAid 5000 and proceeded to shake it gently. "Do you hear that?"

"If there are going to be any ideas around here," Broma shouted, "ZAY TAKE PLAZE IN *MY* DEPARTMENT!"

Scrimshaw looked up from his PowerAid. "Are you saying something? I said, ARE YOU SAYING SOMETHING?!"

"I . . . MAKE . . . ZA IDEAS!" Broma let the blood flow to his face on that one.

"Well, Mr. Ideas, why don't you read this?" Scrimshaw handed him a piece of paper and stormed down the stairs, thinking, *Broma? He hasn't come up with an idea since before the digital hearing aid. Sheesh!*

And so the great cocoa scientist found himself reading one of the rare directives from the offices of Mr. Bea, and as he read the note (which, since written by Scrimshaw, was done in the Western Union Motif), he wondered how much Mrs. Bea knew.

Stop all work. Stop.
Retool for latest idea. Stop.

Chocolate Jesus. Stop.
Report to Conference Room immediately. Stop.

Professor Broma crumpled the paper, stuffed it deep into the pocket of his chocolate research lab coat and climbed down the circular stairs of the catwalk. *She has no idea what that bungler's up to now.*

a tour of the works

irene got up as she always did. at the same time she did every Monday through Friday. The alarm would go off like a gunshot ripping through her dreams, and she'd reach from under the covers, barely aware of the faint early morning light slipping through the thin shades, to hit the snooze bar and slip back ever more deeply and deliciously into the sweet world of dreams under the toasty warmth of her comforter. AND THEN THE ALARM!

She would repeat this process exactly four times: the alarm, the reaching for the snooze bar, the slipping back in, the faint dread of another identical day beginning to gain strength in her consciousness. It was at the first realization of another morning beginning and in the dead of night that she hated the idea the most: *single mom*. It wasn't how she had planned it. She hadn't planned it this way.

Irene padded across the cold hardwood floor to the cold linoleum floor and pushed the button to her coffeemaker, setting her work week in motion. She headed to the room of her little blond-haired boy, to wake him up and get him ready for school two hours early because that's when she had to go to work. Make a quick breakfast, drink a quick cup, make a quick lunch for little Jeffrey, pile into the car, drop him off at the morning day care, pick him up two hours after school let out because that's when she got off work. Maybe she'd get a video tonight after work if she could manage it, pick up a pizza. He liked pizza and she didn't always feel like cooking. Not for just the two of them, sitting at home every night. He's a sweet boy, but . . . it was just not how she'd planned it.

Irene pulled into the lurching traffic after dropping Jeffrey off and jerked along in the bumper-to-bumper nonsense. Today was going to be hectic at work. Today was the day Bea's Candies was unveiling the Chocolate Jesus, just in time for Easter.

Irene Peatmos had worked at the Bea's Candy Works long enough to realize that Mr. Bea was a particularly egotistical and stupid person. She also realized that along with this stupidity came a viciousness, a clumsy, conniving malevolence that she didn't like in the least.

Chocolate Jesus! Who ever heard of such a thing?! This was bound to bring the entire company down, she just knew it. *And even if it does work, out of some sort of dumb luck that seems to follow assholes around (how come I can never get a lucky break?) why on earth hire that guy? Usually Mr. Bea's quite happy to just steal an idea. This Sydney person is . . . nuts. And his brother! What a creep. No,* she thought, picking up speed as the traffic thinned toward the eastern side of town, *something's not right.* You could tell from Day One.

"Irene, could you get a Freeb's Cola-Nated beverage for Sydney?" Mr. Bea was oozing a rather convincing smile along with his own peculiar brand of false charm.

"Decaffeinated if you will," Sydney added. "My delicate metabolic system is unable to withstand the onslaught of jagged caffeine crystals."

". . . Okay." Irene forced a smile. "Sure, decaffeinated. Anything for you?" She turned toward Marty, who was dressed in an ever-so-slightly-too-small suit, sporting a too-wide lapel that had a rather obvious stain on it that he kept wishing would somehow go away.

"I think I'll have the rauschbeir." Marty looked up from his cocktail menu and managed an oily smile. "Maybe we can share a soda later?"

"Mmmm, great." Irene inadvertently flared her nostrils.

"Good choice." Professor Broma smiled as he ordered his usual full liter of southern German festbeir.

Everyone was positioned around the large desk in Mr. Bea's office save for Mrs. Bea, who was in Switzerland receiving blood transfusions from Keith Richards's old doctor.

"Well, Sydney, since you mailed in your suggestion," Mr. Bea began, "and a brilliant idea I might add, we've been kicking a few things around. Care for a butter cream?"

"Oh, why, thank you. Yes." Sydney, quite proud of his accomplishment and at-long-last recognition, reached over to the bowl Mr. Bea offered and delicately chose a milk chocolate confection.

"Marty?"

"Uh, no, I don't eat sweets."

"Well, let's get started. Theo, why don't you show the boys what we've come up with so far."

Heh-heh-heh-hem, Professor Broma cleared his throat. *We.* "Well, my research, as well as basic chocolate physics, tells us that our Jesus can come in any number of sizes, ranging from two-inch miniatures upwards to the limits of the largest known chocolate Santas, bunnies and . . . beyond. You see, in our favor is the compact nature of the typical King of Kings pose—I'm talking hands held in front in your basic prayer pose . . ."

"Well, we're certainly not going to put Him in a diaper and fucking nail Him to a chocolate cross!" Mr. Bea laughed loudly. "Jesus! Besides, that sort of molding—it's cost prohibitive."

Upon hearing Mr. Bea utter the word "fucking," Sydney got the first of what would be many waves of fear that he was in the wrong place, while Marty decided Mr. Bea was all right.

"Umm, yes . . ." Broma continued. "Basically, the Son of God, produced in a columnlike chocolate, will allow for a mold up to fifteen-inches in height and, in a solid version, upwards of a kilo in weight! And with my new enrobing device . . ."

"No way!" Mr. Bea yelled. "We're not going fucking metric here, Theo."

"Zat iss how V vay chocolate," Broma argued, his accent blooming as he grew excited. "I'm a cocoa zientist, Vilbur, not zum zalesmann!"

"All right, calm down." Mr. Bea shoved another butter cream into his mouth. "Go on, go on."

Broma collected himself and continued. "Actually the Christ in Prayer pose is quite cost-effective to produce and lends itself to assembly-line filling and foil wrapping. No long ears that easily break off like the Easter Bunny, no tricky Santa's beards and bags and those impossible tiny boots to try and run through a high-speed assembly line. No, it's almost . . . almost like *He* was made for chocolate. It's . . . it's a miracle."

"It's gonna kick the Easter Bunny's ass!" Marty yelled suddenly, frightening many people in the room, especially Sydney, who thought, *Oh, dear God. He's like a barbarian within Rome's walls.*

"Mmm-hmm." The famed Cocoa Scientist readjusted his thick glasses. "Well, I have a special, a very special tempered semisweet in mind for our Savior. It will give us a high gloss finish that, in my opinion, is perfectly fitting with the image you want for your basic Messiah and this chocolate . . ."

"Semisweet?!" Mr. Bea barked. "Isn't that a little, I don't know, fucking Satanic?"

"No vun likes za weiss chocolate!"

"No one's talking white chocolate, Theo. Calm down." Mr. Bea began to trim a cigar. "The question remains, Do we go with a solid chocolate Jesus, or do we fill the Prince of Peace?"

Sydney swelled with pride over his creation. It was so fascinating. Broma, the Cocoa Master, was all that Sydney had imagined, though he had never pictured the world he now sat in: the big table, the bowl of butter creams, his new, important job. At long last his talents had been recognized. In the excitement, he had an idea. "Why not make an M&M-style candy? Your ad campaign could run along the lines of 'Melts in your mouth, no stigmata on your hands.' "

Marty suddenly felt hot around the collar, thinking, *Oh, shit, my stupid brother's gonna ruin fucking everything on the first fucking day. Thank God that money's already in the bank.*

"Hmmm . . . ?" Mr. Bea's voice closed in on Sydney.

The room was dead silent, everyone seemingly caught in midair, mid-act, the second hand on the wall clock cocked back in anticipation of the next tick forward.

"I like it. This is going to be just perfect." Mr. Bea smiled and shoved another butter cream into his mouth. "That's good. Yeah! Huh? Huh, Theo? Didn't I tell you this young man has some ideas? Yes, I can just see it," Mr. Bea continued, "we do all sorts of Chocolate Jesuses. M&M Messiahs, small foil-wrapped Sons of God, big hollow Easter Basket Saviors." Mr. Bea took a puff on a Macanudo and decided, *I really don't like this brand.* He looked about the room and could hardly keep from laughing aloud. "We take that little guy, the Sweet Lamb I'm talking here, swathe him in some brightly colored foil, do that high gloss temperization you were talking about . . ."

"Chemo-chocolate galvanism," Broma corrected.

"Yeah, whatever, and you gently lay down that little foil-wrapped guy into the lime green depths of an excelsior-lined Easter basket? Now, that's a fucking winner. Huh? Huh?! I can't wait till Christmas--this thing's going to fucking replace nativity sets!" Mr. Bea looked about the room, a huge smile on his face. *Their next meeting will be at the unemployment office. Hah!*

life is sweet

marty was walking a bit taller these days, a little straighter of back and springier of step. He smiled unashamedly at a pretty woman he passed on the street. He no longer jerked his head around, suddenly thinking a surprise beating had found him. The sun was shining and, best of all, he could now reach into his pocket and grab a wad of cash, a fat roll of new bills. His spirit surged with their electricity, his entire being filled with the power of a newly acquired pile of dough. And not just any dough, not the kind of dough he would've had to slave for for hours down at the plant, his hands freezing from loading the boxes of shaved ice and chicken backs, throwing all the heavy cases into the delivery truck, all that fucking traffic. *No, this was made the easy way. Doing almost nothing. Sydney earned most of it, really. What dumb luck. Life is bizarre.*

This is gonna be sweet, Marty thought as he pushed Dutchman's door open and walked in with an implied open-armed, big-smile celebration.

"Ben, my friend. My friend, Ben." Marty took the stool, which practically had his name carved into it.

Ben finished pouring a vodka martini for an old man in a fedora who sat off at the dark end of the bar—Marty always liked the door end of the bar, not the *pissoir* end—and slowly made his way toward him. Marty could see the look on his face: Ben was pissed off about the money he owed, but didn't want to say, them being friends.

Marty peeled out a roll of twenties and began to count them off. "Your house's finest ale, my good man. This should cover my tab and then some."

"Well, well, well." Ben smiled, took up the money and counted it as he tapped a pitcher of Rocko's draft. "Turned to crime now or finally make a winning bet?"

"Me? I beg your pardon. This money was earned off the sweat of my brow."

"Is that right?"

Marty explained his sudden reversal of fortune.

"You're telling me," Ben had to go over it again, "that Sydney sent in some unsolicited candy idea and now they're gonna make a candy shaped like Jesus . . ."

"For Easter."

"For Easter, and now Sydney's working for Bea's Candies?"

"Yeah."

"What does he know about chocolate?"

Marty shrugged. "And not only that, but he's living at the Bea's factory now. I got my place back to myself." Marty smiled and decided to head over to Chaim's after he finished his beer.

"A Chocolate *Jesus*?"

"Mmm-hmm."

"No way."

"I'm tellin' ya. Go check out Short's Drugs. They got

'em there, right next to the fuckin' bunnies and eggs." Marty took a long and oh-so-satisfied drink of that fine Rocko's beer. "Hey, I'm goin' to the track. Wanna come?"

"You're not gonna bet it all away instantly are you?"

"What are you talkin'?"

"Just instantly, huh?" Ben nodded and took a wee sip o' Bushmills. "You are."

"I'm on a roll. Let's go!"

"Don't you think some people are gonna get pissed off about them making a candy bar outta Christ?" Ben asked.

Marty thought about this prospect as though for the first time . . . because it was. He thought about Jesus. Jesus, to Marty, was like a baseball star from the twenties. Say, Tris Speaker. Marty knew he played for the Indians, was some great center fielder, but he couldn't pick him out of a lineup. He wasn't on ESPN.

Same with Jesus. Except for the beard and the robe, I wouldn't know him from Adam. I know he could walk on water supposedly, turned some water to wine, saved a ho, made some lame kid walk and shit, some blind guy see. He was kinda like Tommy without Pete Townsend. And then he got busted by the Romans. And I think Jesus' robe fucked up Richard Burton. Burton made such a good Roman. I always liked the Romans. And then they nailed him to a cross.

"That's what catapulted him. Gettin' nailed to the cross." Marty finished his beer and decided he'd bet $100 against any Cowboys pulling guns or raping through training camp, 15–1, and pray for a miracle.

"Huh?" Ben asked.

"Oh yeah, nailed to a cross, light shines down on him. He's like the only name player ever get nailed to a cross and he says, 'Forgive them, Father, they know not?' and then He's gone! It's like Jim Croce, or Stevie Ray, I don't know."

"I guess." Ben saw Marty's light.

"If ya ask me, I think the things gonna sell," Marty said. "How many people could possibly have a problem with dipping Jesus into dark chocolate anyway?"

jesús's day off

jesús sat in the front seat of the Reverend's chill-ass '59 Fleetwood as the Apocalyptic Handicapper maneuvered the monstrous vehicle down Miracle Mountain's winding road.

It was Saturday. Jesús's day off. The day when the Reverend would drop him off in the south side of town to shop and visit. Willie would drive Jesús down the mountain in that gigantic car, Jesús hardly believing it could negotiate the turns, it was so long and wide, and he would visit his amigo, Salva. Salva worked for a construction company and made more money than Jesús and drove around in a Ford Bronco, highly coveted and revered among the Latinos in Valley, California.

Jesús would meet Salva in the southeast part of town, the Latino section of Valley, where the streets were crowded with people, where the billboards became Spanish, where the taco trucks were parked in the empty lots, where the brown faces replaced the pink-faced *gabachos,* where the produce stood in bins outside the markets. The streets were packed with people, and *musica romantica* drifted out of the cassette store. The smell of food was everywhere and men in white cowboy hats pushed small ice cream carts *"Nieves Michoacán."*

Oh, the food! As soon as Jesús saw Padre Ewilly drive away, he'd practically run to the nearest taco truck and order up three tacos: *una carnitas, una lengua, y una carne asada. Y por favor,* load it up with hot sauce and chopped onions and cilantro. A bite of radish and one of a pickled jalapeno, a drink off the fizzing sweet can of Freeb's and Jesús was in Heaven! Tacos! Carne!

And then he'd hook up with Salva and they'd head off to Los Billares and shoot a couple of games of pool. Drink a beer, maybe two—Jesús didn't dare arrive back at the holy Miracle Mountain smelling of alcohol. They'd shoot their pool, slide dollar bills into the jukebox for some Los Tigres del Norte and Jesús just couldn't get enough. He'd burst into town every Saturday like Fletcher Christian landing in Tahiti.

It was so lonely up there on the mountain all the time. That was the worst thing about his job. For six days a week, Jesús only saw the Reverend, and Padre Ewilly spoke very little Spanish, so it was as though he were alone all the time. Alone with his thoughts and nothing else.

The Reverend spoke some Spanish, oh yeah he did, he'd think as he finished another early morning session of light weights, toweled himself off and offered a tall, cool phenyl-alanine- and guanine-laced wheat grass juice to Jesús. But, really, the Reverend's command of the language consisted of the words *now, here, yes, no, water, yesterday, today.* He spoke nary a *verbo.*

And so Jesús would grow lonely up atop Miracle Mountain. Especially at night with only the stars above, the creaking of the crickets, the whistling of the wind, the occasional patter of rain against his windowpane, a rustling in the brush, a dog barking off in the distance, a coyote howling in the dark. The coyotes would remind Jesús of home, of how far away he was, and then his loneliness would come crashing down upon him and he would light the small, waxy candles of his altar to keep the loneliness at bay and his head would spin with visions of Santa Madre and his sweet wife, Reyna, of the day they might finally be together again. He could see her face, her pretty little face in his mind's eye, but only fleetingly, a quick glance. Whenever he tried—alone up there at night on Miracle Mountain or even now waiting for Salva to line up his shot—to look deep into sweet Reyna's dark, limitless eyes, he would lose the tender thread that held them together.

Jesús dug into his pocket as Salva racked another game. There wasn't much there after the shopping and the tacos, but Jesús decided to spend what little he had on a phone call home. To Uruapan, to talk to Santa Madre and sweet Reyna. *Y una mas cerveza.*

The cherry Caddy pulled into the Reverend's spot atop Miracle Mountain and the two men got out of the huge car.

"Want me to help you with those groceries?" Willie smiled.

"Oh, no." Jesús was quite nervous. "Ease okay. Thaz fine."

"You sure you got it? Lemme help you with a bag," the Reverend insisted.

"Ease okay." Jesús nodded incessantly, his mind stuck on the flank steak he had stuffed in the middle of one of the bags, right next to his contraband cigarettes. Jesús didn't like having to sneak these things, but the Reverend's lifestyle was impossible. All that running up and down Miracle Mountain. In Mexico, a man didn't run once he turned twenty unless thieves or police were after him. And those green drinks and no meat! *Esta loco, solo los Gabachos.*

The Reverend readied himself for another episode of *Sweatin' with the Lord.* It was time to take some calls, gauge the mood of his flock as Armageddon approached. Sort of. *Sweatin' with the Lord* was the toughest half hour of aerobics on TV today, *Men's Health* had claimed. Though the reviewer was turned off by the strident religious tone of the exercise program, no one could deny its seriousness. There was many an agnostic and atheist fitness enthusiast who secretly taped the show and worked out in the solitude of his or her home, privately admitting that Reverend Willie Domingo could probably have kicked Jack La Lanne's ass in a fantasy bout of dizzying proportions.

Willie would have been shocked had he known the extent of his viewership who watched with the sound down and the stereo on (playing God only knows what kind of music), but as the end of the world approached, sort of, even the unbeliever got caught up in the game. The sound came on. Fitness junkies who were waiting to see the Reverend with egg on his face became even more rabid followers than those who held both Jesus *and* a low resting heart rate dear.

Everyone was waiting to see what he was gonna do come Judgment Day.

C: Yeah, Reverend, I think the Lord allowed me through your producer's call screening. I think this may be your last chance to repent to God. You have twisted the word of the Scripture. No man can know the time.

R: Why do you suppose Christ gave signs of abomination, of desolation? False prophets? False Christs will lead us astray. They are upon us as we speak! The signs are so we can prepare.

C: *You* are a false prophet, but there's still time. God is giving you an opportunity to turn back. You have raised your hand against the Scripture.

R: Well, thank you for calling. We walk by faith, not sight, and now let's take another caller. Hello and welcome to *Sweatin' with the Lord.*

C: Yeah, Reverend, would you like to have a debate on the truth of the Bible?

R: What truth is that?

C: There is only one truth.

R: Well, do you have a question?

C: Yeah, Daniel 7:23–25 is not yet fulfilled.

R: Yes, the dividing of the four beasts, mmm-hmmm. This is referring to a final tribulation when Satan is loosed—

C: Yeah, but the laws and times haven't changed. So how has that been fulfilled?

R: Um, I'm sorry we can't agree. Uhh . . . you need to read Matthew 28 in the original Greek, but thank you for calling. And let's take our next caller. Thank you and welcome to *Sweatin' with the Lord.*

C: What about the end of the world? I thought you said the world was gonna end. What happened with that?

R: That's coming. The end is coming. We must have faith. Jesus will return. The question is, are *you* ready? Are you ready to face the Lord, or are your body and soul still polluted? Remember, people, God has a very, very precise program. Now, why don't we

all listen to some beautiful inspiring hymns as we cool
down with a session of stretching.

The Reverend gave Jesús the cue and Jesús cut to an old
tape of some light stretching and the ever-reliable Ray Coniff
Singers *Gospel Hits* album.

Willie Domingo walked out of the studio a dejected
man. He stepped outside to the setting sun and looked down
at Valley from his perch atop Miracle Mountain. The Reverend was a little worried despite his closeness to God that
late afternoon. *Why did I predict the end of the world? What
was I thinking?!*

There were times, though, when the sun was settling
into the vast Pacific, when the air glowed orange and the
smog became beautiful, that the Reverend Domingo really
did wonder if The End wasn't coming. The world had become such a horrible place, full of violence and sin.

He looked down at the city, down through the sickly
air, the sun- and heat-baked day's smog forming a thin, gray
mousse that hung over the region. Willie looked down from
his mountain perch at all the houses in the endless summer's
dusk sitting vague on their common streets, marked only by
the blue glow and incessant babble of a hundred thousand
TVs spilling out onto little green yards. Sprinklers spinning
and chattering each and every long, languid summer evening
over the mirror-imaged postage-stamp plots of neatly
trimmed lawn. A man with a potbelly and white T-shirt, his
dark socks pulled up to his knees, standing in the midst of
his very own bit of repliant lawn, applying his very own set
of lawn care products systems, sipping on a bottle of Freeb's
Cola-Nated beverage. Kids materializing in the cooling dusk
like post-apocalyptic desert creatures. People heading to the

mall in the glazed mental state of consumer junkies pushing baby strollers or shopping carts, marching silently down to the thousand burgermongers for a quick bite, or into a never-closed 7-24 minimart for a quart of Rocko's Malt Liquor and a 'Cono bag of Wad Gompers.

He looked down at all the debauchery he knew was going on that very minute, even if he couldn't make out each and every deplorable act of heinous deviltry. *All the adulteresses, all those drunk with the sins of the flesh, hooked upon the Satanic release of orgasmic lust. The slothful poisoned with their endless burgers, dairy products and sugar. Their systems so toxified they couldn't find the love of the Lord if it bit them on their fat asses. They're all listless and unaware. What if He is coming? A kingdom awaits us.*

Willie looked down upon the town, nearly anxious for the sweet atonement that awaited himself and the chosen few. He looked forward to the wrathful punishment that lay in store for the sinners, the flailing of the flesh, the wailing of lost souls. *Now, that's a spectacle you want front row seats for . . . It is written 2 Paul 3:10: "But the day of the Lord will come as a thief in the night: in which the heavens shall pass away with great noise, and the elements shall melt with fervent heat, the earth also and the works that are therein shall be burned up."* Willie could almost get behind that. *And if not? Isla Basura can't be that bad. Wonder if I'd have to speak Spanish?*

Willie crouched down, pushed his Stetson up his brow and wiped a bit of dust off his Tony Lamas. He thought of Bessie, his long-gone wife. He could feel her right next to him sometimes. Like God almost . . . but even more palpable.

sydney

sydney stretched out at his grand new desk up in the guest room of the north wing of Building #1 and took up his trusted Mont Blanc. An instrument he had let lie for far too long.

He opened up his Journal and began scribbling furiously.

It is with mixed feelings that I pick up my trusty Mont Blanc tonight. It has been far, far too long, my friend. But if Dr. Jenkins could see me now, would even *he* have been able to predict my meteoric rise in the outside world? I think not. I am now a major player in the international chocolate industry! Not only is my first foray into candy design to be found in every candy store across the United States (except for Hawaii—the Family Bea apparently suffered greatly at the hands of our fiftieth and most Polynesian of states and so the fair Islanders are deprived of my sweet design), but I have also been hired on to whip the entire outfit into shape.

While my first weeks here have gone rather smoothly, I can see that my work is cut out for me. It seems that in the final analysis Bea's Candies is run no better than Jack Anvil's Charbroiled

Burgers, and while Mr. Bea is a far more cultured and civilized person than the workingman's buffoon, Miles McPhearson, he is, ultimately, no more qualified a manager. Luckily, they now have me.

My investigations into the inner working of the Bea's Candy Works have already turned up a number of "problem areas." While the production plant seems to be up to modern standards, other areas operate in a forgotten era that perhaps only the near-mythical Mrs. Bea might remember, during one of the brief flashes of coherence her son tells me overcome her every now and again. I accidentally bumped into her late one night. I was heading to the somewhat extensive library at the Candy Works when I came upon a person strapped to a wheelchair making strange sucking sounds. I stopped dead in my tracks, but the "creature" sensed my presence and immediately wheeled about in my direction. It was as though I were in a badly done high school stage version of *Psycho,* the scene where the mummified remains of poor Norman Bates's mother are flashed to a horrified audience. I was thinking it might be some sort of Disneyland animatronic atrocity, one of the many eccentric and expensive whims that seem to occupy the empty, rich life of Mr. Bea, when it spoke to me.

"Wilbur, is that you? Is that you, boy?"

I then realized this was the revered icon and founder of Bea's Candies. She continued making sucking noises as she struggled with a straw to get every last drop out of a rather large cocktail glass decorated with a bright pink umbrella. Luckily, her eyesight is apparantly about as keen as a white rhino's and, combined with the distraction of her drink, it allowed me to slowly back down the hall and slip into my room. I guess I must now limit my library visits to business hours.

I was able, at long last, to meet the famed chocolate scientist, Theodore Broma. The meeting, alas, was like many of his candies: bittersweet. It seems that contrary to what I had believed, the good scientist is no longer at the apex of his creative powers. Frankly, he has come up with nothing since his ingenious Wad Gomper was introduced in the early eighties. Even John Travolta has managed a comeback in such a time frame. Tomorrow we will go over the production of the Chocolate Jesus. Perhaps I might inspire the old Cocoa Master to break through the obvious crust that has formed on many of his synapsal gaps and help him to regain his former glory.

I was able to dodge a potential disaster in the form of my rather coarse sibling, Martin. He actually tried to pass himself off as some sort of manager/agent when I was first contacted by the candy conglomerate. He felt that he was somehow protecting me, when, in fact, it is only through my resourcefulness that he is able to still walk upright. The money I made with the sale of the Chocolate Jesus paid off his quite substantial gambling debt, thereby averting the almost certain kneecapping that awaited him. You'd think this might humble Martin a bit, take the wind out of his sails so to speak, but, alas, such is not the case. He operates under the illusion that it was *he* who made our sudden and good change in fortune possible. Luckily, the fistful of cash Mr. Bea gave him sent him straight back to Apartment 17.

Another stumbling block to the smooth running I have in store for this once-great company is my coworker over in Letters. The bookkeeper, Scrimshaw, I believe may be a direct descendant of the man who inspired Bartleby the Scrivener. He wears hearing aids the size of orange wedges behind both ears yet, mysteriously, claims he can never hear a word I'm saying, and then when he finally does, he yells at me to stop yelling. He has not been at all forthcoming with my requests for the employee records of everyone who has worked here for the last thirty-five years and keeps mentioning antique office machines that I'm not sure ever existed. Luckily, he doesn't understand the workings of the computer at all and I am in the process of placing myself at the helm of Bea's Candies World Wide Web page! The resources that will be at my disposal are mind-boggling.

And that is why I make this entry into my journal with some guilt. My work here at the factory has put my investigations into the Kennedy Assassination on complete hold! If the triggermen only knew, they might breathe a sigh of relief. I know chocolate is not as important as solving America's most important murder case, but lost time will quickly be made up when I turn the resources and search engines of the entire Internet to bear upon solving this tragic crime.

professor broma

professor broma was a small man with an immense nest of insane gray hair that stuck out in all directions from his bespectacled head. He wore the thick wire-rimmed glasses of a type once favored by hippies and evil Nazi scientists, and once on Candy Works grounds he was never dressed in anything save his lab coat, which stretched down to mid-calf. It was thickly starched and white, with "Broma" embroidered over the left breast like a French chef's and it was often spattered with chocolate, nougat, butter cream and the various colors Mr. Bea was always forcing him to experiment with—but not today. This was a Monday morning's chocolatier's lab coat, spotless and white like the one on Sydney, who insisted on spending the day under the tutelage of the famed chocolate scientist.

"German Law, das Schokoladen Rheinheitsgebot, allows four ingredients in the making of fine chocolate," Broma told the rapt Sydney as they made their way down the catwalk that ran above the production line in Building #5. "Number one is cocoa liquor. Lots of cocoa liquor. Number two is vanilla. Real vanilla, no artificial crrr-aaap! Sugar, und force? Ze soy lecithin for da crrr-eamy tegsure!"

"And milk!" Sydney added enthusiastically.

"Milk, hah! Zat ess only für za milk chocolate." Broma put his arm around Sydney, lowered his goggles and led them deeper into the factory. Professor Broma had a great disdain for milk chocolate and explained his position to Sydney. "It's merely an adulterated version of . . . za zemizveet. Und I vill never forgive Henry Nestle! A mere manufacturer of evaporated milk! Ruining everything und zen! Taking all za credit from zis Judas chocolatier, Daniel Peter. It's easier to adulterate, you know."

"Hmm?" Sydney looked up from his notebook.

"Milk chocolate. Up the sugar, lower the cocoa butter, throw in some vegetable fat. Zey ver using lard ven I got here in za late sixties, if you can believe zat!"

"I am shocked, sir." Sydney was on Broma's side. All the way.

"Business. I understand that. The Wad Gomper, it doesn't fall within the Schokoladen Reinheitsgebot, you know."

"No?" Sydney feared for a nation.

Broma felt embarrassment in the face of Sydney's sincere disappointment. Broma's real love was the high-end market. His heart lay in the fine art of chocolate. The Godivas, the Lindts, the Valrhonas of the world. Why be The Gap when you might aspire to Coco Chanel? "This is the first time Mr. Bea's allowed me to make a mass-produced candy out of dark chocolate. The finest chocolate, the kind we will be using for the Chocolate Jesus!" Broma began his self-defense. "Za zemizveet! Von our very own zeigrret plantations of grrrr and crrrr-u crrrrr-iollo cocoa beans. Za crrrrr-iollo is za finest cocoa bean you know, und *zese beans . . .*" He nodded knowingly, as did Sydney in return while scribbling in his notebook.

"What were used for your Chocolate Jesus." *Yes, this Chocolate Jesus will be just the vehicle to put me back on top. Where I belong. Scheisskopf at Hershey. Und Cadbury's . . . shweinhunds!* "My new chemo-chocolate galvanism und patented enrrrr-obing device zat enables detailing beyond any zeen before? Combined vid my prrrr-ivate rrrr-eserve cocoa bean stocks from Oaxaca?! It is a verk of art!

"Chocolate was invented by za Aztecs, you know." Broma led Sydney through the storage warehouse stacked with endless pallets filled with fifty-five-pound burlap sacks of raw cocoa beans. "They were the first chocoholics. Montezuma drank fifty cups a day."

"No!" Sydney was shocked by such excess. "Fifty?!"

Professor Broma nodded. "He was so blitzed on cocoa? He could barely lift a hand against Cortez when he showed up. Sipping all that cold bitter schokoladen in the echoing empty stone corridors deep within his temple in Tenochtitlán. Just one more golden goblet of chocolate flavored with milk and cinnamon as the Spaniards marched, marched relentlessly toward Destiny . . ."

This man is brilliant, Sydney declared in his brain. *Tonight I begin work on the definitive biography of this pioneering chocolate visionary.*

Broma and Sydney were now deep in the chocolate works of the factory, feeling the heat of the giant roasters, the humidity of all the thousands of gallons of molten chocolate.

"Come, let me show you." Broma led Sydney to the roasters. "You see here is where the first manipulation is performed. The raw cocoa beans are slowly, *slowly*, roasted just so."

Sydney was furiously taking notes. "What temperature do *we* roast at?"

"Well, my boy, I like to take it to 214 degrees, just past the boiling point of water. And for just a short time." Broma wagged his finger at Sydney, as though he might one day man the controls. "Just to bring out its hidden brown color, to gently coax the bean to give up its rich aroma, yet still retain its fruitiness and earthy flavors." Broma smiled broadly.

The two men walked past gigantic vats filled with pools of molten chocolate. Huge mechanical arms slowly kneaded the beautiful glossy, dark brown liquid, and the air was rich and warm with chocolate.

"You see? See how it's gently, lovingly kneaded?" Broma was staring deeply into the chocolate, while Sydney studied Broma. Professor Broma had his goggles pulled on and in his lab coat looked more like a WWI flying ace than a world-renowned chocolitician. He peered deeply into an immense vat of molten chocolate held at a constant and unwavering 88 degrees. "Za Virgin Mary didn't tend to Him viz zuch care."

Sydney was both very impressed and very concerned, but didn't dare say anything.

"Za zing viz chocolate," Broma looked up from his Cocoa Lake reverie, "you must first destroy it, und zen?! You recrrr-eate it into zumzing it never vas before. *I* rrr-elease the mysteries of the heavens, rrr-eveal za zeigrets of za Gods . . . Za Food of Za Gods!" Broma looked wide-eyed at Sydney.

a slight

miscalculation

the chocolate jesus worked like a charm. Backed
with a multimillion-dollar ad campaign, the *Time* cover story
on the "Sweet Jesus," and all the available shelf space and
distribution contracts Bea already had in place for the Wad
Gomper, the thing couldn't fail. It was an Easter smash! "Put
the God back in Easter" and "Resurrect a Chocolate Jesus
in your Easter Basket" had proved to be winning ad slogans,
and everyone assembled in the Board Room that afternoon
was as happy as could be, save for one person who was
having a rather difficult time keeping a somewhat uncon-
vincing smile pasted on his face.

"Let's hear the numbers, Fretwell," Mrs. Bea buzzed.

Fretwell flipped through his sheaf of papers, a near
sweat-producing stab of lunch's pesto cream sauce negoti-
ating rather badly a sharp turn in his GI tract. "Woah!" he
inadvertently gasped.

"Hmm?" Mrs. Bea looked concerned.

"No, ohh-umm, here it is." The figures were swimming
before his eyes. *I'm never touching dairy again.* Fretwell flipped
through the pages of his accounting book. It was the size of

a windowpane and as thick as an unabridged Oxford dictionary. Between rooms, Fretwell pulled it along in a special cart Broma had designed one afternoon after coming up empty again on candy bars. "Three million, fi-ohh-fifteen thousand, six hundred and . . . ," using the eraser end of a pencil Fretwell pecked at his calculator with brilliant speed, "sixty-eight units moved in March and April."

"Three million, did you hear that, boy?" Mrs. Bea asked Wilbur. Technically, it was more a taunt.

"Yes, Mother." Mr. Bea didn't look up, pretending to be completely absorbed in a delicate cigar trimming.

"I told you someone off the street could come up with something better than you. Three million units." Mrs. Bea said it as tenderly as one might while using a mechanical voice box.

"It was *my* idea in the first place," Mr. Bea tried. "I picked it."

"*Your* idea, tsk." Mrs. Bea's "tsk" was a quacking mock to Wilbur. "Tell us again, Fretwell."

"Hmm?" Fretwell asked, genuinely moved by the fact that his entire innards had just then melted.

"The sales figures."

"Three million?" Fretwell was sure everyone noticed the gigantic sweat molecules forming on his brow right then.

"Three million," Mrs. Bea repeated. "Three million and you know what?"

"What, Mother?" Mr. Bea could barely contain himself.

"We have this young man to thank." Mrs. Bea wheeled over to Sydney and patted him on the back. "Well, done, boy. Choosing your candy bar is the first decent move my son's made in years."

"Why, thank you, ma'am." Sydney basked in his glory.

"And, Theo, great job on the chocolate. I think it might be your finest work yet."

"Thank you, ma'am." Professor Broma looked up from a pile of articles covering his return to the top of the cocoa heap.

"Yes, yes." Mrs. Bea wheeled toward Wilbur, whose forehead at this point was hotter than the glowing end of his cigar. "Who knows, maybe even *you'll* get inspired to do some decent work, Wilbur. Or I might have to put Sydney here in charge." Mrs. Bea laughed—*raaa-raaa-raaa*. She fired up another cigarette and turned to Scrimshaw. "Orville, it's a beautiful day today. I'd like to see the garden out back."

"Yes, ma'am."

Wilbur Bea sat alone in his office, fuming worse than ever. He set down his Romeo y Julieta Exhibicion #4, the forty-eight-ring gauge being the most pleasing to Mr. Bea's thick, short-fingered hand, and took a drink off his Ramos Fizz, a cocktail Mr. Bea wasn't particularly fond of, but one that is very difficult to make. He was hoping to get a chance to yell at the server, but, alas, the crack cocktail-making team had shined again.

Mr. Bea's Jurassic cerebellum simply couldn't fathom why everything wasn't working according to plan. *How can my plan not be working perfectly? That damn candy was supposed to sink the company, not fucking revive it!* Mr. Bea took a pissed-off puff off the fine Cuban robusto and then ground it out disgustedly.

He got out of his chair and looked through his window at the loading dock, where the next fleet of trucks loaded with Chocolate Jesuses sat. He had the sinking feeling that he was ruined. The company was saved and he was ruined. He was no closer to selling to Frito-Lay, no closer to running the company, and Mother—he shuddered at the thought—was still not only somehow alive but remaining in complete control of Bea's Candies. At that thought, Mr. Bea's mind flew down the last corridor in the far wing, past Letters to Mother lying in her bed, being reattached to her IV. *All those Chocolate Jesuses. Going to all points of the United States. Except Hawaii, of course. Fuck her and that Sydney!*

"Shit!" he said aloud.

Wilbur Bea began his latest installment of "Hating Mother." During his reverie assassinations of Mother's character and parenting skills, Wilbur was always quite adept at conveniently forgetting that it was she who had made him rich. His entire life had basically consisted of fucking around with an ever grander evolutionary trail of toys: Bozo at his eighth birthday party, the fleet of Schwinn bikes, the private prep school with the University of Oklahoma football star grading system, the arrival of the first Jaguar when he turned eighteen, the arrival of the second Jaguar three weeks later after he wrapped the first one around a tree, the trips abroad to Europe and Asia where the young Wilbur Bea took this great educational opportunity to conduct in-depth studies of the world's fleshpots, gaining his first taste for prostitutes (he was quick to realize that where a woman couldn't be wooed—and Mr. Bea's wooing technique could be summed up as clumsy turning quickly caustic—she might be bought).

But still, with Mother there in the wings, the fly in his ointment, Mr. Bea remained more a big kid with one of the world's largest allowances than a Powerful Captain of Industry. *I'm sick of being a fucking puppet!*

Mr. Bea entered his walk-in humidor and hunted out his

most malevolent of smokes: the Royal Jamaica Churchill Ma-
duro, a cigar most men falsely imagined was the same size
as their penis. Mr. Bea sat at his desk preparing the thick,
10½-inch cigar, and tried to formulate the if-I-can't-have-the-
company-no-one-will part of his scheme, his mind creaking
and straining under the weight of thought. A process that
went something like this: *Must win, must win, must destroy
company. How does that saying go? You have to kill the patient
to save it? Mmm, no . . . What's that one about the baby and the
bathwater? . . . Oh! I know! I may have lost the battle, but I
haven't lost the war.* That was as far as Mr. Bea got that
afternoon.

two dudes 11

"**yo, dude.**"

"Whaddup, dude?"

"Nuthin'. Whatchou up to?"

"Not a damn thing." Dude #1 was in the amazing barber's chair that was the centerpiece of his living room if not his entire life. It was from the modern miracle of the barber's chair—complete with hydraulic lift and foot rest, he would have any and all visitors know—that he commandeered much of his waking state.

The chair spun, it lifted, it lowered, it leaned back. It was the closest thing to Kirk's seat on the bridge of the starship *Enterprise* that any of the people the Two Dudes knew possessed, and armed with the TV remote and a can of beer, Dude #1 was good to go, flippin' channels, drinkin' beer, talkin' smack.

"Dude, we need some action!" Dude #2 said as he sat on a slightly mildewed bean bag chair that no one could recall arriving in the corner a few months back.

"Fully, dude," Dude #1 agreed as he sped through the TV channels: 22, 16, 17, 18, 47, 98. Sound up. Sound down.

Click! Click! Click!

C: Earlier you said the date was *exactly* August 15.
R: I never said—
C: Yes, you did. I have it on tape! And now you're saying
   that events will begin to—

Click!

"... *Drink Rocko's. It's Rocko's. It packs a punch, it's got
the gusto. The beer with party-ability* ..."

"Like some, like, chicks, dude," Dude #2 continued.

"Those Rocko-cttes'd be fine, ma brotha."

"Oh, yeah . . . ," Dude #2 agreed.

34, 35, 36, 47, 98.

Click!

"At Jack Anvil's the fries are always crisp and the burger's
always juicy. And this month in honor of Little Big Horn get a Sitting
Bull Sausage Sandwich for only ninety-nine cents—"

Click!

"Item C2239 is the Tonya Harding nine-month calendar. A
signed exclusive from GQV Shopping Network for only $12.99.
Relive with each month the triumphs and tragedies of America's
own trailer park sweetheart—"

Click!

"I'd do Tonya," Dude #1 stated matter-of-factly.

"Shit, dude, Tonya'd be a cool girlfriend. She's got, like,
a pickup and shit."

"Cool."

Click!

"It's like she knew me all my life! She said I'd meet a tall, dark-haired man."

"I asked about children? And you know what? She saw twins!"

"She told me that my new relationship? Not only is it going to continue, but it's going to a higher level!"

"Call now! The first fifteen minutes are free! Don't wait! Our lines are open."

Click!

"Hey, dude, why don't you call them up? Maybe the psychic can tell you if you're gonna get laid this century."

"Fuck you, dude! Like you're getting any. Hey, isn't *Baywatch* on?" Dude #2 asked.

"I'n'know."

"Hey, dude? Have you, like, tried that Jesus candy?"

"That Chocolate Jesus?"

"Chyeah, duh."

"My grandy gave me some for Easter. Kinda gives me the creeps though."

"Yeah, it's a little Christian for me."

"Totally. If I'm gonna be scarfin' up a chocolate bar, I don't wanna be bitin' off Jesus' head."

"No way. But the chocolate's good."

"Dude, the chocolate rules," Dude #1 agreed. "It's a fuckin' Bea's!"

"Hometown chocolate,.."

"YEAH!" they both agreed.

"But, like, I'm getting bored with it, ya know?"

Dude #2 adjusted his stocking cap. "Totally, it's an obvious marketing ploy to grab a chunk of the Easter candy market."

"Fully, with the usual oversaturated and cynical ad campaign."

"Who falls for that anyway, dude?" Dude #2 inquired.

"Not us, dude. Our generation is famed for our resistance to Madison Avenue gimmickry."

"Totally."

"Ya know, dude?"

"What's that, dude?"

"If I was gonna make a candy bar, I'd go with Satan over Jesus."

"Hell yes! Satan rules! Hey, that reminds me, dude."

"What, dude?"

"I seen this show and do you, like, I mean, have you ever heard of, like, this thing called a chubalabra, dude?"

"A *what*, dude?"

"I think it's called, like, chubalabra or something, dude."

"What the fuck is that, dude?"

"I dunno, dude, like some kind of heinous alien type shit, ya know?"

"Like fuckin *X-Files* type shit?"

"Exactly, dude. It's like some fuckin' little critter . . ."

"Oh, dude!" Dude#1 interrupted, as he did ten or twelve times every minute or so. "I saw that episode. It was like these two Mexicans. They got all slimy and shit, but there was this hot Mexican babe in it. Dude, I'd be fully breakin' her shit down."

"Cool, but listen, this thing's like some little fuckin' beast, it's not a fuckin' Mexican. It's got, like, fangs and shit and eats dogs and cats."

"No way, dude."

"Way, dude. It's fuckin' Satanic and shit."

"I never seen one."

"You hardly ever leave that fuckin' chair, that's why you never fuckin' seen one. It'd have to be on TV or come through the fuckin' window before you'd see it."

"Fuck you, dude!" Dude #1 smiled and began stroking the fake red leather arms and lowering and raising the hydraulic lift. "Ever seen a chubby labry? If you can tell me you honestly seen one, I'll let you have The Chair for a whole week, dude."

"I ain't never seen one, dude, but I'm tellin' ya, if we could catch one and kill it, there'd be some money in that. Fuckin' Spock'd be over here in a minute, *Unsolved Mysteries, ET.*"

Dude #1 thought about this for a minute. "Ya know, dude, even though she's hella old and shit? I'd do Mary Hart."

"Dude, you're a fuckin' desperate dawg. Leeza Gibbons is way hotter. I bet she could go on down, dude!"

Dude #1 waved him off.

"Fuckin' Billy Idol was tappin' that shit, dude."

"No way, dude!"

"Way."

special delivery

in the beginning. in those oh-so-sweet days of spring, the predicting of the end of the world had been, to paraphrase Martha Stewart, a good thing. But now that the sun blazed each and every day, now that the rains were long gone and the chaparral had begun to dry, the Reverend could feel the draw of the date approaching. He knew the chances of the world ending were about the same as that of a rich man entering Heaven. What he needed was an escape hatch, a diversionary tactic. He needed somewhere to point the finger, which, really, was one of his religion's true talents.

And so Willie prayed. He prayed long and hard to God. He prayed that God would deliver to him a new scapegoat. The latest sacrificial lamb to rail against, the newest bogeyman to frighten the mob. A convenient enemy to fight: the unbeliever or the flesh-crazed, the drug-addled, the abortion-happy, the brown-skinned, the slanty-eyed, the nappy-haired, the sexually deviant (and this included anything besides eyes-closed, within-the-walls-of-procreating-marriage missionary positionism)—in short, any type of person or lifestyle that couldn't be found in your typical *Family Circus* comic strip. Just somewhere to point the mob he realized his flock would one day transform itself into. And it came to him one day. In the mail.

Please accept this gracious present of our exciting new product. Being a man of the cloth, we at Bea's Candies thought you might enjoy such a gift. Enjoy.

The Folks at Bea's Candies

Reverend Willie Domingo could hardly contain himself as he emptied the bulk-rate box. It was filled with foil-wrapped candies of the Son of God and one 8-inch-tall chocolate figurine of the Messiah. He could barely believe his luck!

"Chocolate Jesus?!" The Reverend crumpled up the paper and looked at Jesús, who was blending the Reverend an early-morning lipidic acid–laced rice bran–guava smoothie. "Yes!"

"Yes, ease fine. How are you?" Jesús smiled at the mention of his name.

"Yes, it's fine," The Reverend smiled broadly, though he was truly concerned with what Jesus (the other Jesus, the famous one) might say if by any chance he did happen to arrive for Armageddon in a few weeks and find a bunch of fat, meat-eating heathens capping off their latest burger dinner with a chocolate graven image of himself. "In fact, it's an abomination!"

In a flash of inspiration, with a profound sense of duty, with an eagerness and clear message such as he hadn't had in weeks, the Reverend switched on his microphone after

Jesús (the Mexican one) gave him the signal to begin a *Sweatin' with the Lord* episode.

"Hello, listeners and welcome to another episode of *Sweatin' with the Lord.* I'm your host, Willie Domingo. Now, folks, as we know, Jesus is coming back in a matter of weeks. His bags are packed, His reservation has been made, the flight's not being canceled. Now, do you think when He arrives ready to do battle with the Devil that He is going to want to see a graven candy image of himself adding to the coffers of an evil whoremonger? Filling the mouths of the suffering children with cavities? You know what I'm talking about. You know the blasphemous confection of which I speak. Cast aside your vile chocolates! Jesus will smote those whose hands carry the sign of His melted chocolate, the blasphemers whose lips are smeared with the Mark of the Beast. The Mark of the Chocolate Jesus.

"Oh, a pox upon those who partake of this evil sweet. Meat, coffee, sugar, chocolate—they are soul defiling habits. How can you worship Him? Your natural life force is enfeebled by these substances. You seek not God in the morning, but only your cherished idol in its steaming cup. Oh look, here comes Satan with free refills. 'Care for some cream and lots of sugar with your coffee?' he asks. 'How about a sweet candy? Look, it's shaped like Jesus.'

"This candy bar is the work of Satan! It's another of his temptations. He's looking for recruits among the unwary, among the weak of flesh. His troops are out and about in anticipation of the Final Battle. Satan's minions are ever watchful, ready to ensnare those not vigilant in the last moments before the return of the Great Redeemer."

The Reverend stared deeply into the camera. "Now, before we start on the abs, let's take some calls."

C: Hey, Reverend! People been making fun of me because I sold the family car. I mean, we won't need cars in the New Kingdom, will we?

R: Of course not. It's a peaceful realm the likes of which we cannot even imagine. Peaceful, serene and thank you for calling. Shall we take our next caller?

C: Uh, yeah, Reverend?

R: Good evening, brother, and thank you for calling.

C: Yeah, well, I been eating these Chocolate Jesuses . . . ?

R: The Chocolate Jesus is an abomination. Cast aside this confection of—

C: Yeah, but listen. I been eating these chocolate Christs? And hey! They real good. I mean the chocolate is real, real good. I think the Lord would be proud to know such quality chocolate was being used on His behalf.

R: Beg forgiveness before it's too late, sinner. Drop on your knees right now! The End Times are upon us. The sweet rapture—

C: Well, that's what I been tryin' to tell ya. Last night I was sittin' on the couch waitin' for the Lord to come like you said he was gonna? And, well, I'm kinda embarrassed to admit it, but I musta ate five or six Chocolate Jesuses. The big ones, too. Bought 'em for gifts for the nieces and nephews . . .

R: There's not much time!

C: Oh, sorry. Well, after I gobbled all them candies up? I had the most peaceful feeling come over me. My wife, Norla? She even said, "Gee honey, you shore look peaceful and all." And I don't know, Reverend, it was like I never felt so relaxed and happy and at peace with the world. Just like you said it would be for The Chosen . . .

R: You're toe up on chocolate, son! Don't you see? It's got your brain all addled. You need to eat fruit. You can't even think straight anymore. That's what Satan wants. He's gathering his forces in readiness for the Final Battle. Armageddon! You think *Satan's* sitting around watching TV all day eating candy? God's Army will not be the only one taking the field on Judgment Day. Only the clearheaded and right minded, only the pure of thought, the fit of flesh and the generous of spirit will be wearing the right jerseys. Only the virtuous few will be delivered.

long odds

chaim poplotnick gave his morning bun a rest for a second and returned to work on his latest brain wave: The Day of Atonement Tote Board. Chaim Poplotnick figured to make a lot of money off the Reverend Domingo's choosing of a date for the end of the world. Not only that, he figured it was a good way to get back at some hard-core Christians. *What good food have they ever come up with anyway? Besides, Domingo's one of those crazed vegetarian fitness nuts.* Chaim shook his head and scratched his ample stomach, glad not to suffer from such eating disorders.

Chaim, his eyes closed and his fingers greedily tickling the air before him, grabbed his chalk and in a flash began to fill the board with Revelations Long Shots.

Seas Turning to Blood? That was good for 175–1, minimum $100 bet.

Redemption of the 144,000? 200–1 there.

Of course! A Scorching of the Flesh of the Blasphemous/ Gnawing of the Tongues Daily Double, 500–1, minimum bet of $500.

The main obstacle to fantastic riches from this betting scheme was that nearly all the over/under money would be going on the world *not* ending. Chaim knew he could count on 52 percent of the Reverend's fanatic flock idiotically betting on August 15. He'd clean up on them, and 34 percent more could be counted on losing their betting slips in the weeks until the event date, but the rest? Poplotnick was going to owe quite a bit of money. Truckloads. In the end, the End of the World didn't add up, but Chaim simply couldn't resist the temptation of all that cash up front.

Luckily he'd also come up with the contingency plan.

Chaim unlocked the top drawer of his desk and pulled out the slick color brochure. Isla Basura, Costa Rica's emerald gem. It was an island paradise, an ecological wonderland; there were pools and tennis courts and ballroom dancing. That was all good and well, but Chaim's main concern was that the Costa Rican cuisine just wouldn't hold up for the many months he'd have to hide out down there to avoid the Day of Reckoning he was sure would be administered to his kneecaps when everyone found out he couldn't pay the winners. *I mean, you can only do so much with plantains, black beans and tortillas. Perhaps I should look into Brazil. Feijoada, now that's a meal!*

Reminded again of food, Chaim eagerly unwrapped another Chocolate Jesus. He held the candy under his nose and took a deep, thoughtful whiff. *Hmmm, what an aroma. Better than your typical candy bar. It's almost reminiscent of a, a . . . Valrhona Manjari if that's possible.*

Chaim took an uncharacteristically dainty bite out of the candy, as though he were a famed chocolate judge at a chocolate contest, and had begun making tiny nibbling motions when he realized the chocolate had immediately melted in his mouth. The sensation stunned him. *The flavor! It's incredible, not the usual overload of sugary sweetness. This stuff's amazing. What chocolate! So rich, so creamy.* In four minutes, without milk, Chaim had scarfed 43½ ounces of the delectable and exciting new candy from Bea's.

"Johnnie, I'm heading out to the store for some more of these chocolates and then to the steambaths. You keep an eye on the place while I'm gone."

"Yeah, all right, all right." Johnnie looked up from his *Big 'N' Busty* magazine. "I got everything under control."

alone at last

marty walked up the stairs to Apartment 17 with a big grin on his face. He had accrued only a minuscule $200 debt to Poplotnick in the past month, and better yet he was heading to the apartment he imagined so deliciously empty— no distractions, no Sydney, no nothing. Finally, he could get on with his life. But as he slipped his key into the slot, as he slowly turned it (for he noticeably slowed as he approached the door for reasons he couldn't have explained), as the tumblers fell with that satisfying click that says you're home, a wave of emptiness swept Marty's very soul to a degree beyond any Marty might have imagined up to that point since he hadn't thought much about having a soul. He stepped inside to a room silent and empty.

Marty sat on the couch, the TV off, with his old buddy, a can of Rocko's DryIceLite. He hadn't yet figured out that his life was killing him. It had been killing him for years, almost since he left high school that warm June night, his mortarboard in place, his degree tucked under his arm, Aunt Sally in the stands of the football field. Marty remembered how eager he had been then for high school to end. Summer was all planned out. The big Road Trip with Ben. Armed with Ben's '66 Fairlane and Marty's convincing fake ID, the boys were ready for adventures that were not to be believed by the buddies they left behind in Valley when they got back, if they ever did . . . and they did. Sooner than anyone hoped, the Fairlane blowing a head gasket outside of Silver Springs.

It wasn't too long before Ben took over the bar, after his old man had the stroke, and Marty began his long and winding road to the present, bouncing from job to job and wandering his way through relationships both vague and distinct.

Marty got up, headed down the hall and looked into Sydney's now-empty room. He saw the thirty-gallon wastepaper basket still filled with wadded balls of yellow paper and empty plastic bottles of Freeb's.

"Decaffeinated. Has to be decaffeinated," Marty said aloud. He couldn't figure it. He'd lived alone for the past five years, since he split with Carla, and it seemed completely normal, but now, a few weeks into his brother's departure, the apartment was more empty than ever. *How the fuck can that be?*

Marty thought of The Night for a moment, the night Sydney thought he always wanted to hear about. He thought of Dad, who in Marty's memory was some sort of lone drifter who passed through the family album long enough to impregnate Mom twice and yell a lot. No family of his own, or at least none anyone had ever seen. He was an apparition, more ethereal than Mom, a cameo fuckup whom Marty always hated. And because he was such an elusive target, so fleeting, he had for many years existed only in a mental confrontation of epic proportions that, over time, had twisted itself into a background soundtrack of self-hate that Marty carried about him, like occasional asthma, or a trick knee that acted up when the weather conditions were just right. Or wrong.

But Mommy, sweet Mommy Marty could picture with great clarity at times like right then in the yellow light of the empty hallway. He could miss sweet Mommy thirty years later as though it had happened yesterday. He took a drink from his can and drained it. Threw it across the room, which he thought of as the fuckin' room right then 'cause he was pretty much in one of those fuckin' moods. He almost felt ashamed. Sydney was like some sort of conscience.

It's all Sydney's fault. Sydney was the final straw. Everybody knew he was fucked up! That withered left leg, the doctor telling sobbing Mommy that he was retarded, the screaming fits at night when Marty lay in his room, the lights out, wishing he were asleep, wishing he were somewhere else, wishing he were *someone* else.

"He's a goddamned cripple!" Dad's voice would boom through the walls, crashing into the darkness of the bedroom Marty shared with the baby Sydney. "And now the doctor says he's retarded?! It's your side of the family, you know. No retarded cripples on my side of the family!"

Marty could remember little snippets of Mom's: "Just stop. Will you please stop. He's just a baby. Why are you so cruel? Don't get another drink, Will . . ."

And Dad: "He's a freak. Who were you fuckin'? You were fucking someone else, weren't you?"

And little Marty, who didn't know what "fucking" meant, knew that when it was mentioned the slapping would start. He'd hear the smack of skin against skin, the banging of furniture, the knocking against walls, the screaming, even louder now. Then the crying, the sad wailing of his mother; the sheer depth and profundity of her sadness and misery slipped unabated through the walls late at night, and it filled Marty with a nameless dread, a shame that would sweep him away, make him pull the covers tightly up against his chin.

There was a special night though. It was a night so profound, and life-altering, packing such an emotional punch that it would never again be mentioned within the family. Never mentioned either sloppy drunk or stone cold sober or any point or moment in between. It was as though it never happened. There wasn't even anything as subtle as the exchange of a knowing glance or the momentary pause to signal a thing unsaid. It was a conspiracy of sorts that existed between Aunt Sally, Uncle K, Marty and Grampa. Sydney, too young to remember, was, in a sense, born an innocent.

But the night existed and it existed no more clearly to anyone in the entire world than it did to Marty Corbet. He was practically a fucking witness. He was there at home that night, and on occasion—such as right now, when he felt sad and lost and sorry for himself and the miserable never-get-a-chance life he felt he'd been dealt—Marty would wheel out the sickly memory. The broken-down super-eight projector, the flickering images, the one shot frozen forever in his mind. It was a great albatross, a ruined relic, a family embarrassment, the secret retarded monster child locked in the basement of Marty's mind. Marty began wheeling out the great clunking, wheezing, fetid, frightening one-act play set in Carlisle. March 1968. The one-act play for the one-man audience. Marty was actor, director, audience and critic for this great moment in his life. Then he thought better of it.

He carefully closed the door to Sydney's room and decided to go and visit Aunt Sally, something he almost never did.

"Did Pierre ever come back?" Marty was sitting at the familiar old kitchen table in the familiar old kitchen.

"I'm afraid Pierre is gone," Aunt Sally said sadly, as she slathered some bright yellow mustard on a slice of bright white bread and laid down some pink fleshy slices of ham. "You just like mustard, right, Marty?"

"Mmm-hmm."

"But now there's some funny little animal coming around."

"What, some stray?"

"No, it's not a dog. It loves the ground chuck I leave for it."

"A coyote?"

"No, I'm pretty sure it's one of, well, wait a minute and I'll get my paper." Aunt Sally came back with the proper issue of the *American Enquirer,* which she had bound in volumes dating back to the Michael Jackson hyperbaric sleeping chamber headlines. "It's one of these. Isn't that so sad about Emmanuel Lewis? He was such a cute boy."

"One of these?" Marty pointed to a picture as he took a big bite out of his ham sandwich.

"Oh, no, that's one of those monsters from that sheep cloning in Scotland. Those scientists don't know what they're doing."

"This?!"

"Mmm-hmm. Except mine's not so ugly. I think it's a girl."

"Yours?!" Marty looked up at Aunt Sally. "You're feeding a Puerto Rican goatsucker ground chuck?"

"Not every night! Jeez!"

to work

sydney cracked his knuckles, positioned his Mont Blanc and with grand excitement began the day's work in his office at Letters.

Dear Distraught and Valued Customer:

First let me express my keenly felt regret at your displeasure with one of our fine line of chocolate dainties. I myself, being not simply a valued employee of Bea's Candies, but also a lifelong connoisseur of quality chocolate, can sympathize with your plight. Rest assured, now that I am in my new position as Bea's Candies Consumer Liaison, along with my extracurricular role in the areas of Quality Control and New Product Development, problems such as the one you encountered will soon be a vague memory from the distant past.

In addition, I would like you to accept these coupons for a total of twenty-five pounds of Bea's Candies. May I suggest you invest a good portion of these monies in the old reliable Wad Gomper as well as the exciting new Chocolate Jesus, a candy, incidentally, conceived by yours truly.

Dear Mr. Weber:

First of all, I'd like to inform you that "cocksuckers" is spelled with three Cs not two, unless you were referring to my cola consumption. I assure you I'm a Freeb's man. I would also like to help you in your sad plight over your candy meltage, and as a true lover of fine chocolates such as those we make right here in Valley at the Bea's Candy Works, I feel your pain over the loss of six 3-pound boxes of Bea's Olde-Fashioned Fine-Timed Butter Creams and Caramels. Unfortunately, most people realize you can't drive from Bakersfield to Salt Lake City via Las Vegas during the Ides of March without negatively impacting a load of boxed chocolates stored in the trunk of your Bonneville (especially given your two-hour layover in the Stovepipe Wells/Furnace Creek area), but since you sound like such an angry and bitter man, I will reward you with the issuance of a coupon for a free Chocolate Jesus in the hope that you might regain a shred of optimism for your fellow Man.

Senator Arlen Specter:

As I am sure you can tell by this letter's masthead, I have climbed the corporate ladder a few flights, and now perhaps you will begin to realize the magnitude of my mettle, and not dismiss me at once as just another lunatic-fringe kook working at a burger outlet. The following attached file is the definitive refutation of the single or "magic" bullet theory that you promulgate so enthusiastically. If I could crack your connection to this cover-up, I feel the answers might begin to fall into place, but rest not, Senator Specter. Not only is this report being "CC'd" to the White House itself, I also want you to know that I now have the full resources of the Internet at my fingertips! Hold that thought the next time you turn off your little bed lamp and tuck it in for the night. A conscience can be a terrible thing. A terrible thing.

Sydney leaned back in his chair, quite pleased with his fledgling efforts. Scrimshaw angled his glasses and over Sydney's shoulder read the last letter.

"You can't be writing letters like that!" Scrimshaw protested.

"And why is that?"

"Hmm?"

"WHY NOT?!"

"Well . . . it's not even candy related!"

"True, but . . ."

"And besides, that's *my* job!" Scrimshaw protested. "*I* answer the letters!"

"I've been here for a month now and I haven't seen you answer one yet!" Sydney countered.

"It takes time. You have no idea." Scrimshaw set down his hearing aid amp. "Some young whipper snapper barging in, fiddling with all the knobs right away, messing everything all up. It takes time."

"I assure you, Mr. Bea has given me carte blanche, as it were, over Communications."

"Carbon what? What the hell are you saying? See, you're not making any sense all of a sudden again."

The two employees stared at each other for a moment. "How about this?" Scrimshaw suggested. "I answer the letters and you get the dolgarned computer. Is that fair?"

Sydney reflected for a moment. "Deal!"

They got along famously after that.

drunk on miracle

mountain

jesús had washed his plate and pot, licking his lips from the hot chile he'd had with the fried eggs, nopalitos and tortillas. He'd finished his short prayer in front of his little altar (St. Luke 4:10: "For it is written, He shall give his angels charge over thee, to keep thee: And in their hands they shall bear thee up, lest at any time they dash thy foot against a stone").

Jesús picked up the new addition to his altar, the small foil-wrapped Jesús Christo, examined it for a moment like a child at Christmas and then set it back alongside the picture of the Virgin de Guadalupe with the crucifix of the lamenting Christ hanging off the frame. He liked the way the flickering light from the candle reflected on the colored foil.

Jesús got up and stepped out into the fresh air. There was no making sense of *Los Gabachos*. Making a candy of Christ. Their churches that looked the same as their banks, their supermarkets that had no smells; everything so wrapped, so clean, their faces so pink.

Jesús stood atop Miracle Mountain, alone with a cigarette and a three-quarters-empty pint of Sauza Hornitos in his hand, his face glowing in the setting sun as he watched rabbits scurry about in the brush outside the grounds proper.

Despite his sincere devotion and true love for Christ as savior and Son of God, despite his worship of this imported Christ in the grand stone churches that stood above the crushing poverty back home, Jesús still believed in demons and spirits that prowled a netherworld both invisible and true. And so, once again, Jesús stood, camera ready, waiting for the little beast. How eager he was to take a picture and sell it to the tabloids, the magazines with the bloody carnage, hellish demons and scantily clad *chicas*. Jesús crossed himself at the thought of the girls and thought instead of love's longing.

He took another swig and a most satisfying drag off his cigarillo, awaiting the Arrival, thinking of sweet Reyna, and by nightfall, by the time he'd had too much of the tequila and thrown the bottle as far as he could down the mountain, not caring if the Reverend caught him, by the time it became obvious the little chupacabra would again not show itself, his mind swam with the thought of her. How badly he wanted to lie next to his dear wife. To have her under the warm blanket, the two of them lying together on their sides, pulling her against his chest, snuggling at her neck, breathing into her ear, whispering softly how he missed her so, telling her all the things she hoped to hear, words to make her feel as safe as he did right then imagining her there with him. How they'd never be apart again. Ever.

But they were! It made him sick and he felt stupid for ever having left her behind. He felt lost in a strange land, an impossible distance between him and a life he now loved so clearly and true. He forgot the lesson of his prayer and began to lose his faith and his mind imagined Emilio back home. *Emilio'd always had his eye on Reyna. Never liked that it was me! Who married her.* Jesús slipped to the deviltry lying in the brush atop Miracle Mountain, became utterly convinced that Reyna was sleeping with Emilio, and his eyes welled with tears. *Oh, how I hate it here. Here where all the money is, but not home! It will never be home.*

Jesús patted the camera in his shirt pocket. He felt it was his only hope. *I need that picture. Donde esta mi chupacabra?*

The rabbit hunting in the thick brush on the steep slopes of Miracle Mountain was some of the finest to be found for miles. And there was water. A broken, dripping sprinkler head and that's why Jesús suspected the regular presence of the beast. El Chupe would check in at Miracle Mountain nearly every dusk to suck at that sprinkler. Every day when the sun slipped into the ocean and the light took on a cool rosy hue, when Night began to take form in the sky to the east, past the Cuyamacas.

Night began in the desert, darkness spread from the east, a comforting cloak for El Chupe. Even in town at night the land woke up and tried as it might, from its gasping death-bed, to reassert itself under the sickly yellow glow of the city street lamps. The crickets competed with the endless whooshing of cars; the smallest of mammals peeked out in great fear.

But out on the mountain, a couple of miles east of town, night still broke big and the rabbits would come out in the cooling dusk, sprinting from bush to bush and then stopping suddenly and crouching motionless, furry statues with twitching noses, their light brown coats disappearing into the land. El Chupe would wait until darkness, for she didn't need to see them. She could smell the rabbits like an overly perfumed woman in a crowded restaurant. She knew exactly where they hid, and would slip up unaware, because it was El Chupe that was hard to spot, much harder than the succulent little rabbits that she'd slip up to as in a dream, upon the gentle breeze in the last light of dusk, the chaparral pungent in the cooling air, a big jack sitting behind a bush, its eyes huge, fully black and absorbing, its nose twitching radar to no avail. Chupe plucked the jack off the ground with her clawed raptor paws, snatched it in one quick motion to her mouth, sinking her teeth deeply into the hot throat, closing down on the soft fur as she drained that warm, reviving blood. Her eyes rolled back in her head, as she connected with the realms beyond. She loaded up as the sun died and her world, the realm of darkness, returned.

She missed the darkness badly. True darkness. For even at the outskirts, up there on the slopes of Miracle Mountain, the night sky was still tinted, tainted, with the mark of the Beast. The Mark of Modern Man. The Machines.

Chupe drifted back in the flush of her meal, blinked her eyes a few times like a cat in the heart of its nap, back to when the first white man came to Valley in the 1750s, back to when the Kumeyaay and Hohokam lived along the coast and the rivers and in the mountains. Back then the chupe—like the land—was strong, her numbers great, and worship was directed at nature and the animals and the stars. Back then, with the strength of Faith, the land wore the rosy cheeks of a well-fed youngster. The air was fresh. Back then the nights were black as pitch, an utter, infinite darkness strewn with the fresh white glow of the stars, the Milky Way, the moon in her various moods, the planets shining headlight true. She remembered the agave-sandaled men, the women in skirts of willow bark, the tiny, crooked ears of corn they grew, the acorns and pine nuts they collected, and then that first cloud of dust kicked up on the southern horizon. Across the endless canyons and mesas it came. The Spaniards. With goats.

fuck you!

sydney hadn't been able to sleep the en-
tire night, his mind spinning endlessly, as he tried not to
think of all the bad things, but they drew him ever closer,
like gravity. He could dismiss the Reverend's rantings as that
of religious fanaticism, but that TV show kept playing over
and over in his mind. It was *Hard Copy*'s usual screaming
sensationalism. The video footage of people melting piles of
Chocolate Jesuses throughout the Midwest and the Deep
South, the angry people being interviewed. And then there
was the Bea's Candies Web Page. They were being inun-
dated with near-hate mail for daring to make such a candy.

How did it turn around? How can the public be so fickle?
Sydney wondered. *Thank God Scrimshaw has no idea how to
use the computer.* But Sydney knew it was only a matter of
time before everyone found out. He felt himself a fake. A
fraud. He was no chocolate design specialist, had no experience in candy marketing. He'd got lucky with a dumb idea,
and now look where it'd got him. In the words of his way-
ward brother, he was in deep shit!

Sydney felt hot around the collar and a bit light-headed,

as though he might faint. The room began to darken and millions of tiny black points danced before his eyes. He was at the precipice looking down into the infinite black, and again had that vague dread, the sour taste of raw fear in the back of his mouth.

He reached into his pocket and fished out the 1-800-JENKINS number he kept on his person at all times, along with a magazine photograph of President and Jackie Kennedy in happier times. He didn't want to have to call the good doctor, but Sydney didn't know what else to do.

"Welcome to the Koala Center Voice Mail. If you know the extension of the person you need to speak with, enter it . . . Now! Or stay on the line and listen to our voice mail menu.

"If you're suffering from Panic Disorder, Agoraphobia, Obsessive-Compulsive Disorder or Acute Stress Disorder, press 1 . . . Now!

"If you suffer from personality disorders including, but not limited to, Paranoid, Schizoid, Borderline, Histrionic or Narcissistic, press 2 . . . Now!

"If you're experiencing a Major Depressive episode or are Bipolar, press 3 . . . Now!

"If you're under eighteen and suffer from Attention Deficit Disorder, Autism or Separation Anxiety, remember you need your parent's permission to use the Koala Center Voice Mail."

Sydney slammed down the receiver. *I know. Martin! He'll help me!*

Marty was sitting in his usual spot on the couch (in a pose so unchanging that Sydney thought a painter from the Dutch School might have best captured it) when Sydney banged on the door and burst into Apartment 17.

"Something's gone wrong!" Sydney announced like Paul Revere. "Oh, why, why couldn't I have just been left alone at the Koala Center to continue my important research?"

"Wha— Jesus Christ!" Marty almost lost grip on his can of DryIceLite. No one had been to the apartment in weeks and Marty's mind instantly went to the piles of dirty clothes and underwear, skid marks to the ceiling, that littered the living room.

"Haven't you been watching TV? People are fomenting. Sales are down. I'm a Kennedy Assassination Scholar, not a candy man." Sydney saw that Panic Attack had followed him all the way back to Oasis, Apartment 17. "What am I going to do!?"

"Hey, you wanna run with the big dogs, boy," Marty (the same Marty who had missed his brother three nights in the past week) said with a sour look and an air of being very put out.

"When Mr. Bea finds out . . ."

"Hey, when the going gets tough . . ."

"You sound like Mr. Bea now. Since when do you employ fractured aphorisms?"

"Whaddaya want from me? I just drive a chicken truck, okay? You're the Big Shot with the Big Job."

Sydney thought about it for a second. His Data/Spock side didn't know what he wanted from Marty. "You're my brother."

"Mmm." Marty took another slug off his beer. "Lotta good that's done me so far. Only bad shit has happened since you came back from Arizona."

"If it wasn't for me, you'd be getting around in a wheelchair," Sydney said with more than a little disdain. "Need I remind you that it was I who saved you from the ruffians that phony rabbi sent after you?"

"Yeah, I know, Syd. You only fucking remind me about every ten minutes. How could I possibly fucking forget?"

"And then I come to you for some help . . ."

Marty shrugged at Sydney.

"You're just jealous. You've always been jealous of me," Sydney decided.

"What?! *Me* jealous? Of *you*?! What are you talking about? Use your head for once."

"I was probably Mother's favorite. Typical sibling rivalry that for some reason you've never been able to get over," Sydney stated matter-of-factly.

"Sydney? You don't know anything about Mom."

"That's because you refuse to tell me anything. It's as though you're hiding something. I think you want to keep any memories for yourself. You know I don't have any of my own."

Marty shook his head. He was trying his best to hold back, but he was never very good at self-control. He couldn't control his temper. He couldn't control his gambling. He couldn't control his drinking, and with the drinks he'd already sucked up (that *special* amount of alcohol that wasn't nearly enough for oblivion, but too much for a happy buzz; an amount that merely made Marty pissy and looking for confrontations), Marty was having trouble holding his tongue. A tongue he'd held for nearly thirty years. He knew he was now going to let it go, and the feeling was intoxicating.

"You're in trouble again, aren't you?" Sydney smelled something.

"Don't, Sydney . . ." Marty began.

"I can't keep getting you out of fixes, you know . . ."

"Come on, Syd, get a fucking grip, huh?"

"Are you already in debt to that bookie again?"

That's it, Marty thought. *There we go.* The bell had rung and now Marty was ready to say all the things that everyone else had said. All the things that Marty had stupidly fought over in defense of his brother. In truth, Marty was kind of an asshole, there was no denying, even though he didn't say as much to himself (the entire affair was converted at some devilish switch deep within the lizard portion of Marty's brain, folded well within the cauliflower convolutions of his gray matter, which roiled right then in a special stew of hormones, electrolytes, chemicals and alcohol). And so he said all the hateful and hurtful things he could think of to his brother right then. He knew the exact coordinates of the most vulnerable targets on the big, white exposed underbelly of Sydney's psyche. Marty knew just how to hurt him. Who better to hurt him?

"Okay, Mom—what do you want to know, Syd? Huh? What do you wanna know about, Mom? Hmm? You wanna hear the story?"

Sydney looked at Marty, somehow knowing it was trouble, remembering all the mean things Marty had done to him as an older brother. The Indian burns. "Why do you have to be a gimp, huh?" Marty would ask after beating up some kid for calling Sydney a gimp. It hurt far worse when Marty said it than when some other kid taunted him openly in front of everybody, in front of all the girls.

Sydney could almost feel himself change right then. His brother looked smaller now. He looked at his own hands; they weren't the hands of a boy anymore. He looked his brother in the eye, straightened himself up, hiked his pants up his skinny hips, and said, "Tell me about Mother."

"You wanna know? She killed herself. That's how she

died. She killed herself after she got a look at you. Okay? You killed our mother. That's why neither one of us has got one. Okay? You happy now?"

"You're lying."

"No. I'm not. I was fucking there, Syd. It's not just you, you know."

Sydney stood frozen, stunned, before his brother for a moment, and then turned and walked out of the room.

Marty found himself walking down Citrus Avenue as miserable as ever and not understanding that he was bringing this misery upon himself. He walked the lifeless sidewalks, his head bent, the sun going down, as miserable and pissed off as he'd been in a long, long time.

But no matter—Marty was miserable and pissed off, but he had decided to have what would turn out to be an unsatisfyingly I'll-show-them kind of drunken night when, out of nowhere, as though a violent guardian angel were smiling down at him, crossing the street up ahead as obvious as could be and totally unaware, walked probably the only person (besides one of the Rocko-ettes throwing down for him) who might snap Marty out of his latest funk. A sort of shuffling therapy session on the street ahead. A thing to help Marty forget his troubles and begin the healing. It was Dude #2.

Marty followed the oblivious Dude #2 from about a half a block back. He followed with that sharp excitement of a predator hot on the trail. Dude #2 turned off Citrus and headed down one of the quiet side streets leading into the canyons that snaked through much of the town.

Marty smiled. He couldn't ask for anything more perfect

and tracked the stocking-capped slacker past the dead end of the cul-de-sac, down the dusty dirt trail and into the open chaparral. He could make out the top of that ridiculous navy blue watch cap as it bobbed down the trail and into the thick, dry brush. Marty followed at what he took to be a bit beyond screaming distance and then picked up the pace, quickly closing the gap between himself and Dude #2.

"Hey, chubalabra, dude," Dude #2 called to the creosote, sage and scrub oaks. "Come on, little buddy. I got some cat food, dude. Psst-psst-psst."

Marty began to run, and just as Dude #2 looked up and turned around, Marty let out a " 'Scuse me!" and landed a running, overhand, full-tilt shot right to Dude #2's face, dropping him to the dusty ground like a sack of horseradish.

Before Dude #2 could even register what had happened, let alone the pain, Marty angrily grabbed him by the collar, sat him on his ass on the ground and delivered a vicious hook that sent the dude's head snapping back in a sickening splat, a clatter of teeth and a spray of blood. Dude #2 was out, but Marty wasn't done.

He kicked at Dude #2's side, jumped up and stomped on his stomach, all the while thinking, *My piece-a-crap life, my stupid brother, dead mother, fuck fuck FUCK!! Fuck 'em all!*

"Fuck with me, huh, punk?" Marty asked rhetorically. "Not so tough now, are you, huh? Fuckin' punk!" Marty sat him up again and sized up a shot to flatten his nose. "Where's your buddy now, huh? Faggot!"

Marty sat there for a moment after delivering the punch that broke the dude's nose, rubbing his knuckles and catching his breath. He tried to calm himself. *Don't kill the asshole, that piece a shit ain't fucking worth it.*

Marty slapped Dude #2 back into a semblance of consciousness, a consciousness mostly comprised of the beginning of some amazing pain involving his broken nose, a couple of loosened teeth and a badly bitten tongue. Dude #2's entire visual world was dominated by the panting Marty Corbet grabbing him by his shirt, a menacing fist poised in front of his bloody face.

"There. You're okay. Hmm? Can you hear me?" Marty asked.

"Uh . . . huh?"

"Good." Marty punched him again on the broken nose, but he pulled the punch, just gave it enough to remind the dude of who was in charge as Marty began to explain some of the deeper tissue damage that was forthcoming if Dude #2 didn't answer a couple of questions to Marty's complete satisfaction.

"Now, listen here, punk. I haven't had the best of days. In fact, my entire life hasn't gone all that well and, well, I really don't want to burden you with my troubles, it's just not my style, you know? But sometimes . . . I don't know, you just get so pissed off, so mad that you wanna take it out on somebody, ya know? I mean, I know it doesn't make things any better, but . . . somehow, I don't know. It does," and Marty punched Dude #2 in the face again, as much as to convince himself of this theory as anything else. "See what I mean?"

Dude #2 nodded meekly, looking around for a rock or stick as rebuttal to this line of thought. Marty rewarded his research by punching him as hard as he could in the stomach.

"No, no ideas. It doesn't suit you. I don't think you're listening. I'm trying to tell you that I don't want to fuck you up even more. Look, I've had some experience here, take my word. I'm fairly certain your nose is broken. That's permanent. Look at mine. They don't grow back straight and is that a front tooth gone there? Huh?" Marty smiled. "Is it? Or is it just loose? I can't tell with all the blood."

Dude #2 shrugged.

"No matter. Anyway, like I was saying, I consider us even now and you should count that as a fucking blessing. All I want is one thing, okay?"

"What's that, dude?"

"Now, what I want to know," Marty began as he let go his death grip, straightened Dude #2's shirt, picked his watch cap off the ground, dusted it off and placed it half-assed on his head. "All I wanna know, pal, is where your little buddy lives. Okay? It's that easy."

What with the lack of honor among thieves and punks, Marty only had to ask once, but before he left he issued one more warning. "Don't ever think of fucking with me again. We're even. Say it."

"We're even."

"Mean it!"

"We're even, dude."

"Good, 'cause if I ever see you anywhere near me again? You're gonna have a permanent limp that'll make my brother look like he's fuckin' Fred Astaire."

"Fred who?"

"Never mind." Marty got up and had two things on his mind: a twelver of Rocko's DryIceLite and a sack of Jax Pounders.

late night at the lab

it was late at night, deep within the factory, and the lights were on in the top secret "Choco" labs of Professor Theodore Broma. Sydney was trying to get through to the Candy Master, who'd had a few too many sips of hot, pure cocoa liquor.

"The Chocolate Jesus is just a start! I have much more in store, candies the world cannot even conceive." Broma smiled.

"Professor, I have some bad news."

"Life ess sveet." Broma had a look on his face that to Sydney appeared near lecherous. "Oh, jah. Jah! Zay wrote mein arse off. Happy, happy! Zey ver ven I couldn't come up viz anysing für a decade. Hah!"

"The media loves to slay the giants," Sydney said soothingly. "But . . ."

"But! I . . . am . . . back! Baaa-beee!" Broma actually broke out into a flash of the Twist, and it was at this moment that Sydney feared for them all.

"Jesus is just the start and I'm not talking mere religious

icons. No, vïr talking schokoladen. It's za food of za gods. Did you know that?"

"Yes. I think you've mentioned it before."

"Come on, Sydney. You know, you're za only pear-son I can really talk chocolate viz. Care für a shot?" Broma took a long swig off an Erlenmeyer flask held in a special high-tech cozy that kept the cocoa liquor at the perfect tempering temperature. He put his arm around Sydney's skinny shoulder and waved the flask.

"Professor, I think you've had enough . . ."

"Come on . . . " the Professor said musically.

"All right, just one." Sydney took a dainty sip of the potent liquor.

"Follow me." The Professor motioned, and the two men, their faces lit by the various Bunsen burners' blue flames made their way past test tubes, vials, beakers and swirling glass tubes of distiller's design (thick, almost black molten liquid coursing through them). On a lab table sat small copper bowls of chocolate held at a constant 88 degrees by digital thermostats so sensitive they were coveted by NASA.

"Oh, not chocolate," Broma corrected. "Pure cocoa liquor. Pure. Crrr-iollo beans. My Oaxacan strr-ain."

"I'm here on more serious business, sir," Sydney began. "Has Mr. Bea told you anything?"

"More important than chocolate? Hah!" Broma took another swig from his flask.

"Professor, a protest is gaining momentum, a groundswell if you will. The Chocolate Jesus . . . Oh, why did I ever send in that idea?" Sydney wondered aloud, but Professor Broma was too hammered from cocoa liquor to follow him.

"I've never shown anyone my latest," Broma confided. "It's qvite bitter, I vorn you now! . . . But Moctezuma,

vell . . ." He picked up a golden ladle from among the chocolate instruments strewn about the table.

Sydney decided it was The Truth Hurts Time. "People
don't care about quality anymore, sir. Can't you see? The
sad thing is, they can't even tell the difference."

"What?! What are you saying?!"

Sydney felt it best to break the news to the deluded
scientist. "The public . . . they're like a mob. Mediocrity won
a long time ago. Most people can't tell the difference between a Groton's and a Mrs. Paul fish stick!" Sydney looked
at the Professor. "Look at what's happened to the chocolate
icing on donuts since the Fall of Saigon. Put that in your
pipe."

Broma stood there for an instance, nearly stunned, a
frozen half-smile frozen on his features . . . but it wouldn't
register. This piece of information was so foreign to all he
lived for (especially right at that moment) that it simply
wouldn't run through the machine. It was a bit of data that
just didn't fit into the slot. So he continued . . .

"Now here, here is my pride und joy, or zoon I hope.
It's not qvite pear-fected just yet." Broma slid his hand,
rather wantonly for Sydney's tastes, along a small two-gallon
vat of experimental cocoa liquor complete with a special
conching device that was constructed in the shape of dozens
of animatronic human hands gently kneading, kneading the
chocolate.

"Zat ess how you brr-ing out za rrr-eal tegsure . . . und
za flavor, too. If I could 'Just Do It' heh-heh, I'd hire out
Third Verld vimmin für ten cents a day like Nike does, but
chocolate being a food, vell . . . U Z, za human hand, zair's
nussing else like it in za verld. I don't care how long zay
fiddle about viz machinery. It'll never be a hummingbird in
flight. Zink about vat I'm tellink hue . . ."

"You're mad, man! *I'm* trying to tell you that the entire company is in serious trouble. There's not much time!" Broma simply stared at Sydney. "Are you listening? This house of chocolate you've created is about to crumble!"

Broma became oddly calm. "Sydney, have you never wanted to do anything that was dangerous? To look beyond the clouds and the stars? To see what changes the darkness to light?"

"Sir, I respect your aims, but the situation long ago escalated far beyond that. Wake up and look the facts in the face."

Broma was too engrossed dipping the golden ladle into the conching chocolate to be listening to anything Sydney had to say.

"Have you lost your mind?" Sydney asked.

Broma looked up. "Oh, I'm astonishingly zane. Here, tays ziss." He offered a piece of wax paper with a smear of hardening chocolate.

Sydney tongued the smear off the wax paper and was swept away as it filled his mouth, his entire consciousness, with a wave of physical flavor and visions of foggy warm mornings atop Monte Albán, jaguars and jade. "That is *some* chocolate."

"U Z?!" Broma cried with glee over Sydney's assent.

"Pull yourself together," Sydney yelled, as much to break the near spell the chocolate had cast over him as to capture the attention of the manic Broma. *Mmm, I'd like another taste of that chocolate* . . . "People are yelling at us on TV. We've become subject material for *Hard Copy* and Jerry Springer. This thing has turned into a monster and it's going to destroy us all!" Sydney declared. "Could I have another piece of that chocolate? It's quite superior."

the end

it was beginning to slip. All the carefully laid plans. Willie just knew it. The due date for the End of the World had crept up so quickly. Sure, it worked fine at first. Ratings had never been higher. The Reverend had thousands of End Time Lovers and Kamikaze Souls, people convinced that in one explosive flash everything they'd slowly learned to loathe would be gone, replaced by all they could ever want. Supreme Peace. Nirvana. Elysium. They were selling their shit, sending him the cash, working out like maniacs in preparation for the Final Battle with Satan. (As the supposed Armageddon approached, fitness levels of the regular viewers had reached fantastic levels. Two marathon runners, an Olympic decathlete and a silver-medal-winning cross-country skier later arose from the soon-to-be scattered ranks of the Reverend's flock.) But for the last few weeks the Reverend Willie Domingo had felt that something bad was slowly catching up to him. It was like one of those dreams where you're running and running but your legs are leaden or the atmosphere is too thick, gravity too much, for any sort of forward progress, and the Devil's Posse is kickin' up dust ever closer. The posse arrived the morning of the supposed end of the world. Jesús found Padre Ewilly wandering through the End Times museum.

"Uh, Padre Ewilly?"

"Yes, Jesus?"

"Hay personas. Ahh, see you."

"People? What people?"

"Oh yes, many. *No estan muy feliz.*"

"What's that?"

"How you say, hoppy?"

"Hmm?" What Jesús was trying to say began to dawn on the Reverend at about the same rate as it would have had he been talking with Lassie. The trouble wasn't at the old mill, but at the gates to Miracle Mountain, where at that very moment a crowd of over five hundred very fit and very pissed off people were demanding immediate deliverance.

As the Reverend approached the locked gates, it finally occurred to him exactly what he had promised. Really, the only man Willie Domingo could possibly turn the mike over to right then was the Sweet Lamb himself in all his two-thousand-years-later Glory. *I don't have Jesus.*

"People, people." The Reverend approached the crowd. "I know today is the day you've all been waiting for. The day we get to meet the Sweet Lamb, and I've carefully examined all the facts, studied the Bible, the many verses therein, and all seems to harmonize and point to the present. We were courageous and we came out and told our loved ones, warned all those we care about, and when we said this, that there were no options, we were scorned, ridiculed, scoffed at because the unsaved, the flabby of flesh, they don't want to hear, they fear the return of our Lord, they feel threatened as game time approaches, the unprepared—"

"Hey, hasn't Satan been loosed yet? Wasn't Satan supposed to have been loosed last week?" yelled one person.

"Yeah! And wasn't the sun supposed to darken by now?" shouted another. "What happened with that?!"

"Yes, well that would have been really nice if the moon had turned to blood last night," the Reverend countered, "but let's not fall into that snare. The time is nigh. We must look to the Bible, not for signs, but—"

"The time is nigh?!" yelled a man far bigger and more ripped than anything you might imagine coming out of the vegetarian wing of humanity. "I thought you said today was the day?! What am I supposed to do now? I quit my job last week. I don't even have a job anymore!"

"Yes, well the Days of Vengeance are a difficult time." The Reverend smacked his hard abs quickly, five times. "Even the churches fear it. It's hard to find a pastor who teaches the Tribulation, who dares mention the Feast of the Tabernacles. But we are strong and we have seen the wonderful things. Can you understand the honor to be living in such times? A new kingdom is soon to rule, in our lifetime. Many have opened their eyes to judgment, and damnation also. Many have received the wake-up call, they've checked the scriptures, and many have cried to God for mercy for the time is close!"

"Close?! Whaddaya mean close?" came one voice.

"I sold my house!" screamed another. "It's in escrow. Where am I supposed to sleep tonight? Where's the New Kingdom you promised?"

"How come the rivers haven't turned to blood yet?" came a third.

A chant arose from the back ranks: "We want Jesus. We want Jesus."

The Reverend could feel it as he stared into the crowd. He knew that what he had on his hands was a mob, and he realized, as all good pastors do, that if he couldn't hand them Jesus, the next best thing was Satan, and if Satan wasn't actually out there in Valley this morning with pitchfork and cloven hoof, if it wasn't going to officially be Satan, it was going to somebody.

Willie Domingo knew what he had to do ("They're a mob," Pastor Ron's voice echoed in his head). He remembered back to the hot, sweaty summer days in Alabama. Green and sticky, the air was thick with the Wrath of God, the heat of Hell glowed round the churches baking under a July 'Bama sun. Willie had seen the laying on of hands, the tension and excitement in the air. The atmosphere became electric with the thunderheads that formed in the afternoon. He'd seen the healing, the sudden possession, the speaking in tongues. (Those were the days. After TV, Disney, after all the fake stuff, you can't even speak in tongues anymore—they're all so jaded and cynical.)

Reverend Willie Domingo dove into an Academy Award–winning, bravura performance as Burt Lancaster in *Elmer Gantry*. It was secretly one of his favorite movies and he'd studied it very carefully for just such emergencies. The thing with Reverend Domingo was that, unlike many less successful preachers, *he* always had a good escape plan.

"Oh, Christ is coming. Doubt it not! FOR IT IS WRITTEN! 'Behold, the day of the Lord cometh, cruel both with wrath and fierce anger.'

"But are you ready? The Lord warned, 'I will punish the world for their evil, and the wicked for their iniquity.' *I'm* ready to face our maker, but what about you and you and you?" He directed his gaze into the eyes of the flock, as though into their souls. "Maybe you should be happy the Savior is a few hours late. It'll give you time to clean up some of the mess. You might start with that candy bar. Made in our very own town. Our hometown, a town many of us grew up in. A candy shaped like Jesus. Look at yourselves. People of Valley. Valley, California. It might as well be Sodom. Aren't you all ashamed?

"What is the Lord going to think when he sees our very own town? Home of the Chocolate Jesus. He's going to think he's in Satan Central. Valley, California, will be the New Babylon. That candy bar is the work of Satan! And what have you done about it? Why is that company still in business? Why have you not shut it down?"

After he'd fired up the crowd with some more fervent vengeful Godisms *and* dangerous levels of free phenylalanine and glucosamine "annointings" at the juice bar, after he'd turned his flock's energies toward the Bea's Candy Works, the Reverend Willie Domingo calmly loaded his packed suitcases into the grand trunk of his beloved 1959 periwinkle Cadillac Fleetwood, placed a fake beard, a passport and $5,000 in cash on the front seat and headed back to the juice bar to get some antioxidants for the trip.

whoops!

mr. bea sat in his office and took a long, satisfied puff off a Santa Damiana, lamenting the decline of a once-fine cigar maker. *They couldn't keep up.* He was supremely, fully, stretching-his-legs-under-his-big-fine-desk-and-wiggling-his-big-toe-in-the-warm-sand-of-Life pleased with himself that afternoon. *There's just no stopping me. And Mother won't be gumming things up this time. The morphine was brilliant. Hah!* Mr. Bea had come up with the brain wave of adding a little something to mother's finely tuned *cuvée* of nutrients, antioxidants, free-radical smashers, painkillers and mood deadeners, which flowed 24-7 into her strawlike veins. So that there'd be no more of the usual interruptions interfering with the very important sinking of the company.

Wilbur Bea looked with true glee at the latest sales reports that Fretwell had dropped off with great alarm. The numbers were in and they were down. Sales were dropping on all Bea's products as a result of an anti-dipping-of-Christ-into-dark-chocolate backlash. It was just what he had hoped for. *This is going to happen faster than I'd imagined. Like a house of cards.* And now, as the King he already pictured himself to be, he could hardly wait for his coronation. *The Wilbur Candy Company. It's got a nice ring to it.* He granted Scrimshaw audience.

"So, what do you have to report, Scrimshaw?"

"I've never gotten so many letters," Scrimshaw complained. "You have no idea, but I think . . ."

"Never mind what you think. The letters. What do these letters say?" Wilbur could hardly keep a straight face. He took a sip off an excellently prepared Bronx, a drink, Mr. Bea decided right then, that best highlighted the distinct flavor of fine gin. In fact, he found the hint of juniper so pleasing that he entertained the notion of not crushing Sydney. *But it'd be nice. Mom's new favorite. Freak anyway. Got that gimpy leg, it's almost useless. How could someone live like that?! Ahh, well . . .* He shuddered, set down the drink and smiled to himself. Mr. Bea was thankful for his superiority. *My . . . perfection.* He dared think it. *Why not?! Such a fine day.*

Scrimshaw looked up from his wheelbarrow of letters and adjusted the angle of his glasses, aiming them straight at Wilbur Bea. "It doesn't look good out there."

"Oh no?"

"Hmm?" Scrimshaw asked.

"What do the letters say?" Mr. Bea asked, smiling.

"Are you *saying* something?" Scrimshaw looked back down at his box and carefully fiddled with a knob. "There we go. This device is very sensitive, you know."

"WHAT . . . DID . . . YOU . . . SAY?!"

"You don't have to yell. I'm not deaf," Scrimshaw yelled, quite pleased with the latest adjustment on his PowerAid 5000 hearing aid amplifier. "I'm trying to tell you that it doesn't look good with the folks outside."

"Outside?! Who are you talking about?" Mr. Bea could

hardly believe it. He was surrounded by incompetents. *Not for long.*

"Hmmm? I'm losing you, wait a dolgarn second there . . ." Scrimshaw shoved his thick old guy's glasses up the bridge of his nose and leaned into the control panel. Mr. Bea decided against hoping for a proper adjustment. He formed his hands into a makeshift megaphone and commenced with screaming. " 'WHO?' I said. WHO?!"

"A bunch of religious nuts. That Reverend guy sent them."

"Our very own Reverend Fucking Domingo?" Mr. Bea smiled. *My plan is so . . . so . . . Machiavellian.* He instinctively reached for his cigar and thought of going to Mrs. Jam's. "And what might their beef be?"

"Beeps?"

"BEEF. WHAT . . . IS . . . THEIR . . . BEEF . . . WITH . . . ME?!"

Scrimshaw looked up from his amplifier—*I'm taking this thing back*—and shot Mr. Bea a quizzical look. "Chocolate Jesus would be my guess."

"YES?! . . . GO ON!"

"They say it's a touch blasphemous?" Scrimshaw continued. "I don't know. Something about graven images and a mockery of the Lord?" Scrimshaw began sorting through a large pile of letters. "Uh . . . Here we go, says the Chocolate Jesus is a, and I'm quoting directly here, 'a mockery of the Lord that could only be carried out by one of Satan's Own.' He's calling for your 'disembowelment' so that, quote, 'the crows of darkness might tear at your whoremongering flesh and pluck the very eyes from your head.' You can probably read some of their signs if you look out the window."

"What is all that fucking noise anyway?"

"That's what I've been trying to tell you."

Mr. Bea's lizard brain, like an old vacuum-tubed television, had finally warmed up and at last made the connection. He walked over to the window that looked out to the factory grounds. By now a rather sizable mob had made their way up to the great locked gates that led to the Candy Works grounds. They were bristling with signs and anger. The worst kind of anger. They were pissed off on behalf of the Lord.

"Why didn't you tell me?! JESUS CHRIST!"

"Oww!" Scrimshaw winced in pain and ripped his two hearing aids from his head like they were suddenly 350 degrees. It was the nasty feedback problem that plagued the PowerAid 5000 design and would later result in a total recall as well as some class-action activity. "Tell you?" Scrimshaw was perplexed. "What do you think I've been trying to do? Sheesh."

"They could tear down the factory. GOD!" Bea was practically ripping the hair out of his head. He fast jammed three butter creams. "I *need* this factory."

"This never would have happened if we'd stuck with the telegraph machine," Scrimshaw concluded nostalgically. "It's that damn computer. Fax, hah! There was nothing wrong with the mimeograph machine *or* the comptometer. They worked perfectly fine. Why'd we ever get rid of them, huh?"

"It's that damn Sydney. That's who they want!" Mr. Bea, in the massive fatal ego syndrome he operated under, decided he would march straight to that gate and straighten everything out. Nip it in the bud, so to speak.

jesus drives a cadillac

it was windy that day, the day the Reverend
had promised the world would end, the day he sent the
angry mob to Bea's Candies, the same day that Jesús Torres
at long last got the glimpse of El Chupe that he'd been
hoping for all summer. Very windy and very hot. The entire
landscape ached with dryness in the heat. It began as many
days will—at the first light of dawn. From the very first
sensation he had of being awake in bed, the sun already
bright even behind the thin drawn curtains inside his little
bungalow, Jesús could tell there wasn't a cloud in the sky.
There hadn't been a cloud in the sky for months. Today was
going to be, as the *gabachos* said down at *Los Billares,* "one
hot mother."

That initial breath of the early morning's breeze slipping
through his curtains, fluttering the thin fabric, already carried
with it the first hint of the heat to come, the first whispers
of the violent winds to come. And as Jesús stepped into the
soft heat he had a feeling. A good feeling.

After the mob left, or "the flock" as Reverend Domingo tried to still think of them, Jesús headed toward the garden shed, smoking a cigarette, thinking he might fit in an hour or so of brush clearing before the afternoon's broadcast of *Sweatin' with the Lord.*

After it had happened (and it happened so very fast), when Jesús tried to remember back to exactly what had happened and how it had happened, but he couldn't really remember how exactly it had happened.

But he would never forget the picture in his head and—oh, how he hoped and prayed—the one in his disposable Kodak camera. The picture of the little beast at long last. Jesús noticed the smell first and then, that's when everything happened so fast.

He noticed the smell as he approached the shed. Like a wet horse blanket coated with rotten eggs, and it flashed in his mind that the day so long ago when he first saw the beast had been hot and windy. Jesús reached into his pocket for the tiny *gabacho* camera that he always carried with him.

There it was! Hunched over a bag of fertilizer, digging away with birdlike claws. It looked up, startled, at Jesús. It seemed sad somehow, to Jesús. Sad, lonely and small as it turned slowly toward him and instinctually began to bare its fangs, but only in a halfhearted manner, as though the beast knew this man meant him no harm, that Jesús came in peace. Suddenly an ancient image of his great-grandfather flashed in his mind and this reminded him to take the picture.

And while Jesús wasn't sure of much after that, he was sure he'd taken one good picture of the little beast, a hand of fertilizer in its raptor claw. And then the Reverend walked in. The Reverend, who Jesús thought had already left, walked into the shed in the now unmistakable heat of day and all hell broke loose.

"Dear Jesus, a Hound of Hell!" the Reverend screamed, pointing at the beast, and everyone was gripped in a terrible fright (Jesús was like a small boy caught, and instinctively tossed his cigarette away). The Reverend screamed like a madman, "You think you can whip me, demon? I fight for God. I've got Jesus as my cornerman!"

The Reverend stripped his light running jacket off and had struck his best Marques of Queensberry pose, ready for some Apocalyptic fisticuffs, when the animal kicked over the canister of fuel for the Weed Whacker and seemed to disappear for a moment, only to reappear wrapped around the Reverend's upper torso region like a pissed-off Marty McSorley, badly tousling the Reverend's always immaculate fine silver hair and digging its hawklike claws deeply into the End Times Specialist's well-preserved yet oddly yellow skin. Then out the window it was gone. As though it had never happened. Except that it had and the Reverend was pretty fucked up.

"No fucking way," Jesús said with the command of a native speaker. He shoved his camera into his shirt pocket and rushed to the side of Padre Ewilly and didn't notice the small fire that had started in the pile of rags, immediately fed by the breeze that was drawn into the shed as though it smelled the possibility.

Jesús rushed to the old man's side, tore off his work shirt and pressed it against the most gaping of the three slices that ran down either side of the old man's face, from cheekbone to chin. His shirt became almost instantly soaked in blood.

"*Ay Dios mío, necisitamos ir al hospital, Padre. Vamos!*" The Reverend wasn't responding. "Oh, sheet. Ease no good."

The Reverend came to as Jesús tried to pick him off the ground. There was blood everywhere from the facial wounds, and actually it was the Reverend who first saw the flames of what was now a small, but intensely raging, inferno in the highly flammable corner of what would soon be known as the former garden shed. The Reverend opened his topaz-colored eyes, clear and untouched, and gazed straight ahead at the tot-sized conflagration.

"Dear God! The Fires of Hell are unleashed!" He passed out for a half a second, then his eyes snapped open again: "The Dogs of Hell have been loosed. The Tribulation has begun. The End Times are upon us."

This seemed to calm the Reverend. He could hardly believe it. *The world is going to end! I was right after all.* And with the security of knowing—what with his face shredded and him probably bleeding to death—that all was to be destroyed and the Kingdom of God was at long last going to deliver him, he was somehow able to stumble, with the help of sweet Jesús, toward the Cadillac.

The Reverend's fine-assed 1959 Fleetwood. The Immaculate Cadillac. Troy McClure had recently offered the Reverend 10Gs cash for it, but the Reverend could never sell her. He'd owned it since back when Bessie was still alive. The car had become "her" over the years, and the Reverend treated that car with the kind of love and attention usually reserved for puppies and newborns.

Jesús opened the back door and shoved the bloody Reverend into the Cadillac's spacious backseat, permanently fucking up the fine leather upholstery to such a degree that an unscrupulous museum operator on some backroad's highway would later saw the top off and claim it was the car Kennedy had been shot in, charging $5 per head (kids $2) to sit in it and another $5 for a photo.

The flames were already burning far out of control. Well beyond the squirting-with-the-garden-hose containment that Jesús had performed for a moment. *No fucking way. Ease no good,* Jesús thought in English in the heat of the moment. *Chingadera Chupecabra! El amigo del Diablo.* Jesús felt bad for having lured it to Miracle Mountain with gifts of food and water. He crossed himself and continued with his Hail Marys and Our Father Who Art in Heavens as he slipped that big Caddy into gear and headed down the now-blazing Miracle Mountain.

Jesús was flying down that mountain! Flying down Miracle Mountain in a gigantic Cadillac. He hadn't driven a car since Tio's old *troca.* The old, beat '49 Ford pickup. The truck with little brakes, back on the dirt roads that ran through the campo in Michoacán, and right then Jesús knew he was going back home. Back to sweet Reyna. With his picture of the little beast. To his new life.

But this car! Such a sweet ride, Jesús marveled. It was immense, like a giant metal raft. The right and left front bumpers seemed to stretch out across the entire road as Jesús wound his way down the spiraling road that wrapped down the burning mountain.

Somehow the Reverend pulled himself back from unconsciousness and the prone position, grabbed the front seat and pulled himself to Jesús's ear.

"The time is nigh!" He grabbed Jesús's shoulder and then caught his bloody reflection in the rearview mirror and began smoothing his shiny silver hair back with a blood-soaked hand.

"Ayy, sheet!" Jesús exclaimed as the Cadillac nearly went off the side of the road.

"Fear God," the Reverend said in a loud voice, "and

give glory to Him; for the hour of judgment is come: and worship him that made Heaven. Ark! Glack!" and he fell back onto the spacious leather seat that was bigger than Jesús's bed.

"Oh, Padre Ewilly. *Qué pasa? Qué pasa?*"

Jesús at last came off the winding mountain road a ways ahead of the fire, and gunned it down Citrus Avenue to the hospital.

The fire ran down the side of the mountain with amazing speed, like the ice cream melting off the Devil's own sugar cone. The wind, drawn in like a hungry dog, whipped at its heels, and the two elements combined with explosive force. And that brush beaten by 150 days of blazing sunshine and no moisture, and for weeks neglected by Jesús, who had to help Padre Ewilly with the End Times preparations? That shit went up like fireworks.

The Reverend came to at a light and began sermonizing. "Babylon is fallen, is fallen, that great city, because she made all people eat of the chocolate . . ." The Reverend fell back onto the seat as Jesús sped on when the light changed. ". . . of the wrath . . . of her fornication. Grrgl. Acckk!"

Jesús screeched to a wild, sliding stop in front of the emergency entrance of the Valley Memorial Hospital, taking out a *USA Today* machine and inadvertently smacking the Reverend's already bloody head against the front seat, causing him to groan loudly. "Ohh, here is the patience of the saints: here are they that keep the commandments of God, and the faith of Jesus."

Jesús pulled the Reverend from the backseat as two attendants came out. The first one at the scene looked at the Apocalyptic Handicapper's bloody face and then at Jesús's brown skin and dark eyes (Jesús naturally recoiled from such a stare and felt at fault) and sized up the situation in a flash.

"What have you done to Bob Barker?!" he yelled angrily at Jesús.

Jesús panicked and, figuring he'd done his part and delivered Padre Ewilly to the doctor, thought he'd best be getting his *pinche nalgas* outta there before *La Migra* showed up. He jumped back behind the wheel of the Cadillac and smacked it into Drive. Besides, he was starting to get the feel of that big Earth Momma Caddy. *Responsive and powerful, yet so very comfortable,* Jesús thought as he raced down Citrus Avenue at about sixty.

He looked a fright as he sped off, tuning the radio to the AM Mexican station and adjusting the rearview. In the mirror he saw the blood smeared on his face from the Reverend's wounds, wounds that would turn out to be superficial but leave some wicked scars that the ever-opportunistic Willie Domingo would parlay into a bit-part character-acting career in pirate and horror movies.

It was then that Jesús noticed the beard lying on the seat. He quickly decided to utilize this Heaven-sent disguise, and when he picked it up, he saw the stack of money lying under it. Jesús simply smiled and looked upward, to God and the firmament that was the ceiling of the 1959 Cadillac Fleetwood. "*Sí!*"

There was only one thing left to do and then he was going home. *Chinga esto lugar.* He first had to warn the people. With that thought he sped up and then realized he was only vaguely aware of where he was going. He had some sort of ill-formed idea of a meeting with some sort of personage of an official nature that wasn't necessarily a cop. A parking meter cop came to mind and Jesús was now on the lookout for their tiny carts.

As he drove on, he saw something up in the distance.

It seemed like . . . a crowd of people. Jesús instinctively adjusted his fake beard, and as he drove closer, he could see that it *was* a crowd. A crowd that seemed to get bigger and bigger as he approached closer and closer. A huge and angry crowd gathered in front of the chocolate factory and blocking the road.

The crowd outside of the locked and barricaded gates of the Bea's Candy Works was swelling with motion and madness. They were pressed against the iron bars of the fence, shaking signs, mob-vicious, justice-ravenous, punishment-hungry and glucosamine- and phenylalanine-buzzing. Their signs bristled in the air, thrusting toward the very heavens. "What do you want?!" an angry voice blasting from an angry face leaned into the wide open Cadillac. Jesús smiled in response. He smiled his beatific smile, the one he'd mastered in his year in Estados Unidos to avoid any confrontations with the *gabachos*. An angelic smile, as pure and good as the man smiling it. Jesús beamed that true smile of peace from the driver's seat of the once-immaculate '59 Fleetwood and began with one of the few non-swearing phrases he had perfected, except for the pronunciation of the J sound. "My name is Jesus."

The man looked at him for a stunned moment. "What?!"

"I say, 'My name is Jesus.' How are you? I am fine, thank you."

The man looked at the blood-smeared face, at the pure smile, at the beard and then at that Cadillac. *What a beaut! It's true. He is here. The Reverend was right. The Rapture!* He turned toward the crowd and yelled, "It's Jesus! Everybody, Jesus is here. Everyone stand aside. Jesus is in a Caddy and he's got to get through."

The words quickly spread through the crowd.

"It's Jesus!"

"Jesus?"

"Jesus! Jesus is here."

"Where's Jesus?"

"In that Caddy."

"That's a beauty!"

"Where's Jesus? I can't see him."

"That's him, in the Caddy."

"Why's Jesus a Mexican?"

"He's not Mexican. He's just been in the desert."

"The Lord works in mysterious ways, brother."

"Jesus, they've made a graven candy bar of you."

"An abomination of chocolate."

"Don't worry, Jesus. We're about to break down their gates and then we're going to burn the factory down and kill the owner all in the name of you, oh, Prince of Peace."

They were all talking way too fast for Jesús to pick up any of it as he nudged the twelve-foot-wide car through the parting crowd.

"*Hay un fuego. Un fuego muy malo,*" Jesús blurted out in the excitement.

"Dear Lord," the man exclaimed and rolled his eyes in orgasmic righteousness. "Hey! Everybody! Jesus is speaking in tongues."

"Dear God, Jesus is speaking in tongues!"

"I still can't see Jesus."

"Jesus is here?"

"He's in the Caddy, speaking in tongues."

"He's not speaking in tongues. It's Spanish. He's a Mexican."

As Jesús's beard and entire mistaken identity began slipping in the face of the crowd, a loud cheer was heard ahead.

"The gates are down."

The crowd immediately surged toward the opening, as if from a lanced boil, and headed toward the corporate offices of Bea's Candies.

Jesús saw his chance. He wheeled the Cadillac deftly to the far right and gunned it down the sweet, open pavement. *Adios,* and Jesús sped down the highway heading south.

marty's brain
on beer

that very same day Marty had started in early on his drinking and though they were still serving Geronimo Breakfasts at Jack Anvil's, he was seated on his usual stool at Dutchman's, already deeply lost in thoughts of the evil night. The night in question, the night that had scarred Marty Corbet, a scar he would only begin to suspect toward the end of our narrative, took place in a time long ago, in a place so distant and foreign as to seem nearly a dream. As though it were the story of another family, a TV movie starring Richard Thomas you could almost recall watching one Wednesday night ten years earlier. Oftentimes it didn't even seem that it had happened at all, and it was very rare that Marty got as far as actually picturing the events of that evil evening. The night the lights went out in his little boy's world. Usually it required even more beers than it did for him to feel Love.

It was the night Dad was last seen, the night Mom ceased to exist, the night the boys became . . . orphans. *Yeah, orphans I guess you could call it.* Marty drained the rest of his beer and looked about the near-deserted Dutchman's.

"Hey, Ben, gimme another Rocko's and a shot a Jack."

"Jack?! Jesus, Marty, it's kinda early, don't you think?" Ben walked over.

"What are you? My fuckin' mother?!" Ben shook his head and poured the drink.

It had been so cold. So very, very cold. He remembered the long walk home from school with his buddy Mike. The light was clear and blinding off the fields of snow, on that one hill behind Bracherst's house. A bunch of kids were out. Chums from boyhood now long lost, they'd been sledding down that perfect slope, whooshing fast and smooth in sprays of snow. The brilliant heat-thin light of the growing sun shone bright, but all its BTUs were absorbed by the still, cold winter air. Refrigerator drafts hung in the shadows above the deep snow.

But that night . . . Marty slammed back the Jack's and chased it with some beer.

That night in the house it was unbearably hot. It was as if a houseguest from southern India were manning the thermostat, trying to find room temperature in Calcutta. Marty could remember tossing in the sheets, finally throwing them off entirely, the sweat beading on his forehead as he heard yet another yelling fight out in the kitchen. He'd heard the same shit so often that he was sick of it beyond his years. Waves of heat radiated out of his body, filling the room, baking the bedroom, while outside was another world. Blue and silver, silent and cold as death, that vast expanse of flat snowfield lay on the other side of his bedroom window, the bare branches of the trees creepily fingering the blue-black of a full moon's night sky. Not a thing moved out there. Cold and silent and still as a photograph, while inside all was hot and frantic, tense and loud. Another crash from the kitchen, a chair against the wall. Her crying—it was practically all he could ever fucking remember of back then, her fucking crying. That and the fucking old man, his booming voice, his whining complaints. Though only nine, Marty was so sick of it that even then he looked forward to the day he'd be big enough to kick Dad's ass. He'd throw his fucking ass out of the house himself.

From Dad's point of view it was a night like so many others, pretty much railing-and-screaming drunk, belligerent and paranoid, Sydney tossing and turning himself in the stifling heat inside the house, trying to kick his own little blanket off with his weak left leg, murmuring, disturbed in some lost, sad dream of half-realizations and misplaced mental imprints. Marty was lying there for what seemed the millionth time, growing an elementary-school-sized ulcer, wishing he was someone else, wishing things were good, wondering why he was being punished, what he had done wrong—when the door slammed as it always did. It was a sound Marty had learned to look forward to, the sound of the front door slamming shut and the car starting up, signaling Daddy's departure to the local tavern to drink it off as it were. Sometimes there followed a few choice screams from Mom, some nasties she saved up for when he was gone, and then it would be quiet at long last, save for the blubbering of his dear sweet dead mother as she lay her head down on the kitchen table.

That was when Marty would sometimes slip out of his room and go downstairs, down to the kitchen, where she'd be crying, all heaped on the kitchen table, slumped in the chair, her shoulders gently heaving in her lonely, hopeless lament. Marty might come up to her and put his small arm around her shoulder, and she'd look up and smile through the tears and hug him as though the little boy were making it better.

But not that night. That night, after the door finally slammed and he heard the starter on the car buzz a few times before the engine caught and it then rumbled off into the distance, there was extra screaming by Mom, it seemed extra bitter. And then complete silence. A strange, heavy silence. Marty was looking out at the silent cold of the silver moonlight on the deep snow when the door slammed again. Except this time it wasn't the door.

There was blood everywhere. The kitchen was impossibly bloody, the wall and even the ceiling splattered. Bright red and dripping and in a pool beside her head, some of it was thick with pieces. Dad's shotgun lay beside her; she had on that apron with the frilly border, like lace. And that look on her face, that agonized look like she'd witnessed the most horrific thing ever known to Man, which was what Marty now witnessed, barefoot and pajamaed, standing over her that night.

"Marty, Marty! Hey! Isn't that the candy factory?" Ben stood right in front of Marty, looking up at the TV, turning up the volume.

Click!

"We have some breaking news. What had been a peaceful protest by Biblical vegetarians out at the chocolate factory has turned ugly. The outbreak of violence is centered at the Bea's Candy Works, where the crowd is in the process of breaking down the gates. A suspect in police custody identified the group as members of the Church of the Returning Vegetarian Christ . . ."

"Huh?" Marty looked up from a lifetime away. He looked up from his millionth pint of Rocko's, his nine hundredth shot of whiskey, looked up from his sickly forays into the sweetened liqueur worlds of Jäger und Schlager, and he saw there on the television screen the live video footage of the riot forming in front of the Bea's Candy Works, and he knew, Marty Corbet knew right then, not just in his head, but as a lump in the back of his throat, a tightness in his chest, a momentary shortness of breath, he knew that Sydney was in trouble. He was in trouble once again, and one side, a deep and true side of Marty's being, thought angrily, *Fuck it!* True and sincere was this easily accessed feeling. He had pictured Sydney living some life of riches and luxury. He pictured Sydney in some fancy room out there at the factory, soaking in a giant tub filled with bubble bath, drinking a Freeb's Cola-Nated beverage out of Waterford crystal, a Ming Dynasty plate filled with his favorite cookie, the discontinued Pepperidge Farms Tahiti, provided special by Mr. Bea, procured from a black-market snacks dealer, held in some sort of freshness cookie humidor so that they crumbled upon bite like a fucking Viennese fantasy. He saw Sydney there, lapping it all up, telling anyone who would listen, First you make the chocolate, then you get the money, then you get the power. *Fuck him. I'm better off without him, without any of them, the whole sorry fucking family. Fuck 'em! Livin' with Aunt Sally! Having to protect stupid fuckin' Sydney from all the kids always making fun of him, pickin' on him, callin' him names, makin' fun of how he talked, his big words and funny shoes . . .*

But on the other hand . . . When he pictured that one shoe of Sydney's, the one with the sole as thick as a steak, his eyes welled up. Gripping the glass of beer firmly, looking up at the TV screen, images swimming before him, he was overcome, overwhelmed with the rallying cry to save his brother. For the first time in months, years even, besides the momentary wash of dreams that filled him right after making a big bet, Marty had a purpose. He had a calling. There was a reason for his existence. He *had* to watch out for Sydney, and he remembered back to the night *she told me to look out for him.*

A blush of shame spread over his face as he felt the great, awful guilt of having let her down, having let everybody down, but instead of slinking away or raging out, instead of sinking as deep into oblivion as possible, Marty knew that this once, just this once at least, he was going to do what he had to do and not let anybody down.

"If anybody's gonna fuck with my brother," Marty suddenly yelled out at the bar, and drained his beer, "it's gonna be me!" And he stormed out the door.

montezuma's revenge

scrimshaw closed the door to his office one
last time, removed his two large hearing aids, dropped them
into an ashtray and headed down the empty hallway. He
placed his usual raspberry cream in his mouth and held it
there as he headed for the last room, adjusting his tie and
checking the tuck of his shirt. He licked his lips and straightened himself up.

In the Last Room, all the way back at the end of the
last corridor, it was quiet and tranquil as could be despite
the mayhem going on at the front gates.

Scrimshaw reached over and removed the IV needle
from Mrs. Bea's arm. He walked over to the closet and
pulled out two suitcases, then sat down in the chair and
waited a moment, taking in the room one last time. Mrs.
Bea soon began to rouse, as though awakening from a sleeping potion. She sat up, smiled at Orville Scrimshaw and
reached her old bony hand toward his old bony hand.

———

Meanwhile down the hall, Sydney was slowly packing his lone suitcase. He didn't know where he might go, but it was gonna be somewhere else. His run as a major player in the chocolate industry was over. Riots were rarely forgiven on a résumé. Maybe he'd go to Aunt Sally's. There was always his research. He would always have that.

Sydney left his room and walked the empty hallway of the last building, down the last corridor, heading slowly toward the door. *The* door. The door to the room of Mrs. H. Bea, revered icon, founder and *still* president of Bea's Candies.

If you asked him later why he walked down that hall that day to Mrs. Bea's room Sydney would not have had an explanation. To this day he could not explain why, and at the time he tried not to think about it at all. He simply headed down that hallway like a king salmon cruising through the Bay and up the Sacramento on destiny's mission.

The door was ajar and the usual nurse long gone. Sydney hitched his polyester slacks up his skinny hips and quietly leaned toward the thin band of faint light coming from inside. As his eyes tried to make out the interior, he was struck by the smell. It was a hospital overlay, not unlike the just-scrubbed linoleum hallways at the Koala, but beneath that, there was mountain lilac and the faint smell of oranges and sage.

Someone else was in the room! Sydney first noticed the fine suit and the tightness of the tie knot. *Scrimshaw! The water cooler gossip is true,* Sydney thought. *Illicit Love.* And for once he wasn't shocked. He smiled slightly.

"Who's that?!" The buzzing was never mistaken. It was Mrs. Bea, who sat in a chair sipping a cup of tea. *She looks marvelous.* Scrimshaw turned toward Sydney. *He looks great!*

"Where did you buy that lamp?" Sydney asked as he tentatively set foot in the room.

"Hmm, what's that?" Scrimshaw asked.

"The light, it's so . . . beautiful."

Mrs. Bea had set down her mike, and in a soft voice, her gentle falsetto, she said, "It's always beautiful and peaceful in here. Why do you think I stay in this room most of the time? Take a seat, Sydney."

"Why, thank you." Sydney lowered himself into a fine antique chair.

"Some coffee?" Orville asked. "Tea?"

"Oh, no, my delicate nervous system," Sydney said and nodded.

"So what brings you here, Sydney?" Mrs. Bea asked.

"Um, well . . ." Sydney felt inhibited, but he swallowed once, for his hands were now different. "I have some terrible news to report. There's a major boycott of Bea's products. People are protesting the Chocolate Jesus."

"Ahhh." Mrs. Bea waved him off and smiled wryly. "It's always something, eh, Orville?"

"Hmm? I suppose. Everyone always fiddling about with the knobs. Can't leave well enough alone."

"You don't seem to understand," Sydney insisted. "This candy bar is going to be your company's undoing."

"You don't know the half of it." Scrimshaw began to laugh.

"Poor Wilbur." Mrs. Bea started cracking up. And now the three of them were laughing heartily, except that Sydney didn't really know why.

Sydney composed himself. "I'd like to tender my resignation."

"Yes, I think that'd be a good idea," Mrs. Bea said. "Orville, why don't you reach into the suitcase and give Sydney a stack for his meritorious service."

"Be glad to, Helen." Scrimshaw leaned forward and handed Sydney a stack of hundies.

Sydney was flabbergasted. "You don't seem to understand . . ."

"Yes, I do," Mrs. Bea said. "You run along now."

"I'd use the back door if I was you," Orville added, but Sydney was gone.

Now, way back when, many pages back—and if you're still following me at all, congratulations—maybe you'll remember what I told you practically everyone had forgotten. Forgotten the days before Mrs. Bea bought the small factory with the large acreage, back in the day when an acre in Southern California wasn't the most valued in all the world.

Everyone had long ago forgotten that Orville Scrimshaw once held title to all that property that stretched at the west, toward the then-small town of Valley, property that now marked the eastern edges of the city's sprawl of condos and tract homes and minimalls, which had slowly covered the land like a spreading fungus. And he still did.

Mrs. Bea knew. She had allowed that nonadvantageous business move to stand, in deference to their more-than-a-shared-butter-cream days. When she and Orville had lived and loved in the golden paradise of postwar Southern California. She *had* loved him once (he had always loved her) and she had hated him for a time and loathed the fact that he kept himself on at Bea's, but in the end, in the not-so-bitter end, she realized (submitting blissfully to the weight of the cosmos right there beside her) that she and Orville were paramount.

"Why didn't you just sell to Frito-Lay?" Orville asked as he finished his cup of Tung Ting Oolong.

"What's the fun in that, Orville? Besides, I hate it when he gets his way. Wilbur didn't deserve it."

Scrimshaw searched his soul for a nanosecond, but found no pity for her son.

There was no love lost between Scrimshaw and Mr. Bea. He just never said so in front of Helen. Didn't think it was right. It was her son after all. But Scrimshaw never did like Mr. Bea. He'd seen him grow up on the candy grounds, rich and spoiled, clumsy and arrogant. Saw Wilbur make the smooth transition from destructive child to bullying adult, saw him grow up into a pushy walking, talking fit of temper. When he wasn't insulting you, he was yelling at you, except for the occasional laugh he'd "share" with you—usually at your expense. Scrimshaw never joined in that mirth. He pretended not to hear. That had served him well all those years.

"Besides, he was trying to pull one over on me." Mrs. Bea angrily set down her cup of Fine Tippy Golden Flowery Orange Pekoe Grade One, Aged. "I could tell. He's always been trouble. Once he grew up? I never trusted him. He was always trying to push me out and he finally got tired of waiting, so he latched on to that ridiculous idea. The way he slumped around? I knew he was up to something. And *no one* gets one over on Helen Bea!"

"The *company's* ruined," Scrimshaw stated flatly.

"Mmmm." They both felt sad for a moment. "Well, thank God . . . ," Mrs. Bea began.

". . . for the Wad Gomper," they said in unison, smiling.

"Well, we really should be going, I didn't like the looks of that mob."

"Has everything been taken care of?" Mrs. Bea looked concerned. "The reservations?"

"Yes, it's all been taken care of. The largest suite Isla Basura has to offer."

"The medical team?" Mrs. Bea asked.

"Yes, in adjoining rooms." Orville shook his head. "There's an entire planeload of medical equipment already en route."

"The hyperbaric sleeping chamber?"

"I didn't forget the hyperbaric sleeping chamber." Orville helped her into the wheelchair and they exited.

By the time Sydney had made his way out of Building #5 with his suitcase, and his front pocket literally bulging with a wad of cash, the crowd had at last broken through the gate and split into two parts. The lead and most foaming part went after Mr. Bea (who for the last twenty minutes had been standing atop a forklift imagining he was defusing the situation, but, in reality, his pleas of "Hey! I'm fucking sick of you holy rollers and your little bitch Jesus" had succeeded only in inflaming the already *very* inflamed group).

"Mother. MOTHER!" Mr. Bea yelled as he jumped from the forklift and broke out into a pseudo-run. He was almost immediately engulfed by the mob, which ran him down like a cheetah might a rickety gazelle. While they didn't go so far as to kill him, you might have wanted to have been Mr. Bea's chiropractor in the coming months—except for the fact that he was financially ruined. So maybe you wouldn't.

A second group caught sight of Sydney and raced toward him. Sydney looked at them, and was trying to make sense of the mayhem when an arm grabbed him from behind.

"Back into the factory!" Broma ordered Sydney. The two men ran into the factory, slamming the door shut. Broma quickly drove a forklift in front of the door as a barricade.

"Up to the catwalk!" Broma yelled.

"I'll never make it," Sydney protested. "My leg. You go."

"I don't know vat zort of a chocolatier you take me für, but I never leave any of my men behind. Mach schnell!" Broma barked out and pulled Sydney by his thin arm.

They made it to the base of the stairs and up to the first level, Broma tugging at Sydney's sleeve, as the door was finally broken down. Broma looked back to the crowd, which was commencing with an enthusiastic blitzkrieg property-destruction tour of the inside of Building #5.

"There they are!" one of the crowd yelled out. "Up there on those stairs."

"It's the candy men!" screamed another.

"Kill the candy men!" Everyone joined in and the crowd dropped, for the most part, their clubbing of inanimate objects and smashing of windows, and redirected their efforts at murder, heading toward the spiraling catwalk stairs. "Let's get 'em!"

"We're not gonna make it," Sydney told Broma. "I just can't climb the stairs fast enough. You go, I'll try and hold off the crowd. Just one thing."

"What's that?"

"Remember me at your induction speech at the Cocoa Hall of Fame."

"How could I not?" Broma agreed tenderly.

A voiced boomed from up near the rafters: "Hey!"

"Look, up there!" one of the crazed vegans yelled. "Another candy-making blasphemer."

There was a man standing atop the catwalk. He had a can of beer in one hand and brandished a wrench over his head with the other.

"It's Martin!" Sydney had a grand smile on his face.

"Whatsamatter?" Marty yelled. "You people don't like a little chocolate?"

"Wer ist dieser Menson?" Broma asked.

"Don't worry," Sydney said. "It's my brother. He knows violence like you know chocolate."

"Ach, scheiss!" Broma cried, still freaked out over the big guy in the mob who kept pointing directly at him and yelling, "You're dead! You are dead!"

"What is it, Professor?" Sydney asked.

"He's got za emergency cocoa blowout falve wrrr-ench. If he vents zose . . ." Broma turned to Sydney. "Zat's molten schokoladen behind zose falves. Thrrr-ee hundred taosend gallons of 115-degree zemizveet. Za sheiss ist loaded viz cocoa liquor, Mann!"

"Here, I got your cocoa, right here!" Marty yelled down at the mob. He took the wrench and uncapped a huge blowout.

"Ach, Gott!" Broma was freaking out. "He's unleashing Moctezuma's Rrrr-evenge! HALT!"

tv dinners for all

click!

"We also have a report, this just coming in, of a massive brushfire in the hills to the east of Valley. The conditions have been perfect for the past week. A heat wave, Santa Ana winds, a *very* dry spring following record January rains provided plenty of dry brush and, combined with the strong, hot easterly winds, it was a recipe that spelled 'disaster.' "

Click!

"I'm just being handed another update. It seems there's been a massive chocolate spill—is this correct? Yes, it seems there are even *more* problems at the Bea's Candy Works. For those just tuning in, a riot has been in progress for the last few hours at the famed local candy factory. You're now seeing helicopter footage from High Sky Live. As you can see, a *large* number of people have filled the factory grounds. The smoke blowing across the scene is from a massive brushfire that you can now see raging completely out of control to the east. At least one structure, a 'religious compound' on Cowles Mountain, has already been reported burned to the ground . . . I'm being told we have a crew at the scene of the riot. Let's cut to some live footage from our Two's News Crews. Yes, Ted, what have you got down there?"

"Bill, I'm having trouble hearing you. I hope I'm coming through. As you can see, it's mayhem here. A group comprised of mostly extremely fit, white men and women are on a rampage here."

"Is there looting going on, Ted?"

"Well, interestingly enough, there's none of the usual looting you'd expect. Cases upon cases of chocolate bars are being completely ignored, but property damage is extensive . . ."

"What is it that the mob, if we can call it that, is after?"

"Oh, it's a mob, that's a fair assessment. Many are screaming to have the false prophets thrown into a, quote, 'Lake of Fire . . .' "

Click!

"In an environmental disaster of momentous proportions, a chocolate spill of over 200,000 gallons of raw cocoa liquor has occurred at the Bea's Candy Works. Containment is not expected before sometime tomorrow. Cleanup crews are hampered by the fire fighting going on simultaneously in the area . . ."

Click!

"It seems a radical arm of the Church of the Returning Vegetarian Christ has taken Wilbur Bea, owner of the Bea's Candy Works, hostage. I also have unconfirmed reports that Mrs. Bea, revered icon and founder of Bea's Candies, rumored long ago dead, was seen driving from the area in the company of an unknown man . . ."

Click!

"Whadda mess!" Marty said in between forkfuls of his first of two Swanson Hungry Man Salisbury Steak dinners.

"These fish sticks are ausgezeichnet," Professor Broma said, complimenting Sydney as he traced one through a mound of tartar sauce.

"Yes," Sydney said proudly. "Mrs. Paul is a stickler for quality."

"Looks like they're not gonna be making much candy there for a while." Marty took a swig off his Rocko's.

"I vorned him about za cocoa." Broma turned to Sydney. "Didn't I vorn him?"

"So, whaddaya gonna do now?" Marty asked Broma.

"Vell . . . viz za Vad Gomper?" Professor Broma had that singularly calm look of a millionaire sitting in front of a TV tray eating Mrs. Paul's fish sticks and OreIda Texas Twisters. "Come on."

Marty nodded in reflection. "You a gambling man, Professor?"

epilogue

santa madre hung up the telephone at the tiny *larga distancia* booth in the back of Abarmotes Guzman, where she had received the call that she could hardly believe. Guzman had told her to return today, for he had called the day before, but she didn't dare believe and told no one. But it was true! And she hurried back the ten blocks, carrying a small load of groceries in her woven plastic shopping bag. It seemed so far under the weight of her great news. She hurried back to the simple house to tell everybody, to see the look on Reyna's face when she told them all,

"Jesús is coming!"